英語 Make Me High 系列

PASS KEY TO

作文致勝關鍵：
寫作範例100
學科能力測驗適用

郭慧敏　編著

WRITING

100

BEST SAMPLES

三民書局

國家圖書館出版品預行編目資料

Pass Key to Writing－100 Best Samples 作文致勝關鍵：寫作範例100／郭慧敏編著.－－初版十三刷.－－臺北市：三民，2023
面；　公分.－－（英語Make Me High系列）

ISBN 978－957－14－5160－2（平裝）
1. 英語 2. 作文 3. 寫作法

805.17　　　　　　　　　　　　　　98002936

Pass Key to Writing－100 Best Samples
作文致勝關鍵：寫作範例 100

編 著 者	郭慧敏
發 行 人	劉振強
出 版 者	三民書局股份有限公司
地　　址	臺北市復興北路 386 號 (復北門市)
	臺北市重慶南路一段 61 號 (重南門市)
電　　話	(02)25006600
網　　址	三民網路書店 https://www.sanmin.com.tw
出版日期	初版一刷 2009 年 3 月
	初版十三刷 2023 年 9 月
書籍編號	S807550
Ｉ Ｓ Ｂ Ｎ	978-957-14-5160-2

三民書局

序

英語 Make Me High 系列的理想在於超越，在於創新。
這是時代的精神，也是我們出版的動力；
這是教育的目的，也是我們進步的執著。

針對英語的全球化與未來的升學趨勢，
我們設計了一系列適合普高、技高學生的英語學習書籍。

面對英語，不會徬徨不再迷惘，學習的心徹底沸騰，
心情好 High！
實戰模擬，掌握先機知己知彼，百戰不殆決勝未來，
分數更 High！

選擇優質的英語學習書籍，才能激發學習的強烈動機；
興趣盎然便不會畏懼艱難，自信心要自己大聲說出來。
本書如良師指引循循善誘，如益友相互鼓勵攜手成長。
展書輕閱，你將發現……
學習英語原來也可以這麼 High！

給讀者的話

相信多數學英文的人在其學習經驗中，多半的時間都耗在背單字、片語，或是學習文法，卻很少有時間學習寫作文。所以即使是英文學習得不錯的人，往往寫作的技能還是很欠缺。一般人的英文寫作最常見的模式就是將中文直譯為英文，寫的是長篇大論，說的是頭頭是道，殊不知完全不符合英文寫作的邏輯。當然，下場就是一碰到考試非死（零分）即重傷（低分）。所以每年學測有高達上萬人作文零分也就不足為奇了。

目前各類考試中常見的作文題型有五種：

◎有提示的自由作文

◎主題句引導作文

◎情境作文

◎書信寫作

◎看圖寫作

針對每種類型，我們加以歸納整理，在《寫作範例 100》中透過不同的主題都有詳盡的說明，包括寫作中最重要的幾點：一是抓住主題，二是時態的拿捏，三是文思布局，四是結論與主題的呼應。所以此書不僅提供各種題材的範文學習，還能進一步掌握描寫文、敘述文、說明文、應用文等不同文體的寫作要點。

感謝三民出版社編輯部同仁的用心與努力，讓此書能順利產出。最重要的是希望《寫作範例 100》一書能對英文寫作能力較薄弱的讀者有所助益。

郭慧敏

2009 年 3 月

Table of Contents

指考篇

Table of Contents

學測篇

1 The Subject I Like Best in School

提示 求學的過程中你最喜歡的科目是哪一科？請以 "The Subject I Like Best in School" 為題寫一篇短文，說明你喜歡該科的原因，並提出你個人的學習心得。

Sample 範文

¹The subject I like best in school is English. ²I like English because it is <u>not only</u> a good tool for entertainment <u>but also</u> an important means of communication. ³For example, when I watch English movies or listen to English songs, I can understand what the lines mean, and this makes me happy. ⁴I have also made many friends from around the world on the Internet. ⁵We all communicate in English, the international language.

⁶Because I like English very much, I pay attention in all of my English classes, and I memorize as many English words as possible. ⁷In addition, I expose myself to this language <u>as much as I can</u> by reading English novels and listening to radio programs in English. ⁸Learning English was not easy at first, but because of my perseverance and interest, I am happy to say that my English keeps on getting better and better every day.

Writing Analysis 寫作精靈

主題： 在學校裡最喜歡的科目

時態： 除非文中提及過去發生的事 (如本文第八句的前半段)，否則談論目前的現況一般多用現在簡單式。

鋪陳： 1. 主旨句：直接點明在學校最喜歡的科目是英文。(Sentence 1)

2. 細節發展：先說明喜歡英文的原因，再接著提出學習英文的心得。(Sentence 2～7)

　(1)原因：英文不只是個能幫助達到娛樂效果的工具，也是重要的溝通方式。

　　舉例：A. 看英文電影或聽英文歌曲時能了解其台詞或歌詞，能帶來樂趣。

　　　　　B. 透過網際網路，使用英文結交世界各地的朋友。

　(2)學習心得：上每堂英文課都很專心、儘可能多背單字、藉由閱讀英文小說及收聽英語廣播節目儘量多接觸它。

3. 結論句：因為有毅力和興趣，現在表現愈來愈好，覺得很開心。(Sentence 8)

注意： 段落寫作中第一個句子通常是主旨句 (Topic Sentence)，接下來的數個句子是支持細節 (Supporting Details)。支持句的主要功能有三：(1)詳述細節、(2)解釋原因、(3)舉例說明，如範文第一段先解釋最喜歡英文的原因 (because...)，接著再舉例說明 (For example, ...)。

🌿 Language Focus 語法重點

I. not only...but also... 不僅⋯還⋯

例 It is not only a good tool for entertainment but also an important means of communication.

例 Mr. Wu is not only a dancer but also a famous writer.

1. 此句型為一平行結構，特別留意 not only 和 but also 後面所接的修飾語詞性須相同。
   - This room is not only dark but also damp. (兩者均為形容詞)
2. not only 可以挪到句首作倒裝句，此時須留意主詞和助動詞的位置是顛倒的。寫作時可以視情況適度運用此種倒裝句，以增加文句的變化性。
   - Not only did Jane offer the emotional support, but she also volunteered to pay Jim's massive medical bills.

📝 TRY IT!

1. Susan 不僅是個才華洋溢的鋼琴家，她還是個有名的畫家。

_____

2. 林先生不僅會說流利的英文，他還精通西班牙文。

_____

II. as + adv. + as one can 盡某人所能⋯

例 I expose myself to this language as much as I can by reading English novels and listening to radio programs in English.

例 Although John ran as fast as he could, he still failed to catch the bus.

1. 此片語一般置於動詞之後，主詞前後須相同。此外，此片語用法等同於 as + adv. + as possible。
   - I will reply to your e-mail as soon as I can.
     → I will reply to your e-mail as soon as possible.
2. 受詞為名詞的情況下，一樣適用於此用法，列法為 as many N(P) as one can/possible，範文中的 I memorize as many English words as possible 即為此例。

📝 TRY IT!

1. 此外，我以每天放學後沿著河邊慢跑，週末時到山區健行的方式，盡可能接觸大自然。

_____

2. 高中生在空閒時間應盡可能多閱讀中文經典著作。

_____

主題寫作　看圖寫作　簡函寫作

3

2 If I Were a Big Movie Star

提示 人常會有不同的幻想，想像自己是國際巨星、運動明星、大企業家、國王、將軍或作家。你可曾有過奇特的想法？寫一篇短文，題目為 "If I Were a(n) _____"，寫出你的幻想，並寫出你想要做的事情有哪些。

Sample 範文

¹If I were a big movie star, I would lead a fantastic life that would be very different from the lives of normal people. ²My life would not <u>consist of</u> only exams and the daily routine. ³Instead, it would be so amazing that each day would be like a new adventure. ⁴I would travel to many different places around the world to shoot movies, and this would give me the chance to experience various cultures. ⁵At the same time, I would show the world the beauty of Taiwanese culture through my movies. ⁶Besides working hard in show business, I would try to create my own products, such as a perfume or a clothing brand, and set new fashion trends. ⁷I would never be just a stereotypical movie star, seeking fame and wealth. ⁸In fact, I would use the money I made from the sales of my own products to improve the lives of people in Africa. ⁹Oh, <u>how wonderful my life would be</u>, if I were a movie star!

Writing Analysis 寫作精靈

主題：想像自己成為名人後所做的事

時態：提出想像的人物角色扮演及其所從事的活動均為假設的狀況，故須使用假設語氣。

鋪陳：1. 主旨句：如果我是有名的電影明星，我的生活會多彩多姿，與平凡人的生活截然不同。

　　　　　(Sentence 1)

　　　　2. 細節發展：先說明幻想中的生活會是如何，再進一步闡述自己會想做哪些事。

　　　　　(Sentence 2～8)

　　　　　⑴幻想中的生活：A. 到世界各地拍電影，並藉此體驗不同的文化。

　　　　　　　　　　　　　B. 透過自己的電影，向全世界介紹台灣文化。

　　　　　⑵想做的事：A. 創造新產品如香水或服飾，藉此開創流行趨勢。

　　　　　　　　　　　B. 利用商品盈餘來幫助非洲的居民。

　　　　3. 結論句：如果我是電影明星的話，我的生活是多麼地美好啊！(Sentence 9)

注意：1. 凡是針對目前的事實提出假設的狀況，可用句型 If + S + were/V-ed..., S + would/should/could/might + V....。

　　　　2. 若針對過去事實提出假設狀況，句型用 If + S + had V-en..., S + would/should/could/might + have V-en....。

✐ Language Focus 語法重點

I. A consist of B　　A 由 B 所組成

例 My life would not consist of only exams and the daily routine.

例 The committee consists of ten doctors and fifteen scientists.

1. 在本用法中，A 表示整體，B 表示組成的個體。
2. 本用法可以改寫成 A be made up of B。
- My life would not consist of only exams and the daily routine.
  → My life would not be made up of only exams and the daily routine.

✐ TRY IT!

1. 這個班級是由 21 個男孩和 24 個女孩所組成的。

_____

2. 這份餐點是由一杯果汁、一個漢堡以及一些薯條所組成的。

_____

II. How + adj. + S + be!　　…真是…

例 Oh, how wonderful my life would be, if I were a movie star!

例 How interesting the show is!

1. 此用法為感嘆句，用來表示讚嘆、驚嘆等強烈的情感，後面一般都使用驚嘆號，而非句點。
2. 感嘆句的主詞與動詞可以省略，更能呈現情感的強烈。
- How wonderful! We can go shopping together!
3. what 所引導的驚嘆句和此用法沒有太大的差別，重點在於 how 後面接的是形容詞，what 後面接的則是名詞。句型列法為 What (+ a/an) + adj. + N (+ S + be/V)!。
- What big eyes Alice has!
- What a cute baby!

✐ TRY IT!

1. 謝謝你提醒我要關燈。你真體貼！

_____

2. 真可惜！你昨晚應該來參加派對的。

_____

主題寫作　看圖寫作　簡函寫作

3 One Thing I've Learned from My Teacher

提示 在我們生活周遭的人們，如父親、母親、師長或朋友，對我們都有某種程度的影響。請以 "One Thing I've Learned from _____" 為題寫一篇短文，敘述他或她曾經做過令你印象最深刻的一件事，並說明這件事對你的影響。

Sample 範文

¹Ms. Klark is my English teacher, and I have learned a lot from her. ²For example, last summer, my class planned a trip to Kenting. ³I couldn't join in because the trip would be too expensive for my parents to afford. ⁴Ms. Klark heard about this and called me into her office. ⁵She took out NT$2,000 and said that she hoped I would be able to join my class on the trip. ⁶It was very touching, but I didn't take the money. ⁷I told her that although I did want to go with my classmates to Kenting, I didn't want to spend someone else's money. ⁸Ms. Klark understood what I meant, but told me that if she could give me a hand in this case, then I could learn to help someone else in the future. ⁹In the end, I accepted the money, and Ms. Klark's words have always remained in my mind. ¹⁰I learned a valuable lesson from my teacher: if I can, I will help those who are in need, and I will ask for nothing in return.

Writing Analysis 寫作精靈

主題：從老師身上學到的人生智慧

時態：敘述一段過去發生的事件，應用過去簡單式。

鋪陳： 1. 主旨句：Klark 小姐是我的英文老師，我從她身上學到很多東西。(Sentence 1)

2. 細節發展：一則故事的描述基本上是由 who、when、why、where 以及 what happened 等五個疑問詞的答案所連結而成的。(Sentence 2～9)

   (1)人物：我和 Klark 小姐

   (2)時間：去年夏天

   (3)發生原因：因為我父母無法負擔到墾丁旅遊的費用，因此我無法參加班遊。

   (4)地點：Klark 小姐的辦公室

   (5)發生經過：Klark 小姐想要給我兩千元，一剛開始我並沒有接受，不過她讓我理解人要互相幫忙的道理。

3. 結論句：我從老師身上學到，當我有能力時，我會幫助那些有需要的人，並不求回報。
   (Sentence 10)

注意：若文中提到對個人影響的篇幅不長，可以接在故事後，以段落寫作的方式呈現；但是若對個人的影響無法用一句話結束，則可以自成一段，結合成一篇短文。

🌿 Language Focus 語法重點

I. for example　舉例來說

例 I have learned a lot from her. For example, last summer, my class planned a trip to Kenting.

例 My family usually dine out on special occasions. For example, last Friday night, we had a dinner at the Friday's to celebrate my grandpa's 80th birthday.

---

1. 寫作時，欲讓讀者了解自己的陳述或主張，舉例說明是最清楚的表達方式，此時便可使用 for example 此詞語。for instance 的用法及意義和 for example 相同，兩者可以替換。

2. 若欲將某人或某事物直接作為例子，用法為 take sth./sb. for example。

• Fruit can be made into different dishes. Take pumpkins for example. There are pumpkin stews, pumpkin pies, pumpkin soup, etc.

✏️ TRY IT!

1. 王太太對她的孩子很嚴格。舉例來說，她要求他們在學校要拿到好成績。

_____

2. Jason 不只是個好爸爸，他也是個好老師。舉例來說，他下班後總是很有耐心地教他女兒數學。

_____

II. those who...　凡是⋯的人

例 If I can, I will help those who are in need, and I will ask for nothing in return.

例 God helps those who help themselves.

---

those who 即等於 the people who，是指「一群具備相同特質的人」。who 在此為關係代名詞，those 可作主詞或受詞使用。

• Those who love others will be loved, too. (those 為主詞)

• I admire those who work hard to realize their dreams. (those 為 admire 的受詞)

✏️ TRY IT!

1. 凡是夠成熟的人都應能分辨對錯。

_____

2. 凡是未滿十八歲的人都不能駕駛車輛。

_____

主題寫作

看圖寫作

簡函寫作

7

4 Whenever I Feel Lonely

提示 我們的心情常因周遭環境或自身心境改變而有所不同，而人們也不喜歡寂寞的感覺。請以 "Whenever I Feel Lonely" 為題，寫一篇短文闡述一種你排遣寂寞的方法。

Sample 範文

[1]As a teenager, I sometimes think that no one can share in my happiness and sorrow. [2]Even though many people around me are chatting and laughing, I still feel alone in the crowd.

[3]However, whenever I feel lonely, I just contact my best friend by phone or by e-mail. [4]By doing so, I can recall the time we spent together in school, when we shared many things and I found happiness. [5]In my memories, we were always carefree, and we did many things together, such as singing songs on the way home from school, playing basketball on the basketball court, and reading comic books at my house. [6]We always had a lot to talk about. [7]Sometimes I didn't even need to speak, and my friend would know exactly what I was going to say. [8]Looking back on those good old days, I am always comforted, and I don't feel lonely anymore.

Writing Analysis 寫作精靈

主題：說明自己如何排遣寂寞

時態：目前的心態用現在簡單式，過去的回憶用過去簡單式來敘述。

鋪陳：1. 主旨句：每當我感到寂寞的時候，我總是會以電話或電子郵件的方式和我最要好的朋友聯絡。(Sentence 3)

2. 細節發展：和最要好的朋友聯絡，總讓我回想起過往美好的時光。(Sentence 4～7)

   (1)每天無憂無慮　　(2)和好朋友一起做很多事　　(3)有很多話可以聊

3. 結論句：回首往日美好時光，我總是感到慰藉，不再感到寂寞。(Sentence 8)

注意：1. 題目的主詞是 I，所提到的一定是自己的生活經驗，切忌用他人 (you/she/he) 的生活經驗，以免離題。

2. 主旨句不一定落在短文的第一句，有可能出現在前言的後面。例如範文一開始先簡單描述作者本身的狀況，讓讀者稍有認識，隨後才切入主題。

3. 談到如何排遣孤獨或寂寞，應舉出數項例子，通常以三項為宜，文章的內容才夠豐富。

🖋 Language Focus 語法重點

(I. even though　雖然，儘管)

例 <u>Even though</u> many people around me are chatting and laughing, I still feel alone in the crowd.

例 I didn't get upset <u>even though</u> Jason declined my invitation.

> 1. even though 的用法等於 although，均為附屬連接詞。even though 後面所接的子句通常為一件事實，讓主要子句的內容看起來更令人驚訝。
> • Even though Ken is a ten-year-old child, he can speak four languages.
> 2. even though 所接的附屬子句可放在句首，也可以放在主要子句之後。
> 3. even if 有「即使，就算…」的意思，和 even though 解釋不同，切記不可混用。

🖋 TRY IT!

1. 雖然沒有人贊同我的想法，我不覺得氣餒。

_____

2. 即使我當時說實話，我想也沒有人會相信我。

_____

(II. such as　譬如，例如)

例 We did many things together, <u>such as</u> singing songs on the way home from school, playing basketball on the basketball court, and reading comic books at my house.

例 Jason is good at playing sports <u>such as</u> baseball, basketball, and golf.

> 1. 若要舉例說明前文的陳述，可以用 such as 連接兩者。一般來說，such as 後面的例子須為名詞，若為動作時，則須以動名詞 (V-ing) 的方式呈現，如範文中的 singing、playing 以及 reading。
> 2. such...as... 是指「像…這樣的…」，such 後面接總稱，而 as 後面則接例子。
> • I have been to many countries, <u>such as</u> Japan, Korea, and Singapore.
> → I have been to <u>such</u> countries <u>as</u> Japan, Korea, and Singapore.

🖋 TRY IT!

1. 在暑假期間，我從事許多戶外活動，例如衝浪、健行以及釣魚。

_____

2. 我喜歡閱讀像《老人與海》這類的勵志小說。

_____

主題寫作

看圖寫作

簡函寫作

5 How the Weather Affects My Mood

提示 請以 "How the Weather Influences My Moods" 為題，寫一篇短文談一談不同的天氣對你的心情所造成的影響。

Sample 範文

¹ The weather plays an important role in my life because it really affects my mood. ²Whenever it is cloudy, the gloomy skies always make me feel that something bad is going to happen. ³Rainy days are no better than cloudy ones. ⁴Raindrops pouring down from the sky make me feel as if I'm going to drown, and I can't concentrate on what I should be doing. ⁵When it's rainy, I feel that I can't do anything but try to survive.

⁶On the contrary, the beautiful sunshine is like water in the desert, showing me that there's still hope in the world. ⁷I can feel the energy of the sun entering my body, giving me the strength to face the challenges of the day. ⁸It goes without saying that I like sunny days rather than cloudy or rainy days, since sunny days always put me in a good mood.

Writing Analysis 寫作精靈

主題：說明天氣對心情有何影響

時態：說明現況宜用現在簡單式。

鋪陳：1. 主旨句：因為天氣能影響我的心情，所以它在我的生活中扮演重要的角色。
　　　　(Sentence 1)
　　　2. 細節發展：說明不同的天氣型態會如何影響我的心情。(Sentence 2～7)
　　　　(1)造成壞心情的天氣：A. 陰霾的天色讓我感覺有不好的事要發生。
　　　　　　　　　　　　　　　　B. 傾盆大雨就像要淹沒我一般，讓我無法專心做事。
　　　　(2)引發好心情的天氣：陽光就像沙漠中的甘泉，給我希望和力量，讓我能面對挑戰。
　　　3. 結論句：因為晴天帶給我好心情，所以我喜歡晴天勝過陰天或雨天。(Sentence 8)

注意：1. 寫作時，可敘述天氣所帶來的好影響與壞影響，藉此產生對比的效果，讓文章更具張力。舉範文為例，先提不好的影響，再利用轉折詞 on the contrary 敘述好的影響。
　　　2. 在結論句的部份，可利用片語 it goes without saying 說明自己比較喜歡哪種天氣型態，並再次強調 weather 與 my mood 的關聯性。
　　　3. 善用譬喻法使讀者更容易了解自己所做的陳述，如範文中的 the beautiful sunshine is like water in the desert。因此平日可多背一些優美的譬喻句子或片語，如：Life is like a journey.、brave like a lion、as sly as a fox 或 as thin as a toothpick 等。

🌱 **Language Focus** 語法重點

I. can't do anything but + V   除了…之外什麼也不能做，只能…

例 When it's rainy, I feel that I can't do anything but try to survive.

例 Being held at gunpoint, this girl couldn't do anything but tremble with fear.

1. 寫作時，若提到「唯一能做的事為…」，即可善用本語法。另外，本語法亦可與 can do nothing but + V 代換。
   - When it's rainy, I feel that I can do nothing but try to survive.
2. can't choose but + V 亦有「除了…之外什麼也不能做」的意思。
   - Because the boss ran out of his money, he couldn't choose but abandon this project.

✏️ **TRY IT!**

1. 隨著期末考即將來臨，我不得不在家用功讀書。

_____

2. 在那場意外之後，他的父母除了接受殘酷的事實之外，什麼也不能做。

_____

II. A rather than B   是 A 而不是 B

例 I like sunny days rather than cloudy or rainy days, since sunny days always put me in a good mood.

例 In my view, Napoleon is a true hero rather than a loser.

1. 本用法強調的重點是 A，而不是 B；此外，rather than 通常可以用 instead of 替換。
2. 在寫作時，與其僅提出肯定的陳述，不如運用 rather than 帶出否定的陳述，一方面可以強化對比的效果，另一方面更可以善用句型，達到文章變化的效果。

✏️ **TRY IT!**

1. 不言而喻，最吸引我的是鄉村生活的儉樸，而不是都市的繁榮景況。

_____

2. 我喜愛的是古典音樂而非鄉村音樂。

_____

主題寫作

看圖寫作

簡函寫作

11

6 The Most Unbearable Thing

提示 以 "The Most Unbearable Thing" 為題，描述一件你最無法忍受的事情，並舉例說明。

Sample 範文

[1]To me, the thing I find most unbearable is that people don't care about being punctual. [2]I think being late not only wastes others' time, but also shows a lack of respect for those who are kept waiting. [3]It's sad to say, but people take it for granted that others will wait for them. [4]They make up excuses for being late and don't realize that they have made others upset or even angry.

[5]Take one of my experiences for example. [6]Once, a club I was a member of decided to hold a meeting at 8:30 on a Saturday morning. [7]I arrived on time, but everyone else showed up after 9:00 a.m. [8]By the time the meeting finally began, I had already been there for more than an hour. [9]I was so upset that I started to yell at others. [10]From then on, all my friends knew better than to be late for an appointment with me. [11]I think everyone should keep Shakespeare's advice in mind: "Better three hours too soon than a minute too late."

Writing Analysis 寫作精靈

主題：說明自己最無法忍受的事

時態：第一段談論自己的想法，用現在簡單式；第二段談過去的經驗則用過去簡單式。

鋪陳：1. 主旨句：對我而言，不守時是我最無法忍受的事。(Sentence 1)

　　　2. 細節發展：內容分為兩段，第一段先說明遲到所帶來的困擾，以及常遲到的人的行為與心態為何。第二段則介紹自己的經驗。(Sentence 2～10)

　　　　(1) 自己的看法：A. 遲到會浪費他人的時間，而且也不尊重等待的人。

　　　　　　　　　　　B. 這種人認為別人的等待是理所當然的，而且會為遲到找藉口。

　　　　(2)自身經驗：朋友未準時出席社團的會議，我發怒之後，從此朋友不敢再遲到了

　　　3. 結論句：我們都應該謹記莎士比亞的建議：早到三小時總比遲到一分鐘好。
　　　　(Sentence 11)

注意：1. 只要題目是談論個人「最…的經驗」，第一句即可利用 To me, the thing I find most...is that... 直接點題。

　　　2. 如果題目的提示字要求舉例說明，提出自身的經驗是非常具有說服力的。可適時運用 Take one of my experiences for example. 這類的用語。

　　　3. 說明原因時，建議至少提出二項理由，會遠比單一理由更具說服力。例如：

■ I don't want to live in big cities. One reason is that the cost of living is higher there, and the other is that people there seem cold and indifferent.

Language Focus 語法重點

I. take it for granted + that-clause   視…為理所當然

例 It's sad to say, but people take it for granted that others will wait for them.

例 Some men take it for granted that their wives should do housework and take care of their children.

1. 本句型是由 take sth./sb. for granted 延伸而來的，take 之後的 it 為虛受詞，代替後面的 that 子句，注意 that 子句不可直接放在 take 之後。
2. 寫作時若提到一般人對某項事物抱持不同的態度，有人認真看待，有人不以為意，則可以用片語 take sth. seriously 以及 take sth. lightly 來表達。
• Not everyone takes honesty seriously. In fact, many people take it lightly.

TRY IT!

1. 我認為好國民遵守法律是理所當然的。

_____

2. 令我驚訝的是，他把我們應該幫助他擺脫困境視為是理所當然的事。

_____

II. know better than to V...   不致於糊塗到…，明白事理而不致於…

例 From then on, all my friends knew better than to be late for an appointment with me.

例 Cindy knows better than to give all her savings to a stranger.

1. know better 表示「能清楚分辨，能明白事理」。
2. to 後面接原形動詞，是指不會也不該去做的事情。

TRY IT!

1. 拿我自己做例子，我不會糊塗到在考試時作弊。

_____

2. 爸爸認真看待法律。他絕不會糊塗到去搶銀行。

_____

7 Something Interesting About a Classmate of Mine

提示 請以 "Something Interesting about a Classmate of Mine" 為題，寫出有關你一位同學的一件趣事。這位同學可以是你任何時期的同學，例如中學、小學或幼稚園的同學。【90 年學測】

Sample 範文

¹Davis is a chubby boy that I will never forget. ²I always remember the first time I met him in junior high school. ³His hair was uncombed, and he was sucking his thumb as he sat at his desk. ⁴For a thirteen-year-old boy, this was not normal behavior.

⁵Like other boys at his age, Davis was also a naughty and mischievous boy who liked to play tricks. ⁶For example, he usually made faces when our teachers turned their backs to write on the blackboard. ⁷Once, he used two pens to push open his eyelids, and then grinned at us. ⁸Suddenly, however, the teacher walked over to see why we were laughing. ⁹Davis tried so hard to hide his face that the pens slipped and almost poked himself in the eyes. ¹⁰Without Davis' funny tricks, my junior high school life would have been very dull indeed .

Writing Analysis 寫作精靈

主題：有關我同學的一件趣事

時態：描述以前的同學用過去簡單式，現在的同學可用現在簡單式；而描述以前所發生的趣事則應用過去簡單式。

鋪陳：1. 主旨句： 我永遠也忘不了 Davis 這個胖胖的男孩。(Sentence 1)
　　　2. 細節發展：第一段先描述第一次看見 Davis 的情景，第二段再講述他的一件趣事。
　　　　(Sentence 2～9)
　　　　(1)第一次看見 Davis 時，他頭髮未梳坐在桌前吸手指。
　　　　(2)發生原因：他與同齡的男孩一樣頑皮且愛惡作劇，他愛在老師轉身寫黑板時扮鬼臉。
　　　　　　發生經過：有一次他用二支筆撐開眼皮，對我們咧嘴而笑。老師冷不防地走了過來，
　　　　　　Davis 為了遮住臉，筆不小心滑下去，差點戳到眼睛。
　　　3. 結論句：若非他的趣事不斷，我的國中生活可能會很無趣。(Sentence 10)

注意：1. 寫作的重點為人物時，切記不可通篇文章都用代名詞 (he 或 she) 來稱呼主角，應該在一開始就先介紹主角的名字，其後才可以用代名詞稱呼。
　　　2. 描述某位人物時 ， 可以運用以下句型以強調其特徵與重要性 ： ...is one chubby/ interesting/... + boy/girl/man/woman that I will never forget.。

🎯 Language Focus 語法重點

I. so + adv./adj. + that-clause 如此⋯以至於⋯

例 Davis tried <u>so</u> <u>hard</u> to hide his face <u>that</u> the pens slipped and almost poked himself in the eyes.

例 Lin Chi-ling is a famous model. She is <u>so</u> attractive <u>that</u> many men want to date her.

> 1. 若前後兩個主詞 (S) 相同時，後面的 that 子句可以與 as to V... 代換。
> • Jimmy is <u>so</u> strong <u>that</u> he can lift a heavy box onto the table with ease.
>   → Jimmy is <u>so</u> strong <u>as to</u> lift a heavy box onto the table with ease.
> 2. 另外一個句型 such + N(P) + that-clause 亦解釋為「如此⋯以至於⋯」，不過 such 後面只能接名詞，不可接形容詞。
> • Tony is <u>such</u> a naughty boy <u>that</u> he is often punished by his teacher.

✏️ TRY IT!

1. 我母親如此專心致志於社區服務以至於她十分受到敬重。

_____

2. 這是一個非常有趣的笑話，以至於觀眾哄堂大笑。

_____

II. Without + N(P), S + would/could (+ not) + have + V-en.... 要不是⋯，某人 (不) 會⋯

例 Without Davis' funny tricks, my junior high school life <u>would have been</u> very dull indeed.

例 Without the stranger's timely help, I <u>would have drowned</u> in the river at that time.

> 1. 寫作中常常會提到往事，在回憶中總有一些遺憾或其他不同的想法，此時運用「與過去事實相反的假設法」就是一種好的表達方式。
> • With a computer, I collected a lot of information on the Internet. (過去的事實)
>   → Without a computer, I couldn't have collected a lot of information on the Internet.
>   (與過去事實相反的陳述)
> 2. 使用此種假設法時務必要注意動詞的時態變化。

✏️ TRY IT!

1. 要不是老師當時給我的忠告，我不會做出正確的決定。

_____

2. 若非有政府給予的經濟援助，這家公司可能已破產。

_____

8 The Most Precious Thing in My Room

提示 以 "The Most Precious Thing in My Room" 為題寫一篇英文作文，描述你的房間內一件你最珍愛的物品，同時並說明珍愛的理由。(這一件你最珍愛的物品不一定是貴重的，但對你來說卻是最有意義或是最值得紀念的。)【91 年學測】

Sample 範文

[1]The colorful beach towel hanging over my couch is the most precious thing in my room. [2]The towel always <u>makes me recall</u> the days I spent with the Case family during the summer I studied abroad.

[3]Right after I had arrived at their home, I was shown to my room by my host mother. [4]<u>The moment I stepped inside</u>, I immediately noticed a spotted beach towel on the bed. [5]There was a card on it that read, "Surprise! We're going to the beach for the Fourth of July holiday. Don't forget to bring this towel with you!" [6]I was deeply moved by the friendliness of the Case family.

[7]Now, whenever I see the towel, it reminds me of that trip to the beach and of my summer abroad. [8]The memories of the good times I shared with the Case family will never vanish as long as the towel is there, hanging over my couch.

Writing Analysis 寫作精靈

主題：我房間中最珍愛的物品

時態：談目前存在的物品用現在簡單式，說明其背後的故事用過去簡單式。

鋪陳：1. 主旨句：我房間中最珍愛的物品是掛在沙發上的一條彩色海灘用毛巾。(Sentence 1)

　　　　2. 細節鋪陳：交代完原因後，接著敘述這條毛巾的故事。(Sentence 2～7)

　　　　　(1)喜愛的原因：這條毛巾總讓我想起暑假出國遊學時與 Case 一家人共度的時光。

　　　　　(2)背後的故事：因為要去海邊度假，Case 一家人幫我準備了毛巾。

　　　　3. 結論句：只要毛巾還掛在那，與 Case 家人的快樂回憶便永不消失。(Sentence 8)

注意：寫作提示可以提供許多下筆的素材。舉本作文題目為例，所謂 precious 意為「珍貴的」，但非著重在物品價格的昂貴，因此建議所寫的物品是看似平凡，但深具意義的物品，才能打動人心。

🎯 Language Focus 語法重點

I. make + sb. + V...　　使某人…

例 The towel always <u>makes</u> <u>me</u> <u>recall</u> the days I spent with the Case family during the summer I studied abroad

例 The brilliant performance <u>made</u> <u>the audience</u> <u>scream and shout</u> for the whole night.

1. make 為使役動詞，屬於不完全及物動詞，同類的動詞尚有 let 和 have。make 後面接受詞時，因語意仍不完整，故受詞後面須再加上補語，以補充說明受詞。
2. 本處的補語為不帶 to 的不定詞，其他補語形式尚有形容詞與過去分詞等。
   - What the student had said made his teacher <u>furious</u>. (形容詞當補語)
   - I found it difficult to make myself <u>heard</u> in this noisy restaurant. (過去分詞當補語)

🖊 TRY IT!

1. 這張明信片使我想到澳洲，那是我第一次騎馬的地方。

_____

2. 聽輕柔的音樂令我很睏。

_____

II. The moment + S + V, ...　　一…就…

例 <u>The moment I stepped inside</u>, I immediately noticed a spotted beach towel on the bed.

例 <u>The moment the principal came in the classroom</u>, all of the students stopped talking.

1. 敘述故事時，若欲強調兩個動作幾乎同時發生，可活用以下兩個句型：
   The moment (that) + S +V..., ...
   As soon as + S + V..., ...
2. 若所發生的動作是依序產生，而非同時進行，則可用 and 連接。
   - After breakfast, Judy took her bag, put on her shoes, and walked out of her house.

🖊 TRY IT!

1. 老師一打開盒子，一隻青蛙跳出來，把她嚇得半死。

_____

2. 我一下飛機就看到幾名警察站在空橋上。

_____

主題寫作

看圖寫作

簡函寫作

9 If I Had Magical Powers, I Would...

提示 英國女作家 J. K. Rowling 所著的 Harry Potter 暢銷套書滿足了許多人的想像力，請以 "If I Had Magical Powers, I Would..." 為題，想像如果你也像書中人物一樣具有魔力，你最想做的改變是什麼？為什麼？

Sample 範文

¹If I had magical powers, I would help my friend Jenny and all the other blind people in the world regain their vision, so they could see this beautiful world again. ²When I was in elementary school, Jenny was my best friend. ³We spent most of our free time together. ⁴We were always having fun and sharing secrets. ⁵Unfortunately, one day Jenny was in a car accident and lost her sight. ⁶From then on, she was full of self-pity, refusing to talk to anyone, including me. ⁷I was so sad to lose such a good friend. ⁸It broke my heart when I imagined her living in total darkness, having to endure so many inconveniences, and being unable to appreciate the beauty of the world. ⁹Therefore, if I had magical powers to do anything, I would make Jenny and all the other blind people able to see again, and she would be my best friend once more.

Writing Analysis 寫作精靈

主題： 在假設自己擁有魔力的情況下，會做些什麼事情

時態： 假設自己是個有魔力的人，故使用與現在事實相反的假設法。

鋪陳： 1. 主旨句：如果我有魔力，我會幫助好友 Jenny 及其他的盲人，讓他們重見光明，再度看見這個美麗的世界。(Sentence 1)

    2. 細節發展：先說明原因，再講述內心的感受。(Sentence 2～8)

      (1)背景：小學時，Jenny 是我最要好的朋友。我們大部分空閒的時間都會待在一起玩樂和分享祕密。

      (2)原因：Jenny 不幸在一次車禍中喪失視力，從此她自怨自艾不與人說話，我也因此失去她這位好友。

      (2)內心感受：想像 Jenny 活在黑暗中必須忍受生活的諸多不便，也不能欣賞世界的美麗，我心都碎了。

    3. 結論句：改寫主旨句，並說出希望 Jenny 能再度成為自己的知己。(Sentence 9)

注意： 構思主旨句時，可以從寫作提示中取材。本文的主旨句即從提示字 If I had magical powers, I would... 所延伸而來的。

Language Focus 語法重點

I. S + V₁..., V₂-ing.... ...並且... (分詞構句)

例 From then on, she was full of self-pity, refusing to talk to anyone, including me.

例 Mary's smile is like an oasis in the desert, giving me the strength to go on.

> 本句型為一分詞構句，是由兩個主詞相同，並以連接詞 and 連接的子句簡化而來的。簡化的方式為省略連接詞與第二個子句的主詞，並將動詞改為現在分詞 (V-ing)。
>
> • Daisy sat down next to me, and she told me that she had broken up with Jim.
>   → Daisy sat down next to me, telling me that she had broken up with Jim.

TRY IT!

1. Sue 傳給我一張紙條，且要求我傳給 Jenny。

_____

2. 我上週打電話給父母，告知他們這個週末我不回家了。

_____

II. including N 包括...在內

例 From then on, she was full of self-pity, refusing to talk to anyone, including me.

例 Eight people, including two children, were injured in the explosion.

> 1. including 為介系詞，作「包括...在內」解釋。除了 including 之外，形容詞 included 亦有相同的意思，但須注意 included 一定要放在名詞後面。
> • My mother had cleaned up the whole house, including the kitchen.
>   → My mother had cleaned up the whole house, the kitchen included.
> 2. including 的相反詞為 except，指「除了...以外」。
> • Everyone went to the party except me.

TRY IT!

1. 媽媽氣炸了，對著客廳中的每個人大吼，包括爸爸在內。

_____

2. 許多的廢紙，包括我的期末報告，被丟到附近的垃圾場。

_____

主題寫作

看圖寫作

簡函寫作

10 Earthquakes

提示 以 "Earthquakes" 為題，敘述你個人遇到地震的經驗，並說明平日應有的準備和地震時的正確應變。

Sample 範文

¹Taiwan has experienced many earthquakes, and the most violent has been the 921 earthquake. ²On the night of this earthquake, I was asleep when a sudden strong shake woke me up. ³I could feel everything in my room swaying back and forth. ⁴Some glass bottles even fell from the cabinet and crashed to the floor. ⁵Then I heard my father telling us to calm down. ⁶He also told us to take shelter under a table and to protect our heads with our pillows. ⁷After the shaking had stopped, my family and I decided to go outside. ⁸However, because we couldn't find a flashlight, we walked very carefully and slowly so that we wouldn't step on any broken glass.

⁹From this experience, I learned that we should always keep a flashlight at hand and that glass bottles should not be stored on high shelves. ¹⁰Most important of all, I learned that when there is an earthquake, we should take shelter under a piece of strong furniture.

Writing Analysis 寫作精靈

主題：談論地震經驗與因應措施

時態：談論所遭遇過的地震經驗應用過去簡單式。

鋪陳： 1. 主旨句：臺灣經歷過多場地震，其中又以 921 大地震最為嚴重。(Sentence 1)

2. 細節發展：第一段敘述自己經歷 921 地震的情景與避難過程，第二段接著說明平日應有的準備工作與地震發生時的應變方法。(Sentence 2～9)

   (1) A. 地震情景：強震使我從睡夢中驚醒，房間裡的物品前後搖晃著，甚至有一些玻璃瓶從櫥櫃上掉落，摔得粉碎。

      B. 避難過程：我和家人躲在桌下，以枕頭保護頭部。等到搖晃停止，我們決定離開屋子；但因為找不到手電筒，只好小心地走，以免踩到玻璃碎片。

   (2) 得到的教訓：平時便要準備好手電筒，玻璃瓶不應放置在高處。

3. 結論句：最重要的是，地震發生時，要躲在堅固的傢俱下方。(Sentence 10)

注意： 1. 有些事件在人的一生中會發生很多次，建議只要提出一次印象最深刻的即可。如範文便僅說明 921 地震發生時的景況。

2. 學習到事前應有的防範，往往都是慘痛經驗之後所得到的教訓，因此第二段可以用記取教訓來代替說理。

🕹 **Language Focus** 語法重點

> **I. has/have + V-en** 現在完成式

例 Taiwan has experienced many earthquakes, and the most violent has been the 921 earthquake.

例 These students have studied English for ten years.

> 現在完成式一般用來表示「從過去到現在事情持續地發生，或截至目前為止的事實狀況」。
> 現在完成式常與 since 所連接的子句搭配使用。
> • I have never seen Ted since he moved to New York three months ago.

✏ TRY IT!

1. 自從那場意外發生後，這個小女孩從未和任何人交談，包括她的家人。

_____

2. Laurence 已經去過許多國家旅行，而印度是他最喜愛的國家。

_____

> **II. From this experience, I learned that...and that....** 從這次的經驗中，我學到…和…

例 From this experience, I learned that we should always keep a flashlight at hand and that glass bottles should not be stored on high shelves.

例 From this experience, I learned that speeding is very dangerous and that I should be more careful when driving.

> 1. 從過往的經驗中學習到的教訓，要用過去式 I learned that...。
> 2. 在主要子句中，第一個 that 可以省略，但第二個 that 不可省略。因作文屬於正式書寫文字，故建議兩個 that 都應保留。
> 3. 寫作時，描述完自己的經驗後，可以適當運用此句型，說明自己從中得到什麼樣的教訓。

✏ TRY IT!

1. 從這次的經驗中，我學會了對陌生人應該要有禮貌，也學到自己不應該對他們說冒犯的話。

_____

2. 最重要的是，從這次的經驗中，我學會了金錢不是萬能的，也學到了家人是世界上最珍貴的事物。

_____

主題寫作　看圖寫作　簡函寫作

11 Making Up with My Sister

提示 人與人之間難免會有誤會或爭執，請以 "Making Up with _____" 為題，描述過去與他人一次誤會或爭吵的經驗，並簡述經過、解決方式以及這次事件帶來的影響。

Sample 範文

¹It's normal for sisters to have fights, and my sister and I are no exception. ²Last week, my sister was angry with me just because I had used her MP3 player without asking her permission first.

³"You should be more generous. I just borrowed it for a little while," I shouted at her. ⁴My sister became furious, and we started to argue very loudly. ⁵Finally, our mother became fed up with our fighting and tried to settle our differences. ⁶She said that we shouldn't be so childish and get into a dispute over such a trivial thing, and that we should be more tolerant of each other. ⁷After a few minutes, I calmed down and realized that I had acted irrationally. ⁸Therefore, I apologized to my sister, and we decided to make up.

⁹After this incident, my sister and I reached an agreement to respect each other's belongings and, at the same time, learn to share.

Writing Analysis 寫作精靈

主題：描述和姐姐吵架的經驗和說明如何解決此次紛爭

時態：舉例說明過去的吵架經驗應用過去簡單式。

鋪陳： 1. 主旨句：姐妹間會發生爭執是正常的，我姐姐和我也不例外。(Sentence 1)

2. 細節發展：首先交待爭吵起因，接著敘述爭吵經過與解決方式。(Sentence 2～8)

    (1)人物：我和姐姐

    (2)時間：上個星期

    (3)發生原因：我擅用姊姊的 MP3 播放器，因此她就生我的氣。

    (4)發生經過：我對姐姐大吼，說她是小氣鬼，這讓她更生氣了，我們倆越吵越兇。

    (5)解決方式：後來媽媽告訴我們不應該這麼幼稚，更不應該為了一點小事而爭吵，我們應該要互相包容。

    (6)結果：冷靜之後，我了解到自己太不理性了，便向姐姐道歉，我們決定要和好。

3. 結論句：事後，我和姐姐達成協議，要尊重彼此的物品，並學習分享。(Sentence 9)

注意： 1. 構思主旨句時，可善用寫作提示中的說明文字。例如本範文的主旨句是以說明文字的第一行中文來點題。

2. 只要是談論會發生在一般人身上的事情，主旨句都可借用範文中的句型：It's normal...,

and... is no exception.

Language Focus 語法重點

I. S + be + no exception 某人也不例外

例 It's normal for sisters to have fights, and <u>my sister and I</u> <u>are</u> no exception.

例 All of the students ought to follow school regulations, and <u>you</u> <u>are</u> <u>no exception</u>.

談到某人也不例外時，表示前面一定有實例的陳述，所以可用連接詞 and 連結二個子句；此外，實例的陳述多半為一般現象，故多用現在簡單式：S_1 + V... (實例), and S_2 + is/are + no exception.

TRY IT!

1. 人們遇到困難時會感到挫折是正常的，而我也不例外。

_____

2. 多數年輕人渴望賺大錢，我想你也不例外。

_____

II. at the same time 同時

例 After this incident, my sister and I reached an agreement to respect each other's belongings and, <u>at the same time</u>, learn to share.

例 The teacher asked us to listen carefully to the CD and, <u>at the same time</u>, take notes in the margin.

1. 欲強調二個動作同時發生，可運用片語 at the same time 連接此兩個動作。除了置於句中之外，此片語亦可放在句末。
 • I'm surprised that the girl looked sad and cheerful <u>at the same time</u>.
2. 假使二個動作是一前一後發生的話，則可改用時間副詞 then。
 • He took a shower, and <u>then</u> had dinner.

TRY IT!

1. 在這次事件之後，John 和 Mary 達成尊重彼此的協議，同時學習控制脾氣。

_____

2. 你最好不要一邊做數學習題，一邊聽音樂。

_____

主題寫作

看圖寫作

簡函寫作

12 A Visit to a Doctor

提示 人生病的時候都應該去看醫生，才能早日痊癒。請以 "A Visit to a Doctor" 為題寫一篇短文，敘述你個人看醫生的經驗，並說明你對醫生這個行業的看法。

Sample 範文

¹Last month, I felt unwell one night, so my parents took me to the emergency room. ²When we got there, the nurse noticed that I had a high fever, so I was quickly taken to a doctor. ³Though it was late at night, the doctor not only examined me carefully, but he also explained in detail what kind of medicine he would prescribe me. ⁴In addition, he kindly told my parents not to worry. ⁵My parents and I felt a lot better after hearing his explanation, and I did get better after taking the medicine. ⁶From this experience, I learned that being a good doctor is not easy. ⁷Great medical skill is not the only thing a good doctor needs; he or she also must have a kind heart and care about the patients.

Writing Analysis 寫作精靈

主題：描述自己就醫的經驗

時態：描述經驗用過去簡單式，發表自己的看法宜用現在簡單式。

鋪陳： 1. 主旨句：上個月的某一天晚上，我感到不舒服，所以父母送我到急診室。(Sentence 1)

　　　 2. 細節鋪陳：先敘述此次看醫生的經過，最後發表感想。(Sentence 2～6)

　　　　(1)身體狀況：因為護士發現我發高燒，因此趕緊請醫生來診療。

　　　　(2)診療過程：雖然已經很晚了，但醫生仍仔細幫我檢查，並詳細說明他會開哪些藥物給我。

　　　　(3)結果：父母和我聽了醫生的話，感覺好多了；此外，我服藥之後真的病情好轉。

　　　 3. 結論句：一個好醫師不只要具備好醫術，他／她更應有好心腸，並能妥善照顧病患。
　　　 (Sentence 7)

注意： 1. 大考中的寫作部分常要應試者談論自身的經驗，因此有一些主題備受青睞，例如 An Unforgettable Experience 或是 A Person I Wanted to Thank Most，都是很常見的題目，建議可以背下來。考試時，如須自行構思文章題目，便可妥善利用。

　　　 2. 欲談論從過去的經驗中得到那些啟示或教訓，可善用第十回所教的句型：From this experience/event, I learned that....。

🌿 **Language Focus** 語法重點

I. Though S + V..., S + V....   雖然…，…

例 Though it was late at night, the doctor not only examined me carefully, but he also explained in detail what kind of medicine he would prescribe me.

例 Though Paula lost her legs in a car accident, she never gave up her dream of becoming a lawyer.

1. though 和 although 都是連接詞，絕不可再與其他連接詞如 but 連用。though 與 but 同時出現在一個完整的句子中，是多數學生寫作時常犯的錯誤，務必隨時注意。
   - Though the family were very poor, but they lived a happy life. (×)
   - Though the family were very poor, they lived a happy life. (○)
2. though 除了放在句首外，亦可置於句中。

✏ TRY IT!

1. 雖然媽媽下班後十分疲憊，她不僅煮晚餐給我吃，還耐心地指導我做功課。

_____

2. 雖然下著滂沱大雨，人群站著不動，並且大聲唱國歌。

_____

II. V-ing...is...   動名詞片語作主詞的用法

例 From this experience, I learned that being a good doctor is not easy.

例 Having enthusiasm for everything is one of his characteristics.

1. 欲以一個動作當句子的主詞時，該動作的一般動詞應轉換成動名詞形式 (V-ing)，而 be 動詞 (am/is/are/was/were) 則一律轉換成 being。
2. 動名詞片語作主詞時，該句應用單數形的動詞。在某些情況下，本句型亦可改寫為以虛主詞 it 開頭的句子。
   - Being a good doctor is not easy.
     → It is not easy to be a good doctor. (it 為虛主詞，真正的主詞為 to be a good doctor)

✏ TRY IT!

1. 從此次的經驗中，我學到光靠運氣是不夠的。

_____

2. 想當一個好父親需要有責任感以及保護孩子的決心。

_____

13 A Special Day to Remember

提示 以 "A Special Day to Remember" 為題，敘述一個特別的日子，並說明這個日子為什麼會特別令你印象深刻。

Sample 範文

[1]To most people, April Fools' Day is a day to play tricks on friends. [2]For me, however, it is not a day for fun, but a day full of sadness.

[3]Four years ago on April Fools' Day, I was like most students who were planning to play tricks on others. [4]While I was enthusiastically talking with my friends about how to play these tricks, I received a phone call from my older sister. [5]In a serious tone, she told me that our grandfather had just passed away in the hospital. [6]Who would believe such news on April Fools' Day? [7]In a playful tone, I answered, "Hey, sis! That's not funny at all. Try something more believable!"

[8]To my surprise, my sister started weeping and said, "I wish that God were just playing a joke on us, but Grandpa really is gone." [9]After hanging up, I sat still in my couch and started to sob. [10]It should be a day to have fun; however, what I really got was sorrow and pain. [11]From that day on, April Fools' Day became a day that I would never forget.

Writing Analysis 寫作精靈

主題：敘述既特別又令人印象深刻的一天

時態：回憶過去的事件用過去簡單式。

鋪陳：1. 主旨句：對我來說，愚人節並不好玩，而是充滿憂傷的日子。(Sentence 2)

2. 細節鋪陳：先敘述愚人節當天所發生的事，最後解釋為何這個節日讓自己永生難忘。
   (Sentence 3～10)

   (1)當天的經過：在四年前的愚人節，當我躍躍欲試地和朋友們分享我的整人計劃，姐姐打電話給我，並以嚴肅的口吻跟我說爺爺剛去世的消息。起初我並不相信，甚至開玩笑地要姐姐講些更容易讓人相信的事。直到姐姐哭著證實這件事，我才相信。掛上電話，我開始啜泣。

   (2)印象深刻的原因：愚人節本是歡樂的日子，但我得到的卻是哀痛。

3. 結論句：自從那天之後，愚人節變成我永生難忘的日子。(Sentence 11)

注意：1. 寫作中可以直接敘述記憶中一個特別的日子，但為了突顯 special 這個字，可以先說出多數人的想法，再進一步說出與眾不同的想法，以吸引讀者的目光。如範文中提到一般人認為愚人節是很有趣的日子，但是對作者來說是充滿悲傷的日子。

2. 回首往事時，文句中常帶有後悔的意味，或是希望事情根本沒有發生過，此時便可善用假設法，如 I wish that... (但願…)。

🖋 Language Focus 語法重點

I. ...not...but...   不是…而是…

例 For me, however, it is not a day for fun, but a day full of sadness.

例 To many kids, pumpkins are not just for eating but for making jack-o'-lanterns.

1. 使用 not A but B 時，須注意 A 和 B 應是對等的字詞。
   • For me, however, it is not a day for fun, but a day full of sadness. (not 和 but 後面都是接名詞片語)
2. 此句型強調的是 B，而不是 A。

🖋 TRY IT!

1. 對觀眾而言，這個電視節目不是教育性的而是娛樂性的。

_____

2. 對我來說，Smith 先生不是個野心勃勃的政客，而是個偉大的教育家。

_____

II. S wish that + S + were/V-ed/Aux. V....   但願或希望…

例 To my surprise, my sister started weeping and said, "I wish that God were just playing a joke on us, but Grandpa really is dead."

例 The ugly girl wishes that she could be a supermodel.

本句型為「與現在事實相反的假設語氣」，用來形容「不太可能或是根本不可能會發生的狀況」。注意子句的動詞時態為過去簡單式，若動詞前方有助動詞 (Aux.)，亦須以過去式呈現；be 動詞則一律以 were 呈現，此為美式用法。

🖋 TRY IT!

1. 我希望這些謠言正漸漸地消失。不過，這似乎是不可能的事。

_____

2. 但願我擁有一個能讓我回到過去的時光機器。

_____

14 A Perfect Day

提示 以 "A Perfect Day" 為題，描述你心中美好的一天會有那些景象，並說明你會如何度過這樣的一天。文章內容可以是依據自身經驗，也可以完全憑自己的想像；而文章時式以過去簡單式或未來式均可。

Sample 範文

[1]For me, last Saturday is a perfect day. [2]My parents decided to take me out for a picnic because they wanted me to take a break from studying for the College Entrance Exam. [3]On that morning, jumping out of bed, I hurried into the bathroom as my mom shouted my name downstairs. [4]I quickly got dressed, and then I rushed into the kitchen, grabbed my breakfast, and dashed into my dad's car.

[5]My father and mother talked about their jobs as we drove, and then I shared my thoughts about the subject I planned to major in at university. [6]As our car headed into the mountains, it suddenly started to rain very hard. [7]Sadly, we had no choice but to turn back home as a result. [8]Though the rain spoiled our trip, I still considered that day to be a perfect day, since I had a wonderful time with my parents.

Writing Analysis 寫作精靈

主題：描述美好的一天

時態：講述過去的經驗應用過去簡單式。

鋪陳：1. 主旨句：對我來說，上週六是美好的一天。(Sentence 1)

　　　　2. 細節發展：先敘述當天的景況，最後再解釋為何這天是美好的一天。(Sentence 2～7)

　　　　　　(1)人物：爸媽和我

　　　　　　(2)計劃的活動：野餐

　　　　　　(3)活動原因：在我努力準備入學考試的期間，父母希望能讓我休息一下。

　　　　　　(4)過程：A. 在家中：起床梳洗後，我跑進廚房，抓了我的早餐再衝進爸爸的車裡。

　　　　　　　　　　　B. 在車上：爸媽聊起他們的工作，接著我也和他們分享上大學後，我打算主修某個科目的想法。

　　　　　　(5)轉折：當車子進入山區，突然下起大雨。我們沒有別的選擇，只好折返回家。

　　　　3. 結論句：雖然大雨毀了我們的出遊，但因為我和父母仍共度美好的時光，所以我還是認為那天是美好的一天。(Sentence 8)

注意：1. 對寫作比較沒有把握的考生，建議選擇敘述自己的親身經歷。這是因為對於發生在自己身上的事，會比較容易發揮。此外，若能善加安排時間、地點、人物及故事情節等四個重要元素，文章會更生動。

2. 美好的一天不一定是事事如意，也可以有少許的遺憾。

🎯 Language Focus 語法重點

I. because 因為

例 My parents decided to take me out for a picnic <u>because</u> they wanted me to take a break from studying for the College Entrance Exam.

例 Ms. Wang is popular with her students <u>because</u> she is patient and thoughtful.

1. because 為一連接詞，解釋為「因為」，後面接原因句。而 so 亦為一連接詞，解釋為「所以」，後面接結果句。須注意兩者不可同時出現在同一個句子中。
2. 在寫作時若需要多次解釋原因的話，建議除了用 because 之外，since 或 as 也是不錯的選擇，適當變換用字可增加文章的變化性。

✏ **TRY IT!**

1. 當時是星期五的早晨，我很緊張，因為我有數學考試。

_____

2. 他匆匆忙忙趕回家去，因為他的家人在等他。

_____

II. consider A (to be) B 認為 A 是 B

例 Though the rain spoiled our trip, I still <u>considered</u> <u>that day</u> <u>(to be)</u> <u>a perfect day</u>, since I had a wonderful time with my parents.

例 Frankly speaking, I <u>consider</u> <u>my mother</u> (to be) <u>the best parent</u> in the world.

consider A (to be) B = regard A as B = view A as B   認為 A 是 B
- A nuclear bomb has long been <u>considered</u> (to be) a destructive weapon.
  → A nuclear bomb has long been <u>regarded</u> as a destructive weapon.
  → A nuclear bomb has long been <u>viewed</u> as a destructive weapon.

✏ **TRY IT!**

1. 即使我成績不好，媽媽仍然認為我是個好女孩。

_____

2. 在他成功解決這場危機之後，鎮上的人都認為他是個英雄。

_____

主題寫作

看圖寫作

簡函寫作

15 My Best English Class Ever

提示 請以 "My Best English Class Ever" 為題，描述從小到大你上過最充實而令你印象深刻的一堂英文課。

Sample 範文

¹Whenever I hear the song "Hero," I always recall the best English class that I ever had in senior high school. ²My junior year was a hard year for me because I not only got poor grades in every subject, but I also had trouble getting along with my classmates. ³This really made me feel worthless.

⁴One day, our English teacher played the song "Hero" for us. ⁵Our teacher explained that a person should have faith in himself or herself because there is a hero living inside each one of us. ⁶This hero will help us find the right way and allow us to handle our frustrations. ⁷She then shared with us her experience of gaining a friend's trust with sincerity. ⁸At that moment, her words and the lyrics of the song made me feel fresh and new. ⁹I felt encouraged, and from then on I had the strength to do what I believed was right. ¹⁰This class helped me overcome the difficulties I was encountering. ¹¹Needless to say, that English class will remain in my mind forever.

Writing Analysis 寫作精靈

主題：我上過最棒的一堂英文課

時態：回憶課堂中的美好人事物用過去簡單式。

鋪陳：1. 主旨句：每當我聽到《英雄》這首歌，我總會想起我在高中上過最棒的一堂英文課。
　　　(Sentence 1)

　　　2. 細節發展：第一段先稍微說明一下自己當時的處境，第二段接著描述這堂英文課，以及自己從中得到什麼幫助及啟示。(Sentence 2～10)

　　　(1)原先處境：我高一時成績不但很差，和同學也處不好。當時覺得自己一點價值也沒有。

　　　(2)課堂經過：有一天，老師在課堂上播放一首英文歌《英雄》。她解說這首歌的內容與意境，藉此鼓勵我們要對自己有信心。同時老師也與我們分享她如何以誠摯的心贏得朋友的信任。

　　　(3)我的收穫：這堂課讓我受到鼓勵，也幫助我解決當時我所遭遇到的困難。

　　　3. 結論句：不用說，那堂英文課會永遠留存在我心中。(Sentence 11)

注意：考量到大考應試時間是有限制的，因此在描寫最棒的一堂英文課時，要盡量避免交代流水帳，建議要從五十分鐘的課堂時間，以濃縮或是擷取精華片段的方式來描述。如範文

是以一首英文歌點題，進而說明這首歌和老師的一席話給了作者什麼樣的幫助。

🎯 Language Focus 語法重點

I. There be + N + V-ing.... 有…

例 Our teacher explained that a person should have faith in himself or herself because there is a hero living inside each one of us.

例 Every Saturday afternoon, there are many children flying kites in this park.

> 1. 本用法中的 be 動詞單複數形是由後方的名詞所決定，假如該名詞為單數形，則搭配單數形的 be 動詞；若該名詞為複數形，則搭配複數形的 be 動詞。
> 2. 本用法很多時候都是以地方副詞結尾，表示「在某個地方有…」的意思。
> • There are several boys playing basketball in the court.

✏ TRY IT!

1. 有幾個警衛站在這間銀行前面。

_____

2. 即使在我眼前有很多阻礙，我仍不放棄我的夢想。

_____

II. Needless to say, S + V.... 不用說…

例 Needless to say, that English class will remain in my mind forever.

例 Jacky is considerate and generous. Needless to say, he will be popular with these girls.

> 1. 此片語用來強調後方的子句是所有人都認可的陳述，與主要子句之間以逗號隔開。
> 2. 此片語除了可以用於結論句外，也可使用於主旨句。
> • Needless to say, everyone has a dream, and I am no exception. (談夢想)

✏ TRY IT!

1. 不用說，它是我所看過最棒的電影之一。

_____

2. 不用說，中國菜受到許多西方人的喜愛，因為它們非常美味。

_____

16 My Experience in Learning Ballet

提示 任何人都有過學習某種才藝、語言或知識的經驗，請以 "My Experience in Learning _____" 為題，寫一篇英文短文說明學習的經過及遭遇的難題。

Sample 範文

[1]As far as I am concerned, I don't view my experience in learning ballet as a good memory. [2]Instead, it was the biggest nightmare of my childhood. [3]My mother, a dance teacher, set a high standard for me. [4]Under her supervision, I had to practice almost every day. [5]I would stretch, raise my legs high, and spin and jump in my toe shoes. [6]If I wanted to take a break, my mother would criticize me for a lack of persistence. [7]Gradually, I lost interest in ballet and decided to quit. [8]My mother was angry, and we had a fight. [9]I could understand her high expectations of me, but I told her that I would never become a good dancer like her.

[10]Now, whenever I see my tutu in the corner of my closet, the unhappy memory of learning ballet always comes to mind. [11]Maybe someday I will find something else I really enjoy learning.

Writing Analysis 寫作精靈

主題：談學芭蕾舞的經驗

時態：談論經驗用過去簡單式。

鋪陳：1. 主旨句：對我來說，我不認為學芭蕾舞是一段美好的回憶。(Sentence 1)

　　　　2. 細節發展：先敘述學芭蕾舞的過程，並說明為何學芭蕾舞會成為童年夢魘，最後描述長大後的心態。(Sentence 2～10)

　　　　　(1)人物介紹：我的母親是一個舞蹈老師，她對我的期望很高。

　　　　　(2)學習過程：我幾乎每天都要練習芭蕾舞，練習內容包括拉筋、抬腿以及用腳尖旋轉跳躍；若是我想休息，媽媽就會批評我是個沒毅力的人。

　　　　　(3)結果：我逐漸失去學習的興趣，於是決定放棄。媽媽非常生氣，我們吵了一架，我能了解她對我有很大的期望，但我不可能成為像她一樣的舞者。

　　　　　(4)目前心態：每次看到衣櫥中的芭蕾舞裙，不愉快的回憶總會浮現心中。

　　　　3. 結論句：也許有一天我會找到自己樂於學習的事物。(Sentence 11)

注意：(1)面對半開放式的寫作題目時，要選擇自己所熟悉的事物。如本文作者選擇小時候學芭蕾舞的經驗。

　　　　(2)寫學習經驗時，除了快樂的回憶之外，也可以寫痛苦的回憶。

Language Focus 語法重點

I. As far as S + be + concerned, S + V....　依某人之見…；就某事物而言…

例 As far as I am concerned, I don't view my experience in learning ballet as a good memory.

例 As far as honesty is concerned, I am of the opinion that it is a good virtue.

> as far as S + be + concerned 通常置於句首，可依主詞不同而作兩種不同的解釋。若主詞為人，則解釋為「依某人之見」，等於 in one's opinion 的用法；若主詞為某事物，則解釋為「就某事物而言」，等於 when it comes to + N 的用法。

TRY IT!

1. 依我之見，我認為 Michael 這本最新的小說將會是一本暢銷書。

_____

2. 就這場表演而言，她的確是一個才華洋溢的音樂家。

_____

II. Instead, S + V....　反之…

例 I don't view my experience in learning ballet as a good memory. Instead, it was the biggest nightmare of my childhood.

例 They didn't go camping with us. Instead, they decided to visit the History Museum.

> 1. 在本用法中，第一個句子是沒有發生的事，而 instead 後方的句子則是有發生的事。
> 2. instead 可放在句首，亦可置於句尾，放句尾時則不用逗點隔開。
> • They didn't go camping with us. They decided to visit the History Museum instead.
> 3. 本用法亦可改寫成 Instead of + V-ing…, S + V…，注意 instead of 後面是接未發生的事。
> • Instead of going camping with us, they decided to visit the History Museum.

TRY IT!

1. 高中畢業後，Paul 沒有出國念書。反之，他在一家汽車修護廠擔任技工。

_____

2. 當父母看到我成績單上的成績很差時，他們並沒有生氣。反之，他們鼓勵我要更用功讀書。

_____

主題寫作　看圖寫作　簡函寫作

17 A Wonderful Person

提示 日常生活中，總可發現好人在我們身邊出現。他 (她) 也許是心地善良，也許是個性好，也許是很有才華，或有其他方面的優點。他 (她) 也可能是我們的親人、師長、朋友，甚至只是公車上幫我們補足車資的陌生人。請以 "A Wonderful Person" 為題，寫一篇短文描述此人及其言行。

✍ Sample 範文

¹My best friend, Amy, is a wonderful person. ²She is humorous, considerate, and optimistic. ³I never get bored when she is around because she always has funny stories that make me laugh. ⁴Her great sense of humor helps her make a lot of friends. ⁵In addition, Amy is a very thoughtful girl. ⁶She always notices any change in my mood, and is ready to offer comfort and help. ⁷Once I did very poorly on a math test and was discouraged. ⁸She came over, patted me on the back, and told me not to lose heart. ⁹She even took time to study with me until I was doing well in math. ¹⁰What impresses me most about Amy is her positive attitude. ¹¹Whatever happens, she always has a radiant smile on her face. ¹²It's amazing how she always looks on the bright side of life.

¹³I really feel lucky to have met such a wonderful person like Amy. ¹⁴She really has set a good example for me to learn from.

🧑 Writing Analysis 寫作精靈

主題：描述一個很棒的人物

時態：若描述現在的人物，形容人格特質宜用現在簡單式，舉例說明他 (她) 過去所為可用過去簡單式。

鋪陳：1. 主旨句：我最要好的朋友 Amy 是個很棒的人。(Sentence 1)

　　　　2. 細節發展：先列出 Amy 的人格特質，接著依序說明這些特質。(Sentence 2～13)

　　　　　(1)幽默：有她在我不會無聊，她總有許多有趣的故事讓我發笑。

　　　　　(2)體貼：她能為人著想，會留意我心情上的變化，隨時準備好給我安慰與協助。有一次我數學考不好，心情沮喪，她不但安慰我，並且花時間陪我讀書。

　　　　　(3)樂觀：無論發生什麼事，她臉上總是保持燦爛的笑容，永遠看到人生的光明面。

　　　　3. 結論句：Amy 的確是我學習的好榜樣。(Sentence 14)

注意：描述該人物的人格特質時，儘量以列點的方式，一方面有利於讀者理解，另一方面也可以使文章更加嚴謹。

⚘ Language Focus 語法重點

I. tell/ask + sb. + not + to V.... 告訴或要求某人不要…

例 She came over, patted me on the back, and told me not to lose heart.

例 My parents asked me not to stay at Nancy's for the night.

1. 本用法屬於間接引句，在此種用法中的動詞除了 tell 和 ask 外，尚有 warn「告誡」、advise「勸告」及 order「命令」等。此處的不定詞片語乃是受詞補語，用來補充說明，以表達完整的意思。
   • My teacher advised me to think again before making any decision.
2. 欲表達「告訴或要求別人不要做某件事」，則應在不定詞片語前加上否定副詞 not，即為範文中的用法。

✎ TRY IT!

1. 他站起來，抓住我的手，要求我不要離開。

_____

2. 警方告誡大家不要酒醉駕車。

_____

II. What impresses me most about sb./sth. + is + N(P).... 最令我印象深刻的是…

例 What impresses me most about Amy is her positive attitude.

例 What impresses me most about her brother is his talent for music.

1. 本用法中的主詞為 what impresses me most about sb./sth.，視為單數主詞，故 be 動詞應為 is。
2. what 在此為一複合關係代名詞，表示 the thing(s) that。
   • What impresses me most about Amy is her positive attitude.
   → The thing that impresses me most about Amy is her positive attitude.

✎ TRY IT!

1. 關於韓國，最令我印象深刻的是泡菜。

_____

2. 關於這位歌手，最令我印象深刻的是她優美的歌聲。

_____

主題寫作

看圖寫作

簡函寫作

_18_ An Act of Kindness

提示 人的一生中總會接受他人的幫忙，請以 "An Act of Kindness" 為題，寫一篇英文短文敘述自己所經歷過的一件善行。

Sample 範文

¹I could never forget that special day when I was in the fifth grade. ²It was hot and sunny in the morning, but just before school had finished, it began to rain heavily. ³I didn't have an umbrella with me, so I had to wait in the hall, like many of my classmates. ⁴I thought the rain might <u>let up</u> after a while, but to my disappointment, it began to rain even heavier. ⁵As time passed, many parents came to pick up their children, and in the end, I was the only one left there. ⁶My parents worked out of town, and they weren't able to come to pick me up. ⁷<u>Just as I began to feel helpless and almost burst into tears, I heard a familiar voice calling my name.</u> ⁸It was my English teacher, Ms. Chen. ⁹She asked me why I was standing in the hall and then kindly offered me a ride as soon as she had learned what an awkward situation I was in. ¹⁰I was so grateful that I was almost speechless. ¹¹I felt so thankful for Ms. Chen's generosity, especially since she had to go out of her way and drive for an extra hour just to take me home. ¹²It was probably the most enjoyable ride I have ever had.

Writing Analysis 寫作精靈

主題：描述一項善行

時態：談論先前的經驗用過去簡單式。

鋪陳：1. 主旨句：我永遠也忘不了五年級時那特別的一天。(Sentence 1)

2. 細節發展：先講述事情發生的經過，接著闡述自己的心情與感想。(Sentence 2～11)

   (1)起因：早上還是艷陽高照，想不到快放學時突然下起大雨。因為我沒有帶傘，只好像其他同學一樣站在走廊等雨停。

   (2)困境：沒想到雨越下越大，而我的父母在城外工作，沒辦法來接我。時間一分一秒過去，許多家長陸續將小孩接走，最後就只剩下我一個人。

   (3)轉折：正當我感到無助，且幾乎要嚎啕大哭時，我聽到一個熟悉的聲音呼喚我的名字，那是我的英文老師陳小姐。在她知悉我的處境之後，主動送我回家。

   (4)感想：我由衷感激，幾乎說不出話。我十分感謝老師慷慨地伸出援手，特別是因為不順路，她得額外多花一個小時開車送我回家。

3. 結論句：這也許是我有生以來最快樂的搭車記。(Sentence 12)

36

🌿 Language Focus 語法重點

I. let up 減緩，減輕

例 I thought the rain might <u>let up</u> after a while, but to my disappointment, it began to rain even heavier.

例 My headache finally <u>let up</u> after I took the pills.

> let up 為不及物動詞片語，通常解釋為「(不好的事情) 減弱或停止」。而 letup 為名詞，意思同 let up。
> • The heavy rain continued without any letup.

✍ TRY IT!

1. 我以為這個謠言也許會停止，但令我失望的是，它卻開始廣泛流傳。

_____

2. 這場雨究竟要下到何時？

_____

II. Just as S + V..., S + V.... 正當…

例 Just as I began to feel helpless and almost burst into tears, I heard a familiar voice calling my name.

例 Just as I decided to leave, Nancy showed up.

> just 本身為副詞，與連接詞 as 連用，表示「正當…，就在…的時候」。此外，just as 一般用來連接兩個同時發生，且發生時間較短的動作。

✍ TRY IT!

1. 正當她開始工作的時候，樓下的警報器響起。

_____

2. 正當我想要放棄時，媽媽激勵的話便出現在腦海中。

_____

主題寫作

看圖寫作

簡函寫作

19 When I Am New to a Place

提示 每個人初到新環境時，往往會有興奮、期待、憧憬、焦慮或恐懼等情緒。請根據個人經驗，以 "When I Am New to a Place" 為題，描述你乍到某個新環境時的感受、調適的過程以及你從中得到的心得或教訓。

Sample 範文

¹I still remember my first day of senior high school. ²I got up very early, since I was afraid that I might miss my bus. ³When I arrived at my classroom, a few students were already there chatting. ⁴To me, they looked sophisticated, and they seemed to know each other well. ⁵This made me nervous because I was a total stranger to this class. ⁶I chose a seat in the back of the room, hoping no one would notice me. ⁷However, in our first class, our English teacher asked each one of us to go to the front of the classroom and introduce ourselves. ⁸I was so nervous that I did not even know what to say. ⁹During the break, I almost burst into tears. ¹⁰Then, Annie walked over and introduced herself. ¹¹She wanted to make friends with me! ¹²With her help, I gradually began to fit in at my school. ¹³I learned from Annie that I should take the initiative next time and try to make friends with others, so that I can save myself a lot of worry and trouble.

Writing Analysis 寫作精靈

主題：描述到一個新環境的經驗與心得

時態：談過往的經驗用過去簡單式。

鋪陳：1. 主旨句：我還記得我第一天在高中上課的情景。(Sentence 1)

2. 細節發展：先敘述第一天上課的情景，接著說明如何解決困難，最後抒發心得與感想。
   (Sentence 2～12)
   (1)上課前：我怕錯過公車，所以起了個大早。到教室時，有一些學生已經在那邊聊天，他們看起來很世故，似乎很熟稔了。這令我很緊張，因為對全班來說，我就像個陌生人一樣。我選了一個後面的座位，希望沒人注意到我。
   (2)課堂上：英文老師要每個人到教室前面自我介紹，我太緊張了，甚至不知道自己該說什麼。
   (3)下課時：我幾乎快哭出來。接著 Annie 走過來並自我介紹，想跟我做朋友。在她的幫助下，我漸漸適應學校生活。

3. 結論句：從 Annie 身上，我學到應該採取主動，並試著和別人做朋友。如此一來，我才能免於許多擔心與麻煩。(Sentence 13)

🌿 Language Focus 語法重點

I. in the back of   在⋯的後方

例 I chose a seat in the back of the room, hoping no one would notice me.

例 Please put these boxes in the back of my study.

> 1. in the back of 指的是「某空間內的後方」，而 in back of 則是「某空間以外的後方」。
> - There is a refrigerator in the back of the kitchen. (冰箱在廚房內的後方)
> - There is a tall locust tree in back of my house. (樹在房子外的後方)
> 2. 另外，in the front of 是指「某空間內的前方」，而 in front of 是「某空間以外的前方」。

✏ TRY IT!

1. 我把傘遺留在你車內後方了。

_____

2. 別站在汽車後方。太危險了！

_____

II. burst into tears   突然大哭

例 During the break, I almost burst into tears.

例 Suddenly, the baby burst into tears. No one knew what was going on.

> 1. burst into sth. 有「⋯突然爆發或發生」的意思，相似的用法尚有 burst into laughter「突然大笑」以及 burst into flames「突然著火」。
> 2. 需留意 burst 為三態同形的動詞。

✏ TRY IT!

1. 當小男孩看到這條蛇時，他當場放聲大哭。

_____

2. 聽完這個笑話後，所有的觀眾哄堂大笑。

_____

主題寫作

看圖寫作

簡函寫作

20 The Most Influential Person in History

提示 讀過中外歷史,誰是你心目中最有影響力的人?請以 "The Most Influential Person in History" 為題寫一篇英文短文,介紹該人物的成就或影響,並說明你個人的看法。

Sample 範文

¹In my opinion, Confucius is the most influential person in history. ²His teachings were collected in a book called the *Analects*. ³In this book, personal and governmental morality, in particular, are emphasized. ⁴Confucius thought that people should live up to specific ethical principles. ⁵That is to say, we should follow certain codes of conduct, respect our elders, and show filial piety to our parents. ⁶We also should strive for virtue, instead of wealth. ⁷For the government of a country, Confucius argued that a leader should govern a country through the natural morality of the people, rather than by using force. ⁸In other words, if people live under strict laws, they may just try to avoid punishment and actually have no sense of shame. ⁹If they are led by virtue, then they will naturally act correctly.

¹⁰In fact, many people's lives and thoughts have been greatly affected by the teachings of Confucius, not only in Taiwan, but also in other East Asian countries. ¹¹Although Confucianism has gone through various stages of transformation and has even been criticized, it still survives today and has become more popular than ever.

Writing Analysis 寫作精靈

主題:介紹心目中最有影響力的歷史人物

時態:雖然歷史人物已經是過去式了,但從現在的觀點來探討此人的成就和影響,文章主要是用現在簡單式。

鋪陳:1. 主旨句:以我之見,孔子是歷史上最有影響力的人物。(Sentence 1)

2. 細節發展:第一段介紹孔子的成就與思想,第二段則說明孔子所帶來的影響。
   (Sentence 1~10)
   (1)《論語》收錄孔子思想,特別記載著個人與政府須遵守的道德規範。
      A. 人民須遵守行為準則、尊敬長輩以及孝順父母,更應追求美德,而非財富。
      B. 一國之主應透過自然的道德準則來治理人民,而非藉由武力。換句話說,在嚴刑峻法之下,人民會設法規避懲罰,自然沒有羞恥心;若以美德循循善誘,人民自然會循規蹈矩。
   (2)在台灣和許多東亞國家,很多人的生活與思想深受孔子的影響。

3. 結論句:雖然孔子思想歷經時代的改變並受到批判,但它仍流傳至今,且比以前更加

受歡迎。(Sentence 12)

🖋 Language Focus 語法重點

I. in particular 特別是，尤其是

例 In this book, personal and governmental morality, in particular, are emphasized.

例 This album is fantastic! I enjoy the first song in particular.

1. 一般來說，in particular 通常放在欲強調的詞語後面，如本單元的第二個例句。但如果此詞語為主詞時，則 in particular 的前後都應加上逗號隔開，如範文的用法。

2. in particular 和 especially 的意思一樣，但是位置略有不同。一般來說，especially 通常都放在欲強調的詞語之前；但是若欲強調的詞語為主詞時，則應置於其後面，前後需加上逗點隔開。

- Mr. Brown loves Chinese dishes, especially fried rice and dumplings.
- All of my sisters are beautiful. My little sister, especially, has won many beauty contests.

🖋 TRY IT!

1. 我特別喜歡 Jay 寫的那一首歌。

_____

2. 這條街上的房子都很貴，尤其是在轉角的那棟。

_____

II. a sense of + N ⋯感

例 They may just try to avoid punishment and actually have no sense of shame.

例 If you still had had a sense of shame, you wouldn't have stolen my money.

a sense of + 抽象名詞，可表示內心的感受或個人的特質，如：a sense of loyalty/humor/responsibility/satisfaction。

🖋 TRY IT!

1. 這個老師很受學生的歡迎，因為他有幽默感。

_____

2. 他被解雇的理由是沒有責任感。

_____

21 When I Am in Trouble

提示 請以 "When I Am in Trouble" 為題目，寫一篇英文作文，說明你常遇到什麼麻煩，以及你會如何應變。

Sample 範文

¹Life isn't always a bed of roses, and people all have trouble in their lives at times. ²I am no exception. ³I usually try to face difficulties because of my personality. ⁴Since I am helpful and outgoing, I often rashly promise to help others, even though they are only acquaintances. ⁵Therefore, I am usually busy keeping my promises to others, instead of studying my lessons. ⁶Sometimes, I feel upset about this and regret what I have done. ⁷When this happens, I usually pause and find a peaceful place to calm down. ⁸I then write down a list of the things that I have to do and decide which ones are more important. ⁹Of course, I will try to finish those things first, and then I can take my time to do the less important ones. ¹⁰Most importantly, I remind myself not to make any more promises without thinking about them more carefully.

Writing Analysis 寫作精靈

主題： 描述自己遇到困難時的應變

時態： 談自己遭遇困難時所持的態度與解決方法是一般現象，故用現在簡單式。

鋪陳： 1. 主旨句：人生無法事事如意，總有遭逢困難的時候。(Sentence 1)

　　　 2. 細節發展：先說明麻煩的起因，再點明是什麼，最後說明應變方法。(Sentence 2～9)

　　　　(1)起因：我愛好助人又外向，因此即使是點頭之交，我也會一股腦地答應要幫忙。

　　　　(2)麻煩：我常常忙著實現對他人的承諾，而非研讀課業。有時候我會心煩意亂，也會很後悔。

　　　　(3)解決之道：我會停下手邊的工作，找個僻靜的地方，好好冷靜一下。接著寫下待辦事件的列表，依據事情的輕重緩急來處理。

　　　 3. 結論句：最重要的是，我會提醒自己在承諾任何事之前，要先仔細思考過。(Sentence 10)

注意： 在本範文中，作者選擇不在文章一開頭就點明自己常遭遇的麻煩是什麼，而是先解釋背景原因，再告訴讀者自己的麻煩為何。這樣的方式可以引起讀者的興趣，鼓勵他們繼續往下讀。

🌿 Language Focus 語法重點

I. not always   未必

例 Life isn't always a bed of roses, and people all have trouble in their lives at times.

例 The richest are not always the happiest.

> 1. always 出現在否定句中表示部分否定，而非全盤否定。
> 2. not necessarily 也表部份否定，解釋為「不見得，不一定」。

✏️ **TRY IT!**

1. 一個有學問的人未必是賺很多錢的人。

_____

2. 好看的食物不見得好吃。

_____

II. be busy + V-ing   忙著…

例 I am usually busy keeping my promises to others, instead of studying my lessons.

例 As a career woman, my mother is always busy working and taking care of us.

> 1. 若 busy 後面是接一個動作時，要留意動詞要改為動名詞 (V-ing)。這是省略了介系詞 in 的結果。
> 2. 若 busy 後面接的是名詞或名詞片語，則以 be busy with + N 表示。如：
> - Don't bother me! I'm busy with my homework.

✏️ **TRY IT!**

1. 近來忙於工作，Miller 很少和妻子一起共進晚餐。

_____

2. 她忙著餵小孩吃飯，所以無法接電話。

_____

主題寫作

看圖寫作

簡函寫作

22 Perseverance

提示 請以 "Perseverance" 為題，描述一段你抱持著堅定的意志，下定決心一定要達成某事的過程。文章須說明過程中發生了什麼事以及最後的結果為何。

Sample 範文

¹Benjamin Franklin once said, "Energy and persistence conquer all things." ²This quote was a gift from my father when I was about to give up ballet. ³At that time, practicing ballet took a lot of time and effort. ⁴Sore legs were the only reward I received from the constant practice. ⁵It was painful for a little girl like me at the age of seven. ⁶I finally collapsed one day and burst into tears, crying that I didn't want to continue practicing anymore. ⁷After my dad shared Franklin's saying with me, I decided that I would stick with it. ⁸Because of the encouragement from my parents and my own perseverance, I kept practicing and was finally chosen as one of the supporting dancers in the ballet *Swan Lake*. ⁹When the performance was over, I felt a sense of accomplishment as I listened to the applause from the audience. ¹⁰Had I given up, I would have never been able to enjoy that moment of glory and happiness. ¹¹Ever since I first heard Franklin's saying, I have tried to live by Franklin's saying, especially during hard times.

Writing Analysis 寫作精靈

主題：談毅力

時態：論述時用現在簡單式，舉過去的例子說明則用過去簡單式。

鋪陳： 1. 主旨句：富蘭克林曾說：「力量與毅力足以戰勝一切。」 (Sentence 1)

2. 細節發展：說明過程中所遇到的困難、解決的方式與結果。(Sentence 2～10)

   (1)欲完成的事：學芭蕾舞

   (2)挫折：練芭蕾舞需要很多時間和努力，從長期練舞中得到的收穫是一雙酸痛的腿。

   (3)轉折：有一天我終於受不了了，哭喊著說我再也不要練習了。在爸爸與我分享富蘭克林說的話之後，我決定要堅持下去。

   (4)結果：有了父母的支持和個人的毅力，我入選為《天鵝湖》伴舞。表演結束時，聽著觀眾如雷的掌聲，我很有成就感。

3. 結論句：從我第一次聽到富蘭克林的名言開始，我就一直努力實踐這個名言，特別是在困境中。(Sentence 11)

注意：本範文是以成功的例子來討論 perseverance 的重要性，同學們也可以分享失敗的例子，並探討失敗的原因以及日後應如何避免類似的情況發生。

🖋 **Language Focus 語法重點**

I. be about to + V 　正要…，即將要…

例 This quote was a gift from my father when I <u>was about to</u> give up ballet.

例 I <u>was about to</u> leave when he called me.

> 1. be about to + V 表示「即將要開始做…」，需留意這個動作是還沒完成的。
> 2. be not about to + V 是指「不願意做…」。
> • Cindy was not about to go out with Jim.

🖋 **TRY IT!**

1. 火車即將離開時，他發現他的小孩不見了。

_____

2. 當其他跑者即將要衝刺時，Lauren 突然昏倒了。

_____

II. Had + S (+ not) + V-en..., S + would (+ not) + have + V-en.... 　如果當時…

例 <u>Had I given up</u>, <u>I would have never been</u> able to enjoy that moment of glory and happiness.

例 <u>Had I had</u> enough money, <u>I would have bought</u> the house.

> 1. 本句型為「與過去事實相反的假設語氣」，用來表示「目前所做的陳述是過去並未發生的事」。
> 2. 本句型是由 If + S + had (+ not) + V-en..., S + would (+ not) + have + V-en.... 演變而來的，省略 if 之後，再將 had 挪至句首，形成倒裝用法。
> 3. 此倒裝用法一般不會在口語中出現，主要是書面用法。

🖋 **TRY IT!**

1. 如果你當時再多一點努力，你一定會得到冠軍。

_____

2. 要是我昨天數學考試沒有作弊的話，我就不會被處罰了。

_____

主題寫作

看圖寫作

簡函寫作

23 My Favorite Retreat

提示 人在繁忙或苦惱的時候，常會找一個地方靜下心來，好好休息或思考，使自己放鬆。請以 "My Favorite Retreat" 為題，描述一個能讓你身心寧靜或放鬆的地方，並且說明在甚麼情況下，你會到這個地方。

Sample 範文

¹It goes without saying that everyone has his or her own favorite retreat to go to whenever he or she feels bad or sad. ²My favorite retreat is a bench under the pines by the playground at my school. ³Whenever I am in a bad mood because of a bad grade or because of a fight with my friends, I will go there to calm myself down. ⁴Sitting under the trees and looking at the other students jogging around the track, I turn my attention to them. ⁵When I see a smiling face, I smile back. ⁶When I see someone frowning, I wonder if that person needs some comfort or help. ⁷Sometimes I just stare at the beautiful sky, thinking of nothing. ⁸Strangely, my mood usually starts to improve. ⁹Though it is just a small corner of the school, my retreat has the magical power to clear my mind and make me feel better.

Writing Analysis 寫作精靈

主題：描述我最喜愛的僻靜處所

時態：說明目前的現況用現在簡單式。

鋪陳：1. 主旨句：我最喜歡的僻靜處所是操場松樹下的長板凳。(Sentence 2)

2. 細節發展：先說明什麼情況下會到這個地方，接著說明自己會在那邊做些什麼事情。

(Sentence 3～8)

(1)時機：當我因考試考不好或和朋友吵架而心情不佳時，我會去那邊讓自己平靜。

(2)行動：A. 我坐在樹下，將注意力轉移到在操場上慢跑的學生。

B. 有時候我會望著美麗的天空，想想過去美好的時光。

(3)影響：我的心情通常會開始好轉。

3. 結論句：雖然這只是校園裡的小角落，但這個處所卻擁有魔力，可以讓我心平氣和。

(Sentence 9)

🎯 Language Focus 語法重點

I. It goes without saying that S + V....　不用說，…

例 It goes without saying that everyone has his or her own favorite retreat to go to whenever he or she feels bad or sad.

例 It goes without saying that regular exercise improves health and reduces stress.

1. 先前在第十五回有介紹過 needless to say 的用法，該片語與本回的 It goes without saying that... 用法相似，可互相替代。
   • It goes without saying that we should take care of our parents when they get old.
     → Needless to say, we should take care of our parents when they get old.
2. 此句型常用於主旨句。
3. 本句型中的 that 可省略。

📝 TRY IT!

1. 不用說，敬人者人恆敬之。

_____

2. 不用說，好國民應遵守交通規則。

_____

II. I wonder if + S + V....　我猜想…是否…

例 When I see someone frowning, I wonder if that person needs some comfort or help.

例 I wonder if Mary is Sam's girlfriend.

wonder 一般可以作兩種解釋，一是文中的用法，表示心裡有疑惑，想弄明白。二是禮貌地提問或是請求，可以解釋為「請問…」，if 後面的子句時態應為過去簡單式。這種用法具有問句的涵義，但不能用問號結尾。
   • I wonder if you were free tonight.

📝 TRY IT!

1. 我猜想他是否會準時抵達餐廳。

_____

2. 請問我可不可以早點離開？

_____

主題寫作

看圖寫作

簡函寫作

24 Music Is an Important Part of Our Life

提示 請以 "Music Is an Important Part of Our Life" 為題,說明音樂 (例如古典音樂、流行歌曲、搖滾音樂等) 在生活中的重要性,並以你或他人的經驗為例,敘述音樂所帶來的好處。【92 年學測】

Sample 範文

¹No matter where we go, we can always find music around us. ²That is to say, music is an important part of our life. ³In a restaurant, for example, classical music is played to create an elegant atmosphere and to help put the diners in a good mood. ⁴In the department stores, pleasant music is used to keep customers staying inside, so that they will buy more. ⁵In a supermarket, pop music distracts us from thinking too much about the decisions we are making.

⁶In fact, music is not only of great importance, but also of benefit to us. ⁷For instance, when we are happy, we often sing or dance to the music we like. ⁸When we are sad, on the other hand, certain songs may help us overcome these feelings of sadness and cheer us up. ⁹Without music, our life would definitely be dull and boring.

Writing Analysis 寫作精靈

主題:探討音樂在生活中的重要性

時態:就事論事或陳述己見時宜用現在簡單式。

鋪陳:1. 主旨句:無論我們去哪裡,總是可以發現音樂在我們周遭。(Sentence 1)

2. 細節發展:文分兩段,第一段舉例說明音樂在生活中的重要性,第二段則說明音樂能帶來哪些好處。(Sentence 2～8)

　(1)重要性:A. 餐廳中,古典音樂創造出高雅的氣氛,讓用餐者心情愉快。

　　　　　　B. 百貨公司裡,愉悅的音樂留住顧客,讓他們消費更多。

　　　　　　C. 超市裡的流行音樂讓我們分心,做決定時不會想太多。

　(2)好處:A. 快樂時,我們常隨著喜歡的音樂哼唱或起舞。

　　　　　　B. 憂傷時,某些歌曲可以幫助我們克服憂傷並使我們振奮。

3. 結論句:沒有音樂的話,我們的生活肯定是乏味且沉悶的。(Sentence 9)

注意:音樂的類型相當廣泛,因此討論音樂在生活中的重要性時,可以說明不同的音樂類型在不同的場合分別扮演什麼樣的角色。

🎯 Language Focus 語法重點

I. no matter where S + V... 無論何處⋯

例 No matter where we go, we can always find music around us.

例 No matter where I go, I won't forget our friendship.

1. no matter where 可以與 wherever 互相代換，兩者的意思和用法是一樣的。
   - No matter where we go, we can always find music around us.
     → Wherever we go, we can always find music around us.
2. no matter 後面可接 where、what、who、when 等疑問詞，形成連接詞，可以用來連接兩個子句，解釋為「無論在何處／是什麼／是誰／何時」。

✏ TRY IT!

1. 無論鑰匙在何處，我一定會找到。

_____

2. 無論你去何處，務必要通知我們。

_____

II. distract sb. from + V-ing/N 使某人分心而無法⋯

例 In a supermarket, pop music distracts us from thinking too much about the decisions we are making.

例 Listening to the music distracts me from my work.

from 有阻止之意，後接名詞或動名詞。

✏ TRY IT!

1. 考試時，焦慮可能會讓我們分心而無法仔細思考。

_____

2. 窗外的噪音令她無法專心做瑜珈。

_____

主題寫作

看圖寫作

簡函寫作

25 How I Usually Spend My Summer Vacation

提示 請以 "How I Usually Spend My Summer Vacation" 為題目寫一篇英文作文，描述你個人在暑假常從事的活動為何。

Sample 範文

¹For many students, summer vacation is a time to relax and have fun. ²For me, it is a time to find a part-time job. ³Usually, I look for a job in a fast-food restaurant because I can learn how to serve customers and get along with my co-workers in this busy working environment. ⁴This can be a valuable experience, especially when I have to deal with unreasonable customers and figure out how to make them happy and satisfied.

⁵Moreover, a part-time job gives me a chance to understand just how difficult it is to make money. ⁶My parents still support me by paying my tuition fees and giving me an allowance. ⁷However, with the part-time job, I realize that I should treasure every dollar I earn. ⁸I believe that the working experience during my summer vacation will surely make me grow up and teach me to be more mature about money.

Writing Analysis 寫作精靈

主題：描述個人暑假常從事的活動

時態：題目中出現 usually 此頻率副詞，因此用現在簡單式說明即可。

鋪陳：1. 主旨句：對我來說，暑假是打工的時間。(Sentence 2)

    2. 細節鋪陳：第一段先說明暑假打工的原因和工作價值，第二段接著說明暑假打工的收穫。(Sentence 3~7)

      (1)打工簡介：A. 性質——通常在速食店打工。

            B. 原因——可以讓我學習如何服務顧客以及如何在繁忙的工作環境中與同事相處。

            C. 價值——這份經驗是很寶貴的，特別當我必須應付無理的顧客，還得想辦法讓他們既開心又滿意。

      (2) 打工收穫：打工讓我了解賺錢是很辛苦的，我也了解我應該珍惜賺來的每一塊錢。

    3. 結論句：我相信暑假打工的經驗一定會讓我成長，並讓我的金錢觀日趨成熟。

     (Sentence 8)

注意：在某些狀況下，文章的時態是可以從作文題目中推斷出的；例如本範文的題目中有 usually 此字，故可以推斷本篇文章應用現在簡單式。

🖋 Language Focus 語法重點

┌───┐
I. For sb., ...is a time to V.... 　 對某人來說，⋯是做⋯的時間
└───┘

例 For many students, summer vacation is a time to relax and have fun.

例 For me, it is a time to find a part-time job.

> 1. 本句的 time 是可數名詞，解釋為「一段時間」，因此主詞基本上應該都是表示時間的名詞，例如 today、this winter 等。
> 2. 在本範文中，因為第一句和第二句的主詞都是 summer vacation，故第二句的主詞可以用 it 代替。

🖉 TRY IT!

1. 對 Larry 來說，周末是陪伴家人的時間。

_____

2. 對他們來說，這是個增廣見聞的時間。

_____

┌───┐
II. how + adj. + it + is/was + to V... 　 ⋯是多麼⋯的事
└───┘

例 A part-time job gives me a chance to understand just <u>how</u> difficult <u>it is to</u> make money.

例 I just don't know <u>how</u> dangerous <u>it is to</u> leave a three-year-old child at home on his own.

> 1. 本用法也是感嘆句的表達方式之一，作為前面主要動詞的受詞。
> 2. 其中 it 是虛主詞，代替後面的不定詞片語。

🖉 TRY IT!

1. 他告訴我他與妻子住在小村莊中是多麼的愉快。

_____

2. 在日本旅遊的經驗讓我了解到學習外語是多麼的重要。

_____

主題寫作

看圖寫作

簡函寫作

26 My Proudest Achievement

提示 雖然人生難免會碰到許多挫折，可是每個人的一生當中也會有令人自豪的表現。請以 "My Proudest Achievement" 為題，描寫你人生中最得意的一件事，及對這件事的感想。

Sample 範文

[1]When it comes to proud achievements, I will never forget the gold medal I received in the lantern competition when I was an elementary school student. [2]I was not that good at art, so it was a surprise when my teacher said that I should make a lantern for the school competition.

[3]Later that day, I was sitting at my desk when an idea suddenly came into my mind. [4]I immediately started to draw a sketch of my lantern. [5]Then, I used bamboo strips to form the shape of a dragon, and I covered this frame with paper. [6]When this dragon lantern was complete, my father and I were stunned by its beautiful appearance. [7]What's more, I won the gold medal in my school's lantern competition! [8]Of course, I was very happy about winning the prize. [9]This is my proudest achievement so far because I learned that as long as I try my best, the outcome will surely be wonderful.

Writing Analysis 寫作精靈

主題：說明個人最引以為傲的成就

時態：回憶過往事件用過去簡單式。

鋪陳：1. 主旨句：講到得意的成就這件事，我永遠也不會忘記當我還是個小學生的時候，得到花燈比賽的金牌獎。(Sentence 1)

　　　2. 細節鋪陳：簡述達到這項成就的過程。(Sentence 2～8)
　　　　(1)開頭：我並不擅長美術，所以我很驚訝老師會指派我製作花燈去參加比賽。
　　　　(2)過程：當天稍晚，我坐在書桌前，突然有了靈感，便開始畫草圖。接著用竹枝做成龍的形狀，並以紙覆蓋。
　　　　(3)結果：爸爸和我看完這盞美麗的花燈後，都瞠目結舌。甚至，我還因此得到校內花燈比賽的金牌獎。

　　　3. 結論句：我從中學到了只要我盡力，結果一定是美好的，因此這是我最得意的成就。
　　　　(Sentence 9)

注意：談成就盡量不要侷限在課業上的表現，也可以寫一些特別的才藝，如本文中提到的花燈比賽便為一例。

Language Focus 語法重點

I. when it comes to + N(P)/V-ing...　提到…，談到…

例 When it comes to proud achievements, I will never forget the gold medal I received in the lantern competition when I was an elementary school student.

例 When it comes to playing tennis, Jimmy is second to none in school.

1. when it comes to... 常見於文章或段落的首句，寫作時可以善加利用。
2. 需注意 to 之後接的是名詞，若為動作要將動詞改為動名詞。
3. speaking of... 的意思與用法和 when it comes to... 相似，但 speaking of 較為口語，一般少出現於正式書寫的文字中。
   • Speaking of music, I prefer rock to country music.

TRY IT!

1. 一談到失敗，我絕無法忘記我上學期英文和數學期末考都不及格的這個事實。

2. 講到異國食物，我認為日本料理非常特別。

II. come into one's mind　某人突然想到

例 Later that day, I was sitting at my desk when an idea suddenly came into my mind.

例 When I was about to fall asleep, the scene of the accident came into my mind.

1. come into one's mind 出現在句子中時，時態通常為過去簡單式，表示已經發生了。
2. 片語 cross one's mind/come to mind/occur to sb. 的意思相似於 come into one's mind。
3. 若突然想起的事情是一個完整的句子，則可用句型 It occurred to me that + S + V....。
   • It occurred to me that he was still waiting for me in the café.

TRY IT!

1. 當他站在祭壇前，六個數字突然浮現在他腦海中。

2. 我突然想起我今天早上把傘遺留在公車上了。

27 The Most Important Role I Play in Life

提示 在一生中，每個人往往同時扮演著很多的角色。例如，你是高中生，同時也是你父母的孩子、兄弟姐妹的手足，並且也是同儕的朋友，角色不一而足。請以 "The Most Important Role I Play in Life" 為題，說明在眾多角色中，哪一個在生命中是最重要且深具影響力的，並解釋原因。

Sample 範文

¹I think that the most important role I can play in life is to be a good friend. ²I am always sincere with all of my friends, and I never lie to them. ³Whenever they are in a bad mood, I try my best to provide a shoulder for them to cry on. ⁴Whenever they need a hand, I always help out and never turn my back on them. ⁵If I find that my friends are behaving badly or foolishly, I try to stop them from making a mistake or doing something wrong. ⁶Because I have done all these things for my friends, I have not had to face any of my own problems alone, since my friends are always willing to help me in the same way that I have helped them. ⁷Therefore, I truly believe that the most important role I play in life is that of a friend.

Writing Analysis 寫作精靈

主題：討論自己在人生中扮演最重要的角色

時態：敘述對自己的看法屬於一般事實的陳述，用現在簡單式。

鋪陳：1. 主旨句：我認為自己在人生中扮演最重要的角色就是做個好朋友。(Sentence 1)

　　　　2. 細節發展：舉實例說明原因以及自己所得到的回饋。(Sentence 2～6)

　　　　　(1)原因：A. 誠懇對待朋友，絕不欺騙。

　　　　　　　　　B. 朋友心情不好時，我會盡力安慰他們。

　　　　　　　　　C. 朋友需要幫忙時，我一定會幫忙，絕不背棄。

　　　　　　　　　D. 朋友行為偏差時，我會設法阻止他們犯錯。

　　　　　(2)回饋：我不必單獨面對自己的困難，因為朋友會以同等的態度回報我。

　　　　3. 結論句：用 I truly believe that... 將主旨句重述一遍。(Sentence 7)

注意：開始寫作前，可試著擬出幾個問題，藉由自問自答的方式幫助構思。

　　　　When your friends are in a bad mood, what will you do?

　　　　When they need a hand, what will you do?

　　　　If your friends are behaving badly, what will you do?

🌿 **Language Focus** 語法重點

I. stop/keep/prevent + O + from + V-ing/N... 阻止某人或某事物…

例 If I find that my friends are behaving badly or foolishly, I try to <u>stop</u> <u>them</u> from <u>making</u> a mistake or <u>doing</u> something wrong.

例 A cup of coffee always <u>keeps</u> <u>me</u> from <u>feeling</u> sleepy in the morning.

> 1. 表示「阻止某人做某事」可用上述字詞，注意介係詞用 from，後可接動名詞或名詞。
> 2. 使用 stop 或 prevent 時，介係詞 from 可省略。
> 3. 其他動詞如 protect「保護」、ban「明令禁止」、forbid「禁止」，亦適用於此句型中。

🖊 **TRY IT!**

1. 如果我發現有人想要考試作弊，我會設法阻止他做這種錯事。

_____

2. 在皮膚上擦防曬乳液能保護它不被太陽曬傷。

_____

II. that/those 那個／那些 (用來取代前面提過的名詞)

例 Therefore, I truly believe that the most important role in life is <u>that</u> of a friend.

例 The students in Class 301 are much taller than <u>those</u> in Class 311.

> 在寫作中，為避免同一個名詞在句中重複出現，第二次出現的名詞可用 that 或 those 取代：單數名詞用 that，複數名詞則用 those。

🖊 **TRY IT!**

1. 他的說話口音跟我們的非常不同。

_____

2. 標示綠標的書比紅標的貴。

_____

主題寫作

看圖寫作

簡函寫作

28 Losing Weight

提示 以 Looking at the junk food on the table.... 開頭，描述圖中主角所經歷的事件，並提供合理的解釋與結局。

 Sample 範文

[1]Looking at the junk food on the table, Fat Tony told himself that he should stop eating it. [2]He had made up his mind to lose weight because he hated the nickname "Fat" Tony. [3]Though the junk food made his mouth water, Fat Tony resisted this temptation.

[4]Besides going on a diet, Fat Tony went to the gym every day. [5]There, he met a chubby girl who also exercised regularly. [6]They quickly became good friends. [7]Both of them wanted to get in shape, so they encouraged each other.

[8]Six months later they had both done it! [9]Fat Tony was not fat anymore, and the chubby girl had become a slender girl. [10]With happy and confident smiles on their faces, they walked out of the gym hand in hand.

 Writing Analysis 寫作精靈

人物：胖湯尼、胖妞

地點：胖湯尼家中餐桌前、健身房

時間：二〇〇六年三月到九月，約六個月。本故事描述過去發生的事，故用過去簡單式。

鋪陳：1. 描述胖湯尼下定決心減重的原因和採取的第一個減肥策略。(Sentence 1～3)

　　　　(1)原因：討厭「胖」湯尼這個綽號。　(2)策略一：節食，不吃垃圾食物。

　　　2. 說明胖湯尼所採取的第二個減肥策略及減重過程。(Sentence 4～7)

　　　　(1)策略二：每天上健身房運動。

　　　　(2)過程：胖湯尼在健身房遇見胖妞，因為志同道合，和她成為好朋友。兩人都想變苗條，所以互相鼓勵打氣。

　　　3. 半年後二人減肥成功，帶著快樂且自信的微笑，手牽手走出健身房。(Sentence 8～10)

注意：為方便敘述，可為圖中的主要人物取名。以範文為例，作者為主角取名為 Fat Tony，後續可用代名詞 he 代替。而胖妞並非主要人物，所以只用 a chubby girl 來描寫。

Language Focus 語法重點

I. V-ing..., S + V....　分詞構句

例 Looking at the junk food on the table, Fat Tony told himself that he should stop eating it.

例 Hearing the fire alarm, we all rushed out of the classroom.

1. 分詞構句是由複句簡化而來，前提是兩個子句主詞相同。本句型形成的步驟如下：
   (1)省略附屬子句的主詞及連接詞。
   (2)判定附屬子句中的動詞為主動用法，將動詞改為現在分詞 (V-ing)。
   (3)若為否定句，則將 not 移至句首。如：Not knowing what to do, the boy started to cry.。
2. 除了簡單句與複句之外，分詞構句更能增加文句的複雜度與變化性。

TRY IT!

1. 請教過醫生之後，爸爸決定要採納他的建議並戒菸。

_____

2. 感到緊張與害怕，這個小女孩連動都不敢動。

_____

II. with + O + OC　以…的狀況

例 With happy and confident smiles on their faces, they walked out of the gym hand in hand.

例 My father was sitting on the rocking chair with his eyes closed.

本用法為表示附帶狀況的獨立分詞構句，其中 OC 為受詞補語。受詞補語的形式有：
(1)介系詞片語 (即範文的用法)。
(2)形容詞 (adj.)。如：You should not take a shower with the door open.
(3)分詞 (V-ing/V-en)。
(4)副詞 (adv.)。如：Jane entered the classroom with her hat on.

TRY IT!

1. 他將額頭放在雙膝間，放聲大哭。

_____

2. 爸爸手持手電筒，衝入地下室。

_____

主題寫作

看圖寫作

簡函寫作

29 Helen Works as a Waitress...

提示 以 Helen works as a waitress... 開頭，描述圖中主角所經歷的事件，並提供合理的解釋與結局。

 **Sample 範文**

¹Helen works as a waitress in a steak house, and the owner there is notoriously mean to his employees. ²One night after work, Helen was caught in a heavy rain. ³She was soaking wet and began to feel sick. ⁴With a high fever, she phoned her boss and asked him for a sick day the next day. ⁵However, to her dismay, her boss insisted that Helen must show up for work as usual. ⁶The next day, feeling dizzy and weak, Helen could barely carry the plates of food to the tables. ⁷When she was trying to serve one customer, Helen sneezed, and the steak she was carrying fell into the customer's lap. ⁸The boss lost his temper and wanted to fire Helen on the spot. ⁹Fortunately, the kind customer accepted Helen's apology and persuaded the boss to let Helen take the rest of the day off. ¹⁰Helen hoped that she would never have a day like that again!

 Writing Analysis 寫作精靈

人物：Helen、老闆、客人

地點：牛排屋、Helen 家中

時間：某天晚上以及隔天。注意敘述過去發生的事用過去簡單式。

鋪陳：1. 敘述 Helen 的工作性質與某天下班後發生的事情。(Sentence 1～3)

　　　　　(1)工作：Helen 是牛排館的女服務生，她的老闆對待員工是出了名的壞。

　　　　　(2)發生的事：Helen 某晚下班後，因為下大雨，她渾身濕透，開始覺得不舒服。

　　　　2. 敘述 Helen 淋雨後的後續動作。(Sentence 4～5)

　　　　　(1)狀況：Helen 發著高燒打電話給老闆，表示明天想請病假。

　　　　　(2)結果：老闆堅持 Helen 一定要照常來上班。

　　　　3. 敘述 Helen 隔天上班的情景。(Sentence 6～10)

⑴突發狀況：第二天上班時，Helen 頭暈無力，幾乎無法將菜送到桌上。當她要幫一位客人上菜時，她打了個噴嚏，手上的牛排掉到客人的大腿上。

⑵老闆的反應：老闆大發雷霆，當場要解雇 Helen。

⑶圓滿結局：幸好這個好心的客人接受 Helen 的道歉，並說服老闆讓她今天休假。Helen 希望這種事情不要再發生。

注意：結局當然也可以是悲慘的，老闆責罵完 Helen 後，她便傷心落淚離開了牛排館。

🌿 Language Focus 語法重點

I. can/could barely + V　幾乎無法…

例 Helen could barely carry the plates of food to the tables.

例 Henry was so sick that he could barely get out of the bed.

1. barely 意為「幾乎不，幾乎沒有」，常與 can 連用，後接原形動詞，表示幾乎不能做該動作。
2. hardly 與 barely 的解釋與用法相同，兩者可互相代換。

✏️ TRY IT!

1. 因為我既訝異又緊張，我幾乎說不出任何話。

_____

2. 第二天早上，那個寡婦感到十分難過，她幾乎不能停止哭泣。

_____

II. lose one's temper　發脾氣　　on the spot　當場

例 The boss lost his temper and wanted to fire Helen on the spot.

例 If my father sees my report card, he will lose his temper on the spot.

1. lose one's temper 表示「發脾氣」之意；若欲表示「忍住不發脾氣」，則用片語 keep one's temper；若要表示「克制怒氣」，則用 hold back one's anger。
2. on the spot 指的是「立刻，馬上」，也就是當場就會發生之意。

✏️ TRY IT!

1. 瞪著這個頑皮的小男孩，Mrs. Li 沒有當場發脾氣，反而帶著她的兒子立刻離去。

_____

2. 那個大個子大發雷霆，當場就想要揍我。

_____

主題寫作

看圖寫作

簡函寫作

30 Last Saturday Morning...

提示 以 Last Saturday morning... 開頭，描述圖中主角所經歷的事件，並提供合理的解釋與結局。

Sample 範文

　　¹Last Saturday morning, my friend Sarah called me and invited me to play tennis with her. ²We have been playing tennis together since junior high school. ³For us, playing tennis is a good way to relax and stay in shape. ⁴After losing the first two sets, Sarah finally defeated me. ⁵She was quite excited. ⁶After our match, we both decided to get something cold because it was so hot that day. ⁷Luckily, a new store had just opened near the court. ⁸We both ordered ice cream and ate to our heart's content. ⁹It was not long after, however, that I began to feel that something was wrong with my stomach. ¹⁰It hurt so much that Sarah had to take me quickly to the hospital. ¹¹The doctor there advised me to stay away from anything but water for the rest of the day. ¹²What a miserable experience!

Writing Analysis 寫作精靈

人物：我、Sarah

地點：家裡、網球場、餐廳、醫院

時間：上星期六早上。描述已發生的事件用過去簡單式。

鋪陳：1. 描述與 Sarah 通話內容與背景介紹。(Sentence 1～3)

　　　　　⑴約會：和 Sarah 一起去打網球。

　　　　　⑵背景介紹：我們從國中開始一起打網球。網球是休閒及保持身材的好方法。

　　　　2. 描述和 Sarah 打球的經過與後續發展。(Sentence 4～6)

　　　　　⑴經過：輸了兩盤之後，Sarah 終於擊敗我，為此她變興奮的。

　　　　　⑵後續發展：因為太熱了，我們決定在比賽後，去吃點冰的東西。

　　　　3. 描述在餐廳發生的事以及結局。(Sentence 7～12)

(1)餐廳：在球場旁邊有一家新開的店。我們兩個都點了冰淇淋，盡情地享用。但不久
之後，我開始覺得胃不舒服，痛到受不了時，Sarah 只好帶我就醫。

(2)結局：醫生告誡我這一天除了水之外，什麼都不要吃，真是慘痛的經驗！

注意：通常吃壞肚子都應去醫院就醫，而醫生也會要求你不要再進食，因此這是很正常的結局。

🌿 Language Focus 語法重點

I. has/have + been + V-ing　現在完成進行式

例 We have been playing tennis together since junior high school.

例 I have been studying English for more than ten years.

1. 現在完成進行式表示「某個動作或事件從過去一直持續到現在，且未來仍可能繼續發生」。
2. 現在完成進行式通常會與 since 或 for 所引導的時間副詞連用。

✏ TRY IT!

1. 史密斯夫婦從第一個兒子出生就住在紐約。

_____

2. 從小學開始我們兩人就一起打籃球，至今已九年了。

_____

II. not long after (+ sth.)　不久之後

例 It was not long after, however, that I began to feel that something was wrong with my stomach.

例 Not long after the wedding, Leon died of cancer.

當內文已有提及明確的時間點時，not long after 可以單獨使用。
• Susan married John in 1982, and their baby was born not long after.

✏ TRY IT!

1. 吃完午餐不久之後，她開始覺得頭暈，而且想吐。

_____

2. 從大學畢業不久之後，他就找到了工作。

_____

主題寫作

看圖寫作

簡函寫作

31 One Day...

提示 以 One day... 開頭，描述圖中主角所經歷的事件，並提供合理的解釋與結局。

Sample 範文

¹One day, something unusual happened to me on my way home from school. ²I was walking through the park, enjoying a leisurely stroll. ³Then, I heard the sound of someone wailing. ⁴A little girl had fallen off her bike and scraped her knee. ⁵She was crying loudly at the sight of the blood. ⁶Rushing to her aid, I helped her stand up and did my best to comfort her. ⁷It was not long before she had stopped crying and started to smile at me gratefully. ⁸As I started to take the girl to a nearby police station, however, a woman ran toward us, waving her hands wildly. ⁹The woman began to blame me for hurting her daughter. ¹⁰It had never occurred to me that I would be mistaken for being a bad person. ¹¹Stunned and speechless, I could do nothing but just watch the woman storm away with the girl! ¹²What a strange experience!

Writing Analysis 寫作精靈

人物：我、小女孩、女孩的媽媽

地點：公園

時間：某天放學之後。描述過去發生的事用過去簡單式。

鋪陳：1. 描述放學返家途中所遇到的狀況。(Sentence 1～5)

(1)故事開頭：某天放學回家的路上，我正走在公園裡，悠閒地漫步著。

(2)突發狀況：我聽到有人嚎啕大哭，原來是一個小女孩摔下腳踏車，膝蓋擦傷，她看到血就大哭。

2. 描述自己如何幫助小女孩：我衝過去幫忙，扶她起來並盡力安慰她。不久她停止哭泣，並感激地對我笑。(Sentence 6～8)

3. 描述和小女孩媽媽之間的誤會。(Sentence 9～12)

(1)誤會：我正要帶小女孩到附近的警局時，一個女人跑過來，氣憤地責怪我傷害她的

女兒。我從未想過會被誤會是壞人。

(2)結局：錯愕到說不出話來，我只能眼睜睜看著那個女人氣呼呼地把女兒帶走。好一個奇怪的經歷！

注意：結局說明人們遭到誤解時，經常無言以對，不知該說什麼；而也有人常不分青紅皂白，就亂指責別人，不給他人說清楚的機會。文章最後以感嘆句結尾。

Language Focus 語法重點

I. It was not long before S + V.... 不久之後⋯

例 It was not long before she had stopped crying and started to smile at me gratefully.

例 It was not long before my parents came to pick me up.

1. 本句型由 before 連接兩個子句，可解釋為「在某件事情發生之前，並沒有經過多少時間」，更明確的說法就是「不久之後，某件事就發生了」。通常可用 soon 來替換。
2. 注意前後動詞時態要一致，通常都是過去簡單式或過去完成式。

TRY IT!

1. 不久之後，這個女孩停止哭泣，臂膀裡抱著泰迪熊就睡著了。

2. 不久之後，生氣的男子冷靜下來，坐下來，然後點了一根菸。

II. can/could do nothing but (+ just) + V 除了只能⋯，什麼也不能做

例 Stunned and speechless, I could do nothing but just watch the woman storm away with the girl!

例 Looking at the blue sky, I could do nothing but only sigh.

1. could do nothing 是指「什麼事都無法做」，而 but 表示「除了」之意。
2. 副詞 just 是用來強調語氣，可以與 merely 和 only 等副詞替換。
3. 本書第五回的第一個句型 can't do anything but V，與本句型的用法與意思均相同。

TRY IT!

1. 這小男孩只能看著妹妹拿走他的巧克力棒，其他什麼都不能做。

2. 發現實情後，男子什麼也不能做，只能安靜地離開。

主題寫作　看圖寫作　簡函寫作

32 One Afternoon...

提示 以 One afternoon... 開頭，描述圖中主角所經歷的事件，並提供合理的解釋與結局。

Sample 範文

¹One afternoon, Bill went into a jewelry shop to buy a birthday present for his girlfriend, Nancy. ²After much deliberation, Bill finally bought a beautiful necklace and put it in a fancy box. ³As Bill walked out of the shop and began to think about how happy Nancy would be, a man with a similar box in his hands rushed around the corner. ⁴The man bumped into Bill, and they both dropped their boxes to the sidewalk. ⁵In the chaos that followed, each of them picked up a box without checking what was inside. ⁶Bill then hurried to the park where Nancy was waiting for him. ⁷When Nancy opened her gift, Bill and Nancy were both very surprised to find that inside the box was not a necklace, but rather a tie! ⁸Instead of being praised by his girlfriend, Bill ended up being scolded for his carelessness.

Writing Analysis 寫作精靈

人物：Bill、女友 Nancy、一男子

地點：珠寶店、店外的街道上、公園

時間：某天下午。敘述過去發生的趣事用過去簡單式。

鋪陳：1. 描述 Bill 到商店購物的情景。(Sentence 1～2)

    (1)購物原因：一天下午，Bill 到珠寶店買生日禮物給女友 Nancy。

    (2)禮物：仔細斟酌後，Bill 最後買了一條美麗的項鍊，並把它裝在很漂亮的盒子裡。

  2. 描述 Bill 購物完，走出店門遇到的狀況。(Sentence 3～5)

    (1)意外：正當 Bill 走出店外，心想 Nancy 會有多麼開心時，一個手持相似盒子的男子從轉角衝出來，他撞到 Bill，兩人手中的盒子都掉在人行道上。

    (2)混亂：在接下來的一片混亂中，兩人都沒有先檢查盒子裡是什麼，就各自拿走。

  3. 描述 Bill 到公園和女友會面的情景。(Sentence 6～8)

(1)驚訝：Bill 匆匆趕到公園，Nancy 正在等他。當 Nancy 打開禮物，她和 Bill 都很驚訝裡面居然不是項鍊，而是一條領帶！

(2)結局：沒有得到女友的稱讚，Bill 的下場是因粗心而受責備。

注意：結局亦可幽默地提到 Nancy 將禮物回送給 Bill，因為下星期是 Bill 的生日，或慶祝 Bill 大學畢業。

Language Focus 語法重點

I. in the chaos that followed, ...　在接下來的一片混亂中，…

例 In the chaos that followed, each of them picked up a box without checking what was inside.

例 In the chaos that followed, the robbers and the police fought fiercely.

1. chaos 指的是「無秩序狀態」，形容場面混亂。
2. 本用法可放在兩個陳述或情節之間，當成轉折語使用，相當於講述故事時會提到的「接著…」。

TRY IT!

1. 在接下來的一陣混亂中，這個笨手笨腳的父親終於幫小嬰兒把衣服穿好。

_____

2. 在接下來的一片混亂中，我不小心把花瓶打破了。

_____

II. Instead of + V-ing..., S + ended up + V-ing....　某人沒有…，反而落得…的下場

例 Instead of being praised by his girlfriend, Bill ended up being scolded for his carelessness.

例 Instead of catching the school bus, I ended up going to school on foot.

1. 在這個用法中，end up 後面通常都是不好的結果或下場。
2. 說明「反而沒有得到預期的好結果」用 instead of + V-ing。

TRY IT!

1. Sam 沒被公開讚美，反而因為說謊而落得被解雇的下場。

_____

2. 他沒有從中獲利，反而落得破產的下場。

_____

33 Sam and His Father...

提示 以 Sam and his father... 開頭，描述圖中主角所經歷的事件，並提供合理的解釋與結局。

Sample 範文

¹Sam and his father were in a boat on a lake. ²They were chatting happily about the fishing competition that they had had the previous Saturday. ³With the fine weather and the beautiful scenery all around them, they were really enjoying themselves.

⁴All of a sudden, they found that their fishing rods were moving. ⁵They quickly pulled their rods up, but it turned out that only Sam caught a big fish, while his father just caught a broken umbrella! ⁶Sam's father was very embarrassed.

⁷As the day ended, Sam's mother began to prepare their dinner. ⁸Of course, the main dish was Sam's big fish. ⁹Besides roasted fish, they also had vegetables, fruit, and cold beer for Sam's father. ¹⁰Sam and his parents had a good time that day at the lake, and they all looked forward to returning there soon.

Writing Analysis 寫作精靈

人物：Sam、爸爸、媽媽

地點：湖邊

時間：描述過去某一天發生的故事，雖未標明時間，仍用過去簡單式。

鋪陳：1. 描述 Sam 和爸爸在湖上聊天的情景。(Sentence 1～3)

　　　(1)聊天內容：Sam 和爸爸在湖上的小船裡，開心地聊著上星期六釣魚比賽的事。

　　　(2)心情狀況：天氣很好，風景優美，他們真的很開心。

　　　2. 描述 Sam 和爸爸分別釣到什麼東西。(Sentence 4～6)

　　　(1)收獲：Sam 釣到一條大魚，而爸爸只釣到一支破傘。

　　　(2)感想：爸爸非常尷尬。

3. 描述 Sam 和爸媽在湖邊用餐的情景。(Sentence 7～10)

   (1)準備晚餐：一天結束後，Sam 的媽媽開始準備晚餐。

   (2)晚餐內容：主菜是 Sam 釣到的大魚。除了烤魚外，還有蔬果和爸爸的冰啤酒。

   (3)結局：Sam 和父母那天玩得很開心，他們期待不久能再回到那邊。

注意：在船上有兩人，所以第二段再次提到他們時，主詞用代名詞 they 即可。

Language Focus 語法重點

I. S + V..., while S + V.... ⋯，而⋯

例 Sam caught a big fish, <u>while</u> his father just caught a broken umbrella!

例 My mom was cooking in the kitchen, <u>while</u> my dad was reading in the living room.

while 為連接詞，解釋為「而；然而」，用來連接兩個子句，使其產生對比。

TRY IT!

1. Peter 已經完成家庭作業了，而我根本就還沒做。

_____

2. Mary 喜歡聽音樂會，而她男友喜歡從事戶外運動。

_____

II. look forward to + V-ing/N 期待，盼望

例 Sam and his parents had a good time that day at the lake, and they all <u>looked forward to</u> returning there soon.

例 I'm <u>looking forward to</u> the trip next weekend.

1. 注意片語 look forward to 後接名詞或動名詞。

2. look forward to 指某人懷抱著愉悅的心情「盼望」某事會發生；而 expect 是指某人「預料」某事將會或可能會發生。兩者的意思略有不同。

TRY IT!

1. 我非常期待你的新小說。何時會出版？

_____

2. 我期待明年和你一起遊巴黎。

_____

34 The CEE Is Coming

提示 以 The college entrance exam is approaching... 開頭，描述圖中主角所經歷的事件，並提供合理的解釋與結局。

Sample 範文

¹The college entrance exam is approaching, and this is the biggest challenge for a high school student like me. ²Every night, I burn the midnight oil, making every possible effort to prepare for this exam. ³Nevertheless, no matter how much I study, it always seems that I never have enough time in one day. ⁴I usually don't go to bed until two or three o'clock in the morning. ⁵Because of this lack of sleep, I often feel exhausted in class. ⁶Even worse, my eyes have started to hurt because of this eyestrain. ⁷Last week, my mother was worried about my failing eyesight, so she took me to the hospital for a checkup. ⁸The doctor told me that I needed to get glasses and have more rest. ⁹Since then, I have tried not to stay up too late. ¹⁰After all, it takes good eyesight to win this long battle!

Writing Analysis 寫作精靈

人物：我、媽媽、眼科醫生

地點：家中、教室、醫院

時間：談現在一般狀況用現在簡單式，去看眼科醫生是之前發生的事，故用過去簡單式。

鋪陳：1. 描述準備大學入學考試的情景。(Sentence 1～4)

　　　　(1)背景簡介：大學入學考試快到了，每個高中生都視其為一大挑戰。

　　　　(2)準備情況：每晚我挑燈夜戰，努力準備。不過，無論讀多少，總覺得一天的時間都不夠用。我常常到凌晨兩、三點才會就寢。

　　　2. 描述缺乏睡眠所帶來的後遺症：上課容易疲倦及眼睛疼痛。(Sentence 5～6)

　　　3. 描述就醫的情況。(Sentence 7～10)

　　　　(1)就醫：媽媽擔心我視力退化，所以帶我到醫院檢查。醫生告訴我要戴眼鏡，也需要

多休息。

　　(2)結局：自此，我設法不要熬夜到很晚。擁有好視力才能贏得這場長期戰爭。

注意：通常圖片僅提供片段資訊，為求敘事流暢且完整，提供額外資訊與故事細節是必要的。

🌿 Language Focus 語法重點

I. burn the midnight oil　熬夜　make every possible effort　盡力努力

例 Every night, I <u>burn the midnight oil</u>, <u>making every possible effort</u> to prepare for this exam.

例 Like many other seniors, I <u>burn the midnight oil</u> preparing for the tests almost every night.

例 We should <u>make every possible effort</u> to preserve the existing rain forests.

> 1. burn the midnight oil 與 stay up 都是指「熬夜」，後面接動詞時需用動名詞 (V-ing)。
> 2. make every possible effort 強調要盡可能努力做事。

✏ TRY IT!

1. 你不該挑燈夜戰，會導致睡眠不足。

　　_____

2. 只要你說好，我會盡可能努力保護你。

　　_____

II. failing eyesight　視力退化

例 My mother was worried about my <u>failing eyesight</u>, so she took me to the hospital for a checkup.

例 I cannot see clearly because of my <u>failing eyesight</u>.

> 1. fail 當動詞用時，表示衰退或變弱之意，如：His health is fast failing over time.。
> 2. 有些現在分詞被視為形容詞，帶有正在進行之意，所以 failing 表示逐漸衰弱中。

✏ TRY IT!

1. 一談到我衰弱的視力，就想到充滿教科書與考試的生活。

　　_____

2. 在逐漸昏暗的光線中，我幾乎看不到前方的任何東西。

　　_____

35 ATM

 Sample 範文

¹One day, as I was working overtime on a project, it suddenly occurred to me that I had to pay my rent that day. ²I rushed out of the office in search of an ATM. ³I quickly found one, but, since I was paying attention to the machine, I failed to notice a man sneaking around just behind me. ⁴As soon as I put the money into my handbag, this man grabbed my bag and rode a scooter away. ⁵I was so shocked that I could only yell "help" over and over again. ⁶Several people walking by heard my yelling, and they ran after the robber. ⁷Though the robber rode fast, he was still caught by these people in the end. ⁸Because of this scary incident, I have learned to stay alert whenever I use an ATM.

 Writing Analysis 寫作精靈

人物：我、搶匪、路人

地點：街上的提款機旁

時間：描述過去某一天發生的事用過去簡單式。

鋪陳：1. 描述在提款機領錢的經過。(Sentence 1～3)

　　(1)提錢原因：我某天加班趕一個計畫時，我突然想起當天要繳房租，於是我衝出辦公室找提款機。

　　(2)狀況：我很快就找到了，可是我專心操作提款機，沒注意後面有人鬼鬼祟祟。

　　2. 描述遭搶的經過。(Sentence 4～5)

　　(1)遭搶經過：我一將錢放進手提包，他馬上搶走我的包包，然後騎機車逃逸。

　　(2)應變：我嚇傻了，只能一直大喊救命。

　　3. 描述搶匪被制伏的情景。(Sentence 6～8)

　　(1)援助：幾個路人聽到我的喊叫聲，就去追搶匪。雖然他騎得很快，最後還是被抓住

了。

　　(2)教訓：因為這次恐怖事件，我學會使用提款機時要提高警覺。

注意：一件意外事件常會讓人學到教訓，所以以此為結尾是很不錯的寫法。

Language Focus 語法重點

I. over and over again　　不斷地，多次地

例 I was so shocked that I could only yell "help" over and over again.

例 I've told him over and over again, but he still made the same mistake.

> 1. over and over again 強調多次重複某個相同的動作，相似於 repeatedly。
> 2. 其中 again 可以省略。

TRY IT!

1. 王先生很健忘，他的太太必須不斷提醒他要準時服藥。

_____

2. 不斷地讀著歌詞，直到你牢記在心為止。

_____

II. people walking by　　路過的人

例 Several people walking by heard my yelling, and they ran after the robber.

例 Many people walking by noticed the beggar, but they didn't give him anything.

> 1. walking by 為簡化形容詞子句之後的分詞片語，用來修飾 people。還原之後應為 people who were walking by。
> 2. by 為一介系詞，表示「經過」之意，如 pass by 或 go by 等。
> * As I passed by Jane's house, I decided to drop in.

TRY IT!

1. 幾個經過的人都嘲笑他，令他很尷尬。

_____

2. 一個路過的女孩對著他笑，然後揮手道別。

_____

主題寫作

看圖寫作

簡函寫作

36 Since Betty's Birthday Party Is Next Sunday...

提示 以 Since Betty's birthday party is next Sunday... 開頭，描述圖中主角所經歷的事件，並提供合理的解釋與結局。

 Sample 範文

¹Since Betty's birthday party is next Sunday, Lucy decided to buy a new dress for this special occasion. ²Therefore, one day after work, Lucy went shopping at a nearby department store, hoping to find the perfect outfit. ³After browsing through the clothes racks of her favorite store, Lucy chose a blue dress that went well with her complexion. ⁴As she tried it on in the fitting room and looked at herself in the mirror, however, she discovered that someone was trying to take her bag! ⁵With a quick move, Lucy grabbed the thief tightly by the arm and made him kneel down to the ground. ⁶All of the store's staff began to cheer for Lucy, since she had helped them solve the mystery of the bags that had gone missing in the store over the past few months.

Writing Analysis 寫作精靈

人物：Lucy、賊、商店員工

地點：百貨公司試衣間

時間：預設為某一天 Lucy 下班後發生的事，用過去簡單式。

鋪陳：1. 描述 Lucy 到百貨公司買洋裝的經過。(Sentence 1～3)

　　　　(1)買洋裝的原因：因為 Betty 的生日派對在下星期天舉辦，Lucy 決定為此買件洋裝。

　　　　(2)挑選經過：一天下班後，Lucy 到附近的百貨公司，希望可以挑到一件適合的服裝。看完店內衣架上的衣服後，她選了一件藍色的洋裝，與膚色很搭。

　　　2. 描述 Lucy 遇到的狀況：在試衣間換上洋裝，正在照鏡子時，她發現有人偷拿她的包包。(Sentence 4)

　　　3. 描述 Lucy 制伏小偷的情景。(Sentence 5～6)

　　　　(1)英勇事蹟：她快步移動，緊緊抓住小偷手臂，並讓他跪在地上。

(2)結局：店內所有員工都為 Lucy 喝采，因為她解開了數月以來店內包包失竊之謎。

注意：結局也可以說這名竊賊竟然是店內員工，令大家吃驚。

Language Focus 語法重點

I. browse through 瀏覽　**go well with** 與⋯相配

例 After browsing through the clothes racks of her favorite store, Lucy chose a blue dress that went well with her complexion.

例 I quickly browsed through the list, and learned that his name was not on it.

例 I like your boots. They go well with your dress.

1. browse 指「(在商店裡) 隨意看看、瀏覽」，through 有「遍及，四處」之意，說明範文中主角是瀏覽遍所有架上的衣服。
2. go with 原指「相配，協調」之意，用副詞 well 修飾，強調非常搭配之意。

TRY IT!

1. 瀏覽書架上的書之後，我拿了一本最厚的書。

_____

2. 這件紅色上衣和這件綠色褲子不搭。

_____

II. kneel down 跪下

例 With a quick move, Lucy grabbed the thief tightly by the arm and made him kneel down to the ground.

例 Sam knelt down and started to cry.

1. kneel down 表示跪下，kneel 為不規則動詞三態變化，過去式與過去分詞為 knelt。
2. make sb. kneel down to the ground 表示使某人跪在地上；若用 kneel down on the mat 則表示跪在墊子上。

TRY IT!

1. 他推了我一把，讓我跪到地上。

_____

2. 我跪在墊子上開始禱告。

_____

37 Walking Out of the Store...

提示 以 Walking out of the store... 開頭，描述圖中主角所經歷的事件，並提供合理解釋與結局。

Sample 範文

¹Walking out of the store with some bags of snacks and food, Johnny and his mother, Mrs. Brown, started to head home. ²Mrs. Brown also bought Johnny a Coke so that he could cool off in the boiling heat outside. ³They chatted as they walked home, and then a big dog suddenly jumped toward them from out of nowhere. ⁴Mrs. Brown was so shocked that she dropped the bag she was carrying to the ground. ⁵Although Johnny had also been surprised by this "attacker," he was more amused than terrified by the cute dog. ⁶The dog seemed to be enjoying itself, as it played with Johnny and ate the food on the ground. ⁷After a while, a young man ran toward them and pulled the dog away. ⁸Offering his apologies, the man said his dog could not resist the smell of food. ⁹Later on, they found out that this man was their neighbor and that he had just moved in a few days earlier. ¹⁰Mrs. Brown and Johnny were very happy when they were invited to his place to play with his dog the next weekend.

Writing Analysis 寫作精靈

人物：Johnny 和媽媽 Mrs. Brown、狗、狗主人

地點：便利超商外面的街道上

時間：寫作提示未特別標示時間，建議敘述故事情節宜用過去簡單式。

鋪陳：1. 描述人物購物後的情景：Johnny 和媽媽走出商店，手上提著一些食物，媽媽也買了可樂給 Johnny 消暑。(Sentence 1～2)

2. 描述人物遇到狗的情景。(Sentence 3～6)

　　(1)突發狀況：當他們邊走邊聊時，一隻不知道從哪邊來的大狗，就突然跳向他們。

　　(2)人物反應：媽媽嚇得把手上的袋子掉在地上，Johnny 則被狗逗樂了。

3. 描述狗主人現身的情景。(Sentence 7～10)

　　(1)狗主人現身：過一會，一個年輕人跑過來把狗拉開並道歉，他說他的狗無法抗拒食物的味道。後來發現這個年輕人是前幾天剛搬來的鄰居。

　　(2)結局：Johnny 和媽媽很開心下週末受邀到他家和狗玩。

注意：可運用想像力創造結局。既然是新鄰居，就有可能會互邀到家中作客。

 Language Focus 語法重點

I. in the boiling heat outside　　在室外的熱浪下

例 Mrs. Brown also bought Johnny a Coke so that he could cool off <u>in the boiling heat outside</u>

例 Don't stay <u>in the boiling heat outside</u>. You might get burned.

1. 動詞 boil 解釋為「沸騰」，而 boiling 為一形容詞，字義延伸為「熾熱的」。boiling 常與 hot 連用，如 a boiling hot day「酷熱的一天」。

2. 類似用法尚有：freezing cold「極冷的」。

✏ **TRY IT!**

1. 我不想待在室外的熱浪下。咱們去附近的戲院看電影吧！

_____

2. 在一個極為寒冷的夜晚，他父親過世了。

_____

II. more adj. than adj.　　與其說是…，不如說是…

例 Although Johnny had also been surprised by this "attacker," he was <u>more amused than terrified</u> by the cute dog.

例 He is <u>more clever than wise</u>.

1. 在本句型中，第一個形容詞要比第二個更加貼切。而中文的說法則會相反。

2. 使用此句型時，無論此兩個形容詞為單音節或多音節，都應用原級，而非比較級。

✏ **TRY IT!**

1. 當我聽到好消息時，與其說我感到驚訝，不如說我開心。

_____

2. 與其說她很美麗，不如說她很有自信。

_____

38 An Unforgettable Baseball Game

提示 以 Yesterday afternoon... 開頭，描述圖中主角所經歷的事件，並提供合理的解釋與結局。

TEAM	1	2	3	4	5	6	7	8	9	R	H	E
兄弟象	0	0	3	0	1	0	0	0	0	4	9	0
興農牛	1	0	0	0	0	0	0	0		1	3	0

TEAM	1	2	3	4	5	6	7	8	9	R	H	E
兄弟象	0	0	3	0	1	0	0	0	0	4	9	1
興農牛	1	0	0	0	0	0	0	0	4	5	8	0

Sample 範文

¹Yesterday afternoon, my brother and I went to a baseball game between the Sinon Bulls, our favorite team, and the Brother Elephants. ²We first bought some snacks and soft drinks, and we then lined up to enter. ³The weather was fine, and we tried our best to cheer for the Bulls during the game. ⁴However, except for a home run in the first inning, the Bulls did not score a run in the following seven innings, which lowered our spirits. ⁵The bulls were behind by three runs in the bottom of the ninth inning, but then they tied the game and later, amazingly, won it with a home run. ⁶Believe it or not, my brother caught that lucky home-run ball. ⁷We were completely overwhelmed with joy and excitement. ⁸There is no doubt that this was the most unforgettable baseball game of my life!

Writing Analysis 寫作精靈

人物：我和哥哥

地點：棒球場

時間：預設為昨天下午，所以注意文章時態需用過去簡單式。

鋪陳：1. 描述從事的活動與事前準備。(Sentence 1～2)

    ⑴活動：我和哥哥去看興農牛和兄弟象的比賽，而興農牛是我們最喜歡的球隊。

    ⑵準備：我們買了一些零食和汽水，接著就排隊入場。

  2. 描述觀看球賽的過程。(Sentence 3～4)

    ⑴聲援：天氣很好，在比賽過程中我們盡力加油。

(2)戰況：興農牛除了在第一局以全壘打得到一分，接下來的七局都沒有得分。

3. 描述球賽的戰況逆轉。(Sentence 5～8)

(1)轉折：興農牛在九局下半落後三分，但先追平比數後，以再見全壘打贏得比賽。

(2)故事高潮：哥哥接到那顆全壘打的球，我們實在是高興極了。

(3)結局：這無疑是我有生以來最難忘的棒球賽了。

注意： 為了強調 unforgettable，故事一定要有戲劇性的轉折，因此情節安排興農牛戰成平手後，再以一支全壘打擊敗對手，同時安排主角的哥哥接到這顆球，使文章更精采。

Language Focus 語法重點

I. except for + N　除了⋯之外 (再也沒有⋯)

例 However, except for a home run in the first inning, the bulls did not score a run in the following seven innings, which lowered our spirits.

例 Except for a ragged suit, there wasn't any clothes in the closet.

except for + N 是指只有這個名詞，再也沒有其他的。

TRY IT!

1. 除了一把鏟子，沿著河岸我們什麼也沒找到。

2. 除了司機之外，公車上沒有任何人。

II. be behind by...　落後⋯分　tie the game　追平比數

例 The bulls were behind by three runs in the bottom of the ninth inning, but then they tied the game and later, amazingly, won it with a home run.

例 At first, our team was behind by two runs, but we tied the game in the seventh inning.

1. 介係詞 by 表示兩者之間的差距，behind 表示落後，若超前則用 ahead。如：

• In the end of the first half, our team was only two points ahead of the guest team.

2. tie 是指在比賽中原本落後，但追平了比數。

TRY IT!

1. 我們以三分之差落後給對手。

2. 洋基隊 (Yankees) 在第二局下半將比分追平。

39 Shopping

提示 以 Shopping was one of Maggie's favorite pastimes... 開頭，描述圖中主角所經歷的事件，並提供合理的解釋與結局。

Sample 範文

¹Shopping was one of Maggie's favorite pastimes. ²Whenever she had free time, she always went to the department stores. ³One weekend, Maggie went shopping again. ⁴She couldn't help touching all the beautiful clothes she saw, and she wanted to take all of them home. ⁵She knew it would cost much more than she could afford, but she decided to buy them with her credit cards. ⁶Later, Maggie went home happily, carrying all the new clothes in several bags. ⁷However, when she entered her room, she saw all of the clothes she had already owned scattered all over. ⁸At that moment, Maggie started to wonder if she had spent too much money on clothes. ⁹One month later, Maggie received her credit card bills. ¹⁰When she found that she had to pay 180,000 NT dollars, she was so upset that she made up her mind not to spend so much money on clothes again.

Writing Analysis 寫作精靈

人物：Maggie

地點：百貨公司、Maggie 的房間

時間：某個週末以及一個月後，都是已經過去的時間，文章時態宜用過去簡單式。

鋪陳：1. 說明 Maggie 最愛的休閒活動以及一次購物的經過。(Sentence 1～5)

　　　⑴休閒活動：購物是 Maggie 最愛的休閒活動，她有空就會去百貨公司。

　　　⑵購物經過：某個週末她又去購物，忍不住想買看到的每件漂亮衣服。雖然她知道無法負擔這些支出，但還是刷卡買了這些衣服。

　　　2. 描述 Maggie 購物返家後的景象與想法。(Sentence 6～8)

(1)景象：她開心地帶著新衣服回家，但是一進房間就看到滿地的衣服。

(2)想法：在那一刻，她懷疑自己是不是花太多錢買衣服了。

3. 描述 Maggie 收到帳單後的想法：當她發現必須繳 18 萬的卡費，她下定決心不再花這麼多錢在衣服上面。(Sentence 9～10)

注意：結局發展可以朝向 Maggie 因此得到教訓，從此不敢再亂花錢了。

Language Focus 語法重點

I. can't/cannot help + V-ing/N　忍不住…

例 She couldn't help touching all the beautiful clothes she saw.

例 A: Stop complaining! B: I can't help it!

1. can't/cannot help 後面接動作時，需留意動詞要改為動名詞 (V-ing) 的形態。

2. 本用法也可以改寫為 can't/cannot help but to V。如：

• She couldn't help but to touch all the beautiful clothes she saw.

TRY IT!

1. 每當我看見 Nancy 的時候，我總忍不住臉紅。

2. 看見爸爸受重傷的樣子，我忍不住哭了。

II. make up one's mind + (not) to V　下定決心 (不) 去…

例 She was so upset that she made up her mind not to spend so much money on clothes again.

例 He made up his mind not to be late for school again.

表示「下定決心要做某事」用片語 make up one's mind，後接不定詞；亦可改寫為 be determined to + V。若表示「下定決心不做某事」，則將否定詞 not 置於不定詞的前面。

TRY IT!

1. 為了要增進聽力，我決心從現在起每天收聽英文廣播節目。

2. 看著成績單，Jack 決心不再瞎混。

40 Drunk Driving

提示 以 Last night... 開頭，描述圖中主角們所經歷的事件，並提供合理的解釋與結局。

Sample 範文

¹Last night, Joe and his good friends from college had a party in a small bar. ²They were very happy to get together because they hadn't met since graduating from school. ³As they drank beer and wine, they began to talk excitedly about their old college days.

⁴At eleven o'clock, Joe got a call from his wife, telling him it was time for him to go home. ⁵Joe said goodbye to his friends and stumbled toward his car, not realizing that he was drunk and that he shouldn't drive.

⁶Unfortunately, ten minutes later, Joe's car hit a tree on the side of the road. ⁷Joe was lucky that he was only slightly injured. ⁸However, he didn't even know that he had been in an accident until he found he was at the police station. ⁹Having regained consciousness there, Joe was very embarrassed and promised that he would never drink and drive again.

Writing Analysis 寫作精靈

人物：Joe 和其好友

地點：小酒吧、路上、警察局

時間：故事發生在昨天晚上，文章時態應該用過去簡單式。

鋪陳：1. 描述 Joe 和朋友在酒吧裡的情景。(Sentence 1～3)

　　　(1)活動：昨晚 Joe 和大學的好朋友在酒吧聚會，因為畢業後就沒見過面了，所以他們非常開心能夠聚在一起。

　　　(2)過程：在喝酒的時候，他們興奮地聊著大學時光。

　　2. 描述聚會尾聲的情景：Joe 的太太來電要他回家，於是和朋友道別，便搖搖晃晃地走向車子，渾然不知自己喝醉了，不該開車。(Sentence 4～5)

　　3. 描述 Joe 酒後開車發生意外的過程與結局。(Sentence 6～9)

　　　(1)意外：不幸地，十分鐘後他的車就撞到路旁的樹，所幸他只有輕傷。他不醒人事，

直到發現自己人在警局，才知道出了意外。

(2)結局：恢復意識之後，Joe 很尷尬，也承諾他絕不會再酒後開車了。

注意：雖然最後一張圖的地點是在街道上，也可以接著將情節延伸到警局裡。

Language Focus 語法重點

I. S + had (+ not) + V-en...since + V-ing.... 　自從…就 (從未) …

例 They hadn't met since graduating from school.

例 He had never left his room since breaking his legs.

本句型為過去完成式，表示「在過去某一時刻之前持續的動作或狀態」。而句型列法原本為 S + had (+ not) + V-en...since + S + V-ed....，因為前後兩個子句的主詞相同，故可省略第二個子句的主詞，並將動詞改為現在分詞 (V-ing)。

TRY IT!

1. 自從搬到美國之後，他從未回去家鄉。

2. 自從目賭謀殺案，她從未開口與家人說話。

II. It is/was time + for sb. + to V.... 　是某人該…的時候了。

例 At eleven o'clock, Joe got a call from his wife, telling him it was time for him to go home.

例 It is time for children to go to bed.

1. It 在此為虛主詞，真正的主詞是句末的不定詞片語。

2. 本句型也可改寫為 It is/was time + that + S + V-ed....，須注意 that 子句中的動詞為過去式。

• It is time that children went to bed.

TRY IT!

1. 八點半時，我接到老師的電話，告訴我該用電子郵件寄作文給他了。

2. 該是我們為自由而戰的時候了！

41 Typhoon

提示 以 Last weekend... 開頭，描述圖中主角所經歷的事件，並提供合理的解釋與結局。

 Sample 範文

¹Last weekend, the Lin family couldn't go anywhere. ²They had to stay home because a typhoon was going to hit Taiwan. ³The child had never experienced such a strong typhoon before. ⁴She watched TV with her mother to find out the latest news about the typhoon, and her father checked the doors and windows of the house to make sure that they had all been securely fastened.

⁵Suddenly, there was a blackout, and they couldn't see anything. ⁶Mr. Lin found a candle and lit it. ⁷He turned on the radio and listened to the news with his family. ⁸They all hoped the typhoon would soon leave Taiwan.

⁹On Monday, the violent typhoon was gone. ¹⁰The Lin family went outside, and they were shocked to find that broken branches had fallen on the roof of their car and that there was garbage all over the streets. ¹¹However, they were glad that the whole family were safe after the terrible typhoon.

 Writing Analysis 寫作精靈

人物：林家人 (爸爸、媽媽、小女孩)

地點：家裡、街上

時間：預設為上個週末，所以動詞時態用過去簡單式。

鋪陳：1. 描述林家人在颱風來襲時，躲在家裡的狀況。(Sentence 1～4)

　　　　(1)原因：上周末林家人哪都沒去，因為有颱風侵襲台灣，所以他們得待在家裡。

　　　　(2)活動：小女孩和媽媽一起看颱風的最新消息，爸爸則檢查門窗是否關緊。

　　　2. 描述停電時的情況與應變：(Sentence 5～8)

　　　　(1)突發狀況：突然間停電了，什麼都看不見。

　　　　(2)應變：林先生點起蠟燭，打開收音機，和家人一起聽新聞，希望颱風可以趕快離開。

3. 描述颱風過後的情形。(Sentence 9～11)

    (1)街景：林家人看到街景很震驚，樹枝壓在他們的車頂上，街上到處都是垃圾。

    (2)結論：他們很高興全家人都安然無恙地度過這場可怕的颱風。

注意：颱風與地震屬於台灣常見天災，可多背誦與這主題相關的字詞。

Language Focus 語法重點

I. make sure (that) S + V...　確認…

例 Her father checked the doors and windows of the house to <u>make sure</u> that they had all been securely fastened.

例 Call Tom to <u>make sure</u> that he will show up on time.

> 1. make sure 後面可以加子句，表示要確定的事，that 可省略。
>
> 2. make sure 之後亦可加不定詞片語，如：Make sure to lock the door.。

✎ TRY IT!

1. 睡覺之前我檢查所有的插頭，確認都已經拔掉了。

_____

2. 打電話給 David 以確認他已經安全抵達目的地。

_____

II. turn on...　打開…

例 He <u>turned on</u> the radio and listened to the news with his family.

例 Let's <u>turn on</u> the TV to watch the show.

> 1. turn on 是指用按鈕或轉盤等方式使機器或電器用品開始運轉，常用在收音機、電視、電燈、電腦等物件上。
>
> 2. 相反詞為 turn off，指關掉該機器或電器用品。

✎ TRY IT!

1. 因為房間很暗，他把燈打開。

_____

2. 別忘了把爐子關掉。

_____

主題寫作

看圖寫作

簡函寫作

42 A Stray Dog

提示 以 Late one night, Lisa... 開頭，描述圖中主角所經歷的事件，並提供合理的解釋與結局。

Sample 範文

¹Late one night, Lisa was on her way home. ²She was riding her scooter and didn't notice a stray dog in front of her, and she accidentally hit it. ³The dog was injured, and it howled in pain. ⁴At first, Lisa panicked, but she calmed down and immediately took the dog to the vet.

⁵Luckily, the dog wasn't seriously hurt. ⁶The vet told Lisa that with good care, the dog would recover in a week. ⁷On hearing it, Lisa felt relieved, and she decided to take the dog home. ⁸Lisa took good care of the dog, and the dog seemed to like her. ⁹Lisa was happy to see the dog recover and decided to keep it.

¹⁰Now, they often play frisbee together in the yard happily. ¹¹The dog is no longer a poor stray dog but Lisa's beloved pet.

Writing Analysis 寫作精靈

人物：Lisa、一隻流浪狗、獸醫

地點：路上、動物醫院、家中庭院

時間：前半部描述人物在某天夜晚遇到的狀況，動詞時態宜用過去簡單式；而後半部說明目前現況，用現在簡單式即可。

鋪陳：1. 描述 Lisa 某晚騎摩托車回家遇到的意外。(Sentence 1～4)

　　　　(1)意外：她騎摩托車時沒注意到前方有隻流浪狗，撞到了牠。牠受了傷，痛苦地哀嚎。

　　　　(2)應變：一開始 Lisa 很慌張，但她冷靜下來，立刻帶狗到獸醫院。

　　　　2. 描述 Lisa 帶狗看診與照顧牠的經過。(Sentence 5～9)

　　　　(1)看診：所幸狗傷得不重，獸醫告訴 Lisa 好好照顧牠，便可在一星期內復原。聽完獸醫的話，她鬆了一口氣，並決定帶狗回家。

(2)照料：Lisa 妥善照顧狗，而狗似乎也喜歡她。看見牠恢復健康，Lisa 決定飼養牠。

3. 描述 Lisa 平時和狗相處的情景。(Sentence 10～11)

(1)相處：他們經常在院子裡開心地玩飛盤。

(2)結論：狗兒不再是可憐的流浪狗，而是 Lisa 心愛的寵物。

注意：寫作時若必須同時處理過去的經驗與現在的狀況，轉換時態要特別小心。

Language Focus 語法重點

I. On + V-ing/N..., S + V....　一…就…

例 On hearing it, Lisa felt relieved, and she decided to take the dog home.

例 On her arrival at the airport, Nancy sent a text message to her parents.

1. 這個句型表示一個動作產生之後，另一個動作便隨之發生。
2. 介系詞用 on 或 upon 皆可，後接動名詞或名詞。

✎ TRY IT!

1. 一聽到比賽的結果，大家興奮地大聲歡呼。

2. 一看到兒子平安無事回家，那位母親喜極而泣。

II. seem + to V...　似乎…

例 Lisa took good care of the dog, and the dog seemed to like her.

例 The man seemed to want to attack the lady next to him.

1. seem 後面若接動作，則動詞須轉為不定詞，表示「似乎要做…事」。
2. 本句型也可改寫為 It seems/seemed that + S + V....。
• Lisa took good care of the dog and it seemed that the dog liked her.

✎ TRY IT!

1. 這個小孩似乎很想吃桌上的蛋糕。

2. 這個記者似乎知道這件醜聞背後的祕密。

主題寫作

看圖寫作

簡函寫作

43 Quit Smoking

 提示 以 Arnold was... 開頭，描述圖中主角所經歷的事件，並提供合理的解釋與結局。

 ## Sample 範文

¹Arnold was a chain smoker. ²His wife and son had tried very hard to get Arnold to quit smoking because they were worried about his health. ³Arnold, however, didn't care about their concerns and continued to smoke every day. ⁴His wife was very angry, and his son once even held a "No Smoking" sign in front of him.

⁵One day, Arnold coughed a lot and felt a severe pain in his chest. ⁶He went to see a doctor, and the doctor said, "Smoking has really damaged your lungs. If you don't stop smoking, you will probably develop lung cancer some day."

⁷After he heard what the doctor had said, Arnold got very angry with himself. ⁸He went home and threw all his cigarettes into a trash can. ⁹For the sake of his own health and his family, Arnold made up his mind never to smoke again.

Writing Analysis 寫作精靈

人物：爸爸 Arnold、兒子、媽媽、醫生

地點：家中、醫院

時間：提示句的時態採過去簡單式，故全篇文章宜統一為過去簡單式。

鋪陳：1. 描述 Arnold 抽菸的情形與家人的態度與反應。(Sentence 1～4)

    (1)抽菸情形：Arnold 抽菸抽很兇，即便家人因為擔心他的健康而力勸他戒菸，他仍不理會家人的關心，繼續每天抽菸。

    (2)家人反應：他的太太因此非常生氣，他的兒子有一次在他面前舉起禁菸標誌。

  2. 描述 Arnold 身體不適就醫的過程。(Sentence 5～6)

    (1)身體不適：有一天他咳得很嚴重，而且胸部嚴重疼痛。

    (2)就醫：醫生說抽菸已對他的肺造成傷害，若不戒菸的話，可能會演變成肺癌。

  3. 描述 Arnold 就醫後的反應與決定。(Sentence 7～9)

(1)反應：聽完醫生的話後，他很氣自己。回家後他把所有的香菸丟到垃圾桶裡。

(2)結論：為了自己的健康以及家人著想，Arnold 下定決心不再抽煙。

注意：撰寫文章時，可特別著墨在 Arnold 就醫前後心態上的轉變，文章會更吸引人。

Language Focus 語法重點

I. quit + V-ing/N　戒除、停止…

例 His wife and son had tried very hard to get Arnold to quit smoking.

例 The doctor suggested that the patient quit drinking.

> 1. quit 為及物動詞，其後接受詞，若受詞為一動作，則動詞應加上 -ing 形成動名詞。
> 2. 此處的 quit 也可用 give up 替換。

TRY IT!

1. 他的父母努力讓他戒除毒品。

2. 你應該努力戒除壞習慣，然後就可以改頭換面。

II. for the sake of + N　為了…著想

例 For the sake of his own health and his family, Arnold made up his mind never to smoke again.

例 For the sake of his future, he attended the night school to learn how to cook.

> for the sake of 後面可以接事物或人，兩者的意義稍有不同。如範文中的 for the sake of his own health 是指「為了維持自己的健康」，而 for the sake of his family 則可解釋為「為了家人著想」。

TRY IT!

1. 為了維持他們小孩的健康，王姓夫妻決定搬到鄉下去。

2. 為了家人，也為了生意，Allen 買了一輛新的小貨車。

主題寫作

看圖寫作

簡函寫作

87

44 Garbage Sorting

提示 以 After dinner, Nancy was in the kitchen... 開頭，描述圖中主角所經歷的事件，並提供合理的解釋與結局。

 Sample 範文

¹After dinner, Nancy was in the kitchen sorting her garbage. ²She was conscious about the environment, and she always did a good job recycling. ³Nancy put her plastic bottles in a bag, stacked the waste paper in a box, and then collected the kitchen waste in a bucket for leftovers.

⁴Outside Nancy's house, the garbage truck had already arrived. ⁵At that moment, Nancy was so busy sorting her garbage that she was not aware of the truck outside. ⁶All of her neighbors, with the help of the garbage men, were busy throwing their garbage into the truck.

⁷Unfortunately, Nancy was late, and the garbage truck had already started to move when she finally got there. ⁸She ran after the truck with the bag full of plastic bottles, the box full of paper, and the bucket of leftovers in her hands. ⁹The truck, however, didn't stop, so Nancy had no choice but to take all her trash back home.

 Writing Analysis 寫作精靈

人物：Nancy、鄰居、清潔隊員

地點：廚房、屋外巷道中

時間：晚飯後清理垃圾，預設是已發生過的事件，動詞時態用過去簡單式。

鋪陳：1. 描述 Nancy 於晚餐後在廚房做垃圾分類。(Sentence 1～3)

(1)態度：Nancy 是個環保意識很強的人，她總是認真做垃圾分類。

(2)過程：她將塑膠瓶裝成一袋，並將廢紙放在紙箱內，接著將廚餘放在桶中。

2. 描述垃圾車的抵達與鄰居倒垃圾的情景。(Sentence 4～6)

(1)意外：因為 Nancy 忙著做垃圾分類，完全沒注意到垃圾車已經來了。

⑵街景：所有的鄰居都在清潔隊員的協助下，忙著將垃圾丟進垃圾車裡。

3. 描述 Nancy 因晚到而追趕垃圾車的情景。(Sentence 7～9)

　⑴追趕垃圾車：不幸的是當 Nancy 抵達時，垃圾車正駛離此處。Nancy 拿著大包小包的垃圾追趕垃圾車，但車子並沒有停下來。

　⑵結局：Nancy 別無他法，只好帶著所有的垃圾回家。

注意：結局也可以發展成清潔隊員後來停下車讓她倒垃圾，Nancy 感激地向他們道謝。

Language Focus 語法重點

I. be aware of + N　察覺到…，意識到…

例 Nancy was so busy sorting her garbage that she was not aware of the truck outside.

例 She walked quicker when she was aware of a man following her.

1. 本用法也可以改寫為 be aware that + S + V...。
* She walked quicker when she was aware that a man was following her.
2. be aware of 也可解釋為「知道，明白」，若要表示完全清楚了解之意，可用 be fully/well aware of。

TRY IT!

1. 他非常專心看漫畫，以至於未察覺有人接近他。

_____

2. 你確信政府已明瞭我們的問題嗎？

_____

II. have no choice but + to V...　別無選擇只好…

例 Nancy had no choice but to take all her trash back home.

例 In fact, you have no choice but to take the doctor's advice.

have no choice 表示沒有其他的選擇，but 之後固定用不定詞。本用法也可改寫為 leave sb. no choice but + to V...。

TRY IT!

1. 輸了比賽，我們除了接受失敗之外別無選擇。

_____

2. 既然她決定離開，我們除了祝她好運外別無選擇。

_____

主題寫作　看圖寫作　簡函寫作

45 Being Late for School

以 It was eight o'clock, but Jack hadn't woken up yet... 開頭，描述圖中主角所經歷的事件，並提供合理的解釋與結局。

Sample 範文

¹It was eight o'clock, but Jack hadn't woken up yet. ²The sun shone brightly into his room, and when he finally opened his eyes, it was 8:20. ³Jack was shocked to <u>learn what time it is</u> because he had a very important exam at 8:30 that morning.

⁴Jack put on his uniform in a hurry, grabbed his school bag, and rushed to the bus stop <u>as fast as he could</u>. ⁵Unfortunately, the bus had already left by the time he got there.

⁶When he arrived at his classroom at 8:50, all of his classmates were taking the exam and the teacher was monitoring them. ⁷Feeling so embarrassed, Jack dare not go into the classroom. ⁸However, the teacher noticed him and told him to sit down and take the exam. ⁹Jack was relieved and grateful, and he also promised his teacher that he'd never be late for school again.

Writing Analysis 寫作精靈

人物：Jack、同學、老師

地點：房間、公車站、教室

時間：星期一的早上，提示文字已標明動詞時態用過去簡單式。

鋪陳：1. 描述 Jack 早上睡過頭的情景。(Sentence 1～3)

　　　(1)狀況：Jack 到早上八點都還沒起床。陽光照入房間，當他醒來時已經八點二十分了。

　　　(2)反應：他知道時間後很震驚，因為他早上八點半有一個很重要的考試。

　　　2. 描述 Jack 趕公車的情景：Jack 匆忙地穿上制服，拿著書包，儘快衝到公車站。不幸的是，他抵達時公車已經開走了。 (Sentence 4～5)

　　　3. 描述 Jack 到校之後所發生的事。(Sentence 6～9)

　　　(1)教室外：當他在八點五十分時抵達教室時，他的同學已經在應試了，而且老師也正

在監考。他覺得很尷尬,不敢進教室。

⑵老師的反應:老師注意到他,並告訴他坐下來考試。

⑶結局:Jack 鬆了一口氣,除了感謝老師,他也向老師保證再也不會遲到。

注意:結局也可以是老師對於 Jack 遲到感到相當生氣,讓他在走廊罰站,之後再讓他補考。

🌿 Language Focus 語法重點

I. ...what (+ N) + S + be/V... 間接問句

⑩ Jack was shocked to learn what time it is.

⑩ Please tell me what you want to eat.

1. 疑問句作為動詞的受詞時,須改為間接問句,句型列法為「疑問詞 (+ 名詞) + 主詞 + 動詞」。
2. 若間接問句作主詞時,視同單數主詞,後接單數動詞。
- What we need is your support.

📝 TRY IT!

1. 你應珍惜所擁有的一切。畢竟,你比其他許多人幸運許多。

_____

2. Lucy 知道父母在哪時感到很震驚,因為她以為她是孤兒。

_____

II. as + adv. + as one can/could 盡某人所能

⑩ Jack put on his uniform in a hurry, grabbed his school bag, and rushed to the bus stop as fast as he could.

⑩ I'll write to you as soon as I can.

1. 本用法置於一般動詞的後面,注意 as...as 中間應置放副詞。
2. 本用法亦可改寫為 as + adv. + as possible。

📝 TRY IT!

1. 醫生建議我每天要盡可能多運動。

_____

2. Emma 闔上教科書,拿出鉛筆,儘快回答所有的問題。

_____

46 Abandoned Dogs

提示 以 One day, a puppy was abandoned... 開頭，描述圖中動物主角所經歷的事件，並提供合理的解釋與結局。

 **Sample 範文**

¹One day, a puppy was abandoned by its owner and left in a paper box near a trash can. ²It was the first time that the puppy had been left alone on the roadside, and he didn't understand why his owner had done this to him.

³From that day on, the poor puppy became a stray dog. ⁴He had to look for food in the garbage dump, like all the other stray dogs. ⁵In order to survive, these stray dogs had to fight for food and eat people's leftovers.

⁶It was hard, however, for the stray dogs to survive. ⁷Some people thought that they were a big problem and wanted to get rid of them. ⁸One day, near the garbage dump, a man with a net got out of the car, trying to catch them. ⁹The stray dogs were all scared, and they ran away as fast as they could, wondering why people had kept them at first, but abandoned them in the end.

 Writing Analysis 寫作精靈

人物：小狗 (puppy)、垃圾堆旁的流浪狗、捕狗人員

地點：路邊、垃圾堆

時間：敘述一隻小狗所經歷的事，發生在過去的某一天，動詞時態用過去簡單式鋪陳。

鋪陳：1. 敘述小狗被遺棄的情景：一隻小狗被主人遺棄在垃圾桶旁的紙箱內，這是牠第一次獨自被遺留在路旁，牠不知道為什麼主人要這麼做。(Sentence 1～2)

2. 描述牠的流浪生活：從那天起，牠成為流浪狗，必須在垃圾堆中覓食。為了生存，這些流浪狗必須爭奪食物，以人類的廚餘為食。(Sentence 3～5)

3. 描述小狗和其他流浪狗遭受人類的威脅。(Sentence 6～9)

(1)險境：有些人覺得流浪狗是一大問題，想要除掉牠們。一天在垃圾堆附近，一個人帶著網子走下車，想要抓牠們。

(2)結論：這些狗兒嚇壞了，在牠們全力逃走的時候，心想為什麼人們一開始要飼養牠們，但最後卻又拋棄牠們。

注意：本文以流浪狗的角度來看待人類的作為，十分發人省思。

Language Focus 語法重點

I. In order to + V..., S + V....　為了…

例 In order to survive, these stray dogs had to fight for food and eat people's leftovers.

例 In order to get good grades, Susie burned the midnight oil studying.

1. 為了達成某種目的而做某事，此種目的用 in order to + V 表示，可置於句首，而所做的事則為主要子句，放在逗點之後。
2. in order to + V 可簡化為 to + V。

TRY IT!

1. 為了要發展新市場，經理要求整個團隊更加努力。

_____

2. 為了擴充字彙量，你必須要盡可能多讀書。

_____

II. ...at first...but...in the end...　起初…最後卻…

例 The stray dogs wondered why people had kept them at first, but abandoned them in the end.

例 He wanted to order a steak at first, but he changed his mind and had a pork chop in the end.

1. 本用法具有前後對比的效果，表示一開始是某種狀況，但最後事情產生變化。
2. at first 亦可與 in the beginning 替換。

TRY IT!

1. 起初他不喜歡英文，但最後英文成為他最愛的科目。

_____

2. 我想知道為什麼他們一開始彼此相愛，最後卻沒有結婚。

_____

47 Offering Seats

提示 以 This morning I took the bus to school... 開頭，描述圖中主角所經歷的事件，並提供合理的解釋與結局。

Sample 範文

¹This morning I took the bus to school. ²As time went on, the bus got more and more crowded. ³Luckily, I already had a seat.

⁴Later, I saw an old lady about seventy years old getting on the bus. ⁵I knew it was dangerous for the elder to stand in such a crowded bus, so I stood up and offered my seat to her. ⁶The old lady smiled at me, telling me that I was very kind and sweet.

⁷Just as I was feeling proud of myself, the bus driver suddenly slammed on the brakes. ⁸I wasn't holding on to anything, so I fell down to the ground. ⁹All the passengers looked at me with their mouths wide open. ¹⁰I stood up immediately, and I felt a little embarrassed. ¹¹However, I didn't regret giving my seat to the old lady because I knew I had done a good deed.

Writing Analysis 寫作精靈

人物：我 (I)、老婆婆、司機、其他乘客

地點：公車上

時間：今天早上發生的事件，動詞時態用過去簡單式。

鋪陳：1. 敘述公車上的景況：今天早上我搭公車上學，隨著時間經過，公車越來越擠，很幸運地我還是有位子坐。(Sentence 1～3)

2. 敘述讓座給老婆婆的經過。(Sentence 4～6)

  (1)原因：對長者來說，站在擁擠的公車上是很危險的，於是我起身讓座給老婆婆。

  (2)反應：老婆婆對我微笑，說我人真好。

3. 敘述讓座之後遇到的狀況。(Sentence 7～11)

  (1)意外：正當我洋洋得意時，司機突然煞車。我沒抓住任何東西，於是摔倒在地。所

有乘客都張大嘴巴看著我。我馬上爬起來，覺得有些難為情。

(2)結論：我不後悔讓座給老婆婆，因為我知道我做了一件好事。

注意：結局也可以是其他乘客看見主角摔倒，紛紛過來關切，以「溫情滿天下」的概念結尾。

Language Focus 語法重點

I. It is/was + adj. + for sb. + to V.... 做…對某人是…

例 I knew it was dangerous for the elder to stand in such a crowded bus.

例 It is impossible for a three-year-old child to realize the true meaning of life and death.

> 1. it 在此為虛主詞，句子後面的不定詞片語才是真正的主詞，句型列法亦可改寫為 To V... + is/was + adj. + for sb.。
> 2. 本句型中的形容詞是用來形容事物的，而非形容人，常見的形容詞有 possible、necessary、important、essential、difficult、convenient 等。

TRY IT!

1. 維持規律的作息時間對每個人來說是重要的。

2. 你和大衛今晚七點到我家來方便嗎？

II. regret + V-ing... 後悔…

例 I didn't regret giving my seat to the old lady because I knew I had done a good deed.

例 He regretted having sold his villa.

> 1. regret 後若接一個動作時，動詞須改為 V-ing，表示該件事已經做了，而當事人也後悔不已。
> 2. regret 尚可解釋為「遺憾」，後面接不定詞 to tell、to inform、to say 等。
> • We regret to inform you that your request has been rejected.

TRY IT!

1. 我不後悔借錢給他，因為我知道我幫助了一位有前途的年輕人。

2. 我真後悔說謊話。我早該三思的。

主題寫作　看圖寫作　簡函寫作

48 A Letter to My Mother

提示 請寫一封信給某人，可以是你的親人或友人，也可以是你不認識的人，如偶像歌手、知名作家或甚至歷史人物，寫下你想對他或她說的話。

Sample 範文

Dear Mother,

¹I am writing this letter to apologize to you. ²Yesterday, you got mad at me because I returned home after midnight. ³Actually I went to a movie with my classmates, but I didn't let you know in advance. ⁴At first, I was mad at you, too, since you decided to ground me for the weekend. ⁵Unable to hold back my anger, I just slammed the door and did not say anything. ⁶Later, as I lay in bed, I kept thinking about your worried face, and I began to feel guilty about what I had done. ⁷For so long, you have done so many things for our family and me. ⁸All you ask of us is to take good care of ourselves. ⁹I feel so bad that I have never properly expressed my gratitude to you. ¹⁰Please forgive me. ¹¹I promise I will never make you worry again.

Your son,
Roger

Writing Analysis 寫作精靈

主題：寫給母親的一封信
時態：表明現在的感受用現在簡單式，敘述過去發生的事件用過去簡單式。
鋪陳：1. 寫信目的：向母親道歉。(Sentence 1)
　　　2. 事件經過：昨天午夜過後我才回家，你生我的氣。因為我和同學去看電影，沒事先告訴你。起初我也很氣你，因為我週末會被禁足，無法消氣之下，我甩門不做任何解釋。(Sentence 2～5)
　　　3. 表達歉意：稍後我躺在床上，不斷想到你擔憂的臉孔，我開始覺得內疚。長久以來你為家人付出很多，唯一要求的回報就是要我們好好照顧自己。我從未適當地向你表達感激之情，我覺得好糟。(Sentence 6～9)
　　　4. 結論：請原諒我，我保證絕不再讓你擔心。(Sentence 10～11)
注意：1. 一般來說家書是屬於私人信件，故格式較為精簡。信件的第一行通常是稱呼語「Dear 名字或稱謂」，後方需加上逗號。
　　　2. 寫完內文之後，在下方加上結尾詞，如 Your father、Your son 等，最後再署名。

Language Focus 語法重點

I. get + adj. 變得…，處於…狀態

例 Yesterday, you got mad at me because I returned home after midnight.

例 Don't stand in the rain. You'll get wet.

1. get 在此為連綴動詞，後面接形容詞，get 在此的用法和意義與 become 相同。
2. get 亦可解釋為「使…處於某種狀態」，句型列法為 get + O + OC (adj.)。
   • Don't stand in the rain. You'll get yourself wet.

TRY IT!

1. 昨天晚上，因為我不小心把爸爸心愛的杯子打破了，所以他就生我的氣。

2. Linda 幫兒子穿好衣服之後，便帶著他外出吃早餐。

II. hold back 抑制 (怒氣或淚水等)

例 Unable to hold back my anger, I just slammed the door and did not say anything.

例 Julia held back her tears, walking away without saying anything.

1. 片語 hold back 表示「不顯露自己的情感或想法」，後面常接 anger 或 tears。hold back 亦可與動詞 contain 替換。
2. hold back 尚可解釋為「妨礙進展或發展」，如：
   • You could have been an excellent athlete, but your laziness held you back.

TRY IT!

1. Tim 強忍怒火，避免了一場爭吵。

2. Susan 強忍淚水，決定好好照顧那些可憐的孩子們。

主題寫作 ｜ 看圖寫作 ｜ 簡函寫作

49 A Letter to Dad

提示 請以英文書信格式撰寫一封家書，信中敘述你過去所犯的一個嚴重錯誤，並詳述其原因。同時告訴你的父母你要如何彌補這個過錯。信件開頭的稱呼語用 Dear Mom 或 Dear Dad，內文以 I'm sorry that I... 開頭，信末請署名 Wendy 或 David。

Sample 範文

Dear Dad,

    ¹I'm sorry that I shouted at you last night when you told me to stop watching TV and to study in my room. ²I know I should spend more time on my lessons. ³However, as the college entrance exam approaches, I am getting more and more nervous, and sometimes I can't concentrate at all when I try to sit at my desk. ⁴What's more, the lessons are getting harder and harder for me, and it seems that I cannot read through all my textbooks and make sense of everything in them. ⁵Dad, I hope you understand how much pressure I'm under right now. ⁶Please allow me to have some time to relax. ⁷As you know, after I get some rest, I feel refreshed, and I can study more effectively. ⁸I promise that I will try to manage my time better and be a responsible student. ⁹I hope that you can trust me.

Love,
Wendy

Writing Analysis 寫作精靈

主題：寫一封致歉信給父親

時態：敘述過去犯下的錯誤用過去簡單式，談論目前的心態用現在簡單式。

鋪陳：1. 致歉：昨天你叫我不要看電視，該進房間讀書時，很抱歉我對你大吼。(Sentence 1)

　　　2. 解釋原因：我知道我該多花時間在課業上。但隨著大考接近，我愈來愈緊張，有時無法專心坐在書桌前。再加上課業愈來愈難，我讀不完也無法完全理解所有的東西。
(Sentence 2～4)

　　　3. 請求：希望你能了解現在我的壓力很大，請允許我有放鬆的時間。如你所知，休息會令我神清氣爽，讀書更有效率。(Sentence 5～7)

　　　4. 結論：我保證我會設法做好時間管理，當一個負責任的學生。希望你能信任我。
(Sentence 8～9)

注意：親子或家人之間因為關係親密，信末的結尾詞可用 Love。

🎯 Language Focus 語法重點

I. read through 讀完全部　make sense of... 理解…

例 It seemed that I cannot read through all my textbooks and make sense of everything in them.

例 Please read through the contract carefully before you sign it.

例 Although I have read this paragraph ten times, I just can't make sense of it.

> 1. read through 表示「從頭到尾讀得很徹底」之意。
> 2. make sense of 表示「理解 (困難或不清楚的文字或概念)」。另外，片語 make sense 則解釋為「合理，有道理」，如：
> • What you just said doesn't make any sense.

✏ TRY IT!

1. 在考試前要我讀完所有的教科書是不可能的。

_____

2. 你能理解老師正在教授的東西嗎？

_____

II. some time 一些時間

例 Please allow me to have some time to relax.

例 I usually spend some time reading every night.

> 1. some time 表示一段時間。而 sometime 表示過去或未來的某個時間，如：
> • I'll call you sometime tomorrow.
> 2. sometimes 是頻率副詞，解釋為「有時候」，如：
> • Sometimes, my father takes me to the amusement park.

✏ TRY IT!

1. 我們已經走了一段時間了，但是沒有人想停下來休息一下。

_____

2. 上星期的某個時候我的確在機場遇見他。

_____

50 A Letter to a Friend

提示 寫一封信給一位好友 ，包含日期 、 稱謂 (salutation) 、 結尾 (closing) 及署名 (signature)。第一段描述你的近況，第二段寫目前的感想和未來的計畫。

Sample 範文

June 14, 2006

Dear Helen,

[1]How have you been? [2]It has been a year since you moved to America. [3]I guess you have got used to life there. [4]As for me, my life is still full of textbooks and tests. [5]Imagine having to review everything you've learned over the past two years! [6]It means piles and piles of books for me to read and review. [7]To get good grades, I have to burn the midnight oil almost every night. [8]Thank God I don't have to go to cram school—at least I can arrange my schedule myself and have some free time during the weekends.

[9]In fact, I don't think this is a miserable life. [10]Instead, I think of it as a challenge, knowing that if I can overcome all these difficulties, I will be able to accomplish my goal of getting into the college of my choice. [11]You know that I want to be a lawyer, and you can be sure that I'll work as hard as I can to make my dream come true. [12]Well, I hope I will hear from you soon and that you will share your experiences in America with me.

　　　　　　　　　　　　　　　　　　　Sincerely,
　　　　　　　　　　　　　　　　　　　Annie

Writing Analysis 寫作精靈

主題：寫信告知朋友近況與未來計畫

時態：談近況用現在簡單式，未來計畫則用未來式。

鋪陳：1. 問候朋友並描述自己的近況。(Sentence 1～8)
　　　　　(1)問候：近來好嗎？你搬到美國已經一年，我猜你已適應當地生活。
　　　　　(2)近況：我的生活中充滿課本與考試，有一大堆書要讀。為了拿到好成績，我幾乎每晚挑燈夜讀。幸好我不必補習，可以自己安排時間，週末也有空閒時間。
　　　　2. 說明自己對目前生活的想法與未來的計劃。(Sentence 9～11)
　　　　　(1)對現狀的想法：我不覺得這種生活很悲慘，反而是一種挑戰。如果能克服萬難，我就能進入最想就讀的大學。

(2)未來的計劃：你知道我想當律師，而且我會努力用功讀書讓夢想成真。

　　3. 結論：希望不久就能收到你的回信，與我分享你在美國的經驗。(Sentence 12)

注意：1. 朋友之間寫信，第一句通常是問候近況，例如 How have you been?。

　　　　2. 正式的結尾詞可用 Sincerely 或 Sincerely yours 等。

🖋 Language Focus 語法重點

I. get used to N/V-ing　　習慣…

例 I guess you have <u>got used to</u> <u>life</u> there.

例 I haven't <u>got used to</u> <u>staying</u> up so late these days.

> get used to 後面可以接名詞或動名詞，表示「習慣 (做) 某事」。注意不可與 used to 混淆，used to 後面接原形動詞，表示「以前習慣做某事」。

🖉 TRY IT!

1. Mike 發現要習慣早上六點起床是困難的。

_____

2. 我以前會在週末和朋友打網球，但是我現在沒有時間從事這個運動。

_____

II. accomplish one's goal　　達成目標　　**of one's choice**　　自己最想選擇的…

例 If I can overcome all these difficulties, I will be able to <u>accomplish my goal</u> of getting into the college <u>of my choice</u>.

例 If you want to <u>accomplish your goal</u>, just stick to it.

例 Study harder, and you can get into the school <u>of your choice</u>.

> 1. 目標可用「完成」或「達成」作為搭配動詞，除了 accomplish 之外，亦可用 achieve。
> 2. …of one's choice 是指「某人最想選的事物」。

🖉 TRY IT!

1. Jack 努力賺錢，希望在五十歲以前完成環遊世界的目標。

_____

2. 只要你盡全力，要進入最想選擇的大學並不難。

_____

主題寫作　　看圖寫作　　簡函寫作

指考篇

1 On TV

提示 請以 "On TV" 為題，寫一篇短文敍述你對電視的看法。第一段寫電視帶來的好處，第二段寫看電視所帶來的壞處。

Sample 範文

¹Without a doubt, ever since television was invented, it has had a tremendous effect on people's lives. ²TV has certainly made life more convenient. ³With TV, people have quick and easy access to the latest information and news from around the world. ⁴In addition, television's various programs offer new knowledge and entertainment much faster than other types of media. ⁵TV can reach large audiences, and it is a medium that greatly appeals to many people.

⁶However, the disadvantages of TV should not be ignored. ⁷Watching too much TV might harm a person's eyesight. ⁸Moreover, the sex and violence found in some television programs might have a negative effect on children. ⁹Lastly, if children become couch potatoes, then they will spend less time reading and thinking independently, which hinders their intellectual development. ¹⁰All of us should be aware of the pros and cons of TV and choose the programs we watch wisely.

Writing Analysis 寫作精靈

主題：談論電視所帶來的好處與壞處

時態：針對某事件討論現狀用現在簡單式。

鋪陳：1. 主旨句：毫無疑問，自從電視被發明後，它對人們的生活帶來極大的影響。
　　　　　(Sentence 1)

　　　　2. 細節發展：分成兩段說明電視帶來的好處與壞處。(Sentence 2～9)

　　　　　(1)好處：A. 電視讓生活更便利，人們能迅速獲得全世界最新的訊息及新聞。

　　　　　　　　　　B. 比起其他媒體，多樣化的電視節目能更快速地提供新知與娛樂。

　　　　　　　　　　C. 電視的觀眾群大，而且能吸引許多人。

　　　　　(2)壞處：A. 看太多電視可能會有損視力。

　　　　　　　　　　B. 某些含有色情與暴力的電視節目可能對孩子造成負面的影響。

　　　　　　　　　　C. 如果小孩整天坐在沙發上看電視的話，他們閱讀與獨立思考的時間便會減少，阻礙智力發展。

　　　　3. 結論句：我們都應深知電視的優缺點並慎選觀看的節目。(Sentence 10)

注意：1. 若說明某事物有兩項以上的特點時，則可善用轉折詞如 in addition、moreover 以及 lastly 等，使段落更有組織。

2. 若欲將文章分為兩段，藉以說明某事物的正反兩面時，則可在第二段首句使用轉折詞 however。

Language Focus 語法重點

I. With + N(P), S + V....　有了…，…

例 With TV, people have quick and easy access to the latest information and news from around the world.

例 With an MP3 player, you can go jogging and listen to music at the same time.

1. with 在此為介系詞，後面接名詞或名詞片語，表示「有了…」。
2. 本用法一般將 with + N(P) 放置於句首，逗號的後面接主要子句。

TRY IT!

1. 有了數位相機，人們不用使用底片就可以快速且輕鬆地拍照。

_____

2. 有了她的幫忙，我在三天之內完成了這份報告。

_____

II. spend less time + V-ing...　少花時間…

例 If children become couch potatoes, then they will spend less time reading and thinking independently.

例 You should spend less time playing online games.

1. less 為比較級形容詞，解釋為「較少的」；若欲表示「較多的」，則用 more。注意 spend less/more time 後面接一動作時，需用動名詞 (V-ing)。
2. spend 後面亦可接明確的時間名詞，如 two days 或 one year 等。
• Lisa spent one hour cleaning her room.

TRY IT!

1. 如果 John 沉迷於漫畫，他將會少花時間讀書。

_____

2. 我花了兩個月適應日本的都市生活。

_____

2 Travel Is the Best Teacher

提示 請以 "Travel Is The Best Teacher" 為主題,寫一篇至少 120 個字的英文作文。第一段針對文章主題,説明旅行的優點,並在第二段舉自己在國內或國外的旅行經驗,以印證第一段的説明。【93 年指考】

Sample 範文

¹In my opinion, travel not only brings pleasure to us but also broadens our horizons. ²We may read a lot about the world in newspapers, books, or magazines, but only real experience can leave a deep and lasting impression on our minds. ³Not until we have walked along the Great Wall will we realize how spectacular it is.

⁴When we travel, we also need to deal with cultural differences that may not have been mentioned in the books we have read. ⁵For example, my parents and I traveled in India last summer. ⁶On our first night in Mumbai, we decided to try the local cuisine at a famous restaurant. ⁷After we were all seated, we were surprised to see that most of the diners ate their meals with their hands rather than chopsticks or forks. ⁸Although we had read many articles about Indian culture, we knew little about Indian dining etiquette. ⁹From this special experience, I have learned that table manners vary from culture to culture. ¹⁰In short, travel is not just a way to relax; it is also a way to learn about the real world we live in.

Writing Analysis 寫作精靈

主題: 旅行的重要性

時態: 第一段談論一般人的認知用現在簡單式,第二段敘述親身經歷則用過去簡單式。

鋪陳: 1. 主旨句:旅行不僅帶來樂趣,它還能擴展我們的眼界。(Sentence 1)

　　　　2. 細節發展:第一段說明讀萬卷書不如行千里路的道理,第二段以經驗證明旅遊亦是學習之道。(Sentence 2~9)

　　　　　(1)親身經驗的重要:雖然從書報雜誌中可學到很多,但真實經驗才會留下深刻印象。例如,要到長城一遊才能知道它有多壯觀。

　　　　　(2)旅遊經驗:我和爸媽去年夏天到印度旅遊,在孟買的第一天晚上,我們決定要嘗嘗印度料理。在餐廳就座之後,我們很驚訝大部分的顧客都是以手就食,而非用筷子或叉子。即使我們讀過很多有關印度文化的報導,但對印度的餐桌禮儀所知不多。從這次的經驗中,我學到各個文化的餐桌禮儀是不同的。

　　　　3. 結論句:旅遊不僅是放鬆的方式,也是認識真實世界的方式。(Sentence 10)

注意: 1. 說明主題句時,要儘量使用具體的例子或是個人經驗來加以陳述,以增加說服力。

2. 提示文字要求以個人旅行經驗加以說明主題，切勿以第三者的角度含混籠統帶過。

🎯 Language Focus 語法重點

I. Not until S₁ + V₁... + Aux. + S₂ + V₂....   直到…才…

例 Not until we have walked along the Great Wall will we realize how spectacular it is.

例 Not until Judy stormed out of the room did her brother realize that he had offended her.

本倒裝句型是由 S₂ + Aux + not + V₂... until S₁ + V₁.... 轉化而來的，注意將 not 和 until 挪至句首後，第二個子句需倒裝。

• We won't realize how spectacular the Great Wall is until we have walked along it.

→ Not until we have walked along the Great Wall will we realize how spectacular it is.

✏ TRY IT!

1. 直到我站在玉山山頂，我才了解到它有多高。

_____

2. 直到你寫完回家作業之後，才可以看電視。

_____

II. from N to N   各個…，從…到…

例 I have learned that table manners vary from culture to culture.

例 The salesman went from house to house asking if anyone wanted to buy this new product.

1. 注意 from 和 to 後面均用單數形名詞，名詞前不加任何冠詞。

2. 類似的搭配用法尚有 from school to school「各校」、from country to country「各國」以及 from door to door「挨家挨戶」。

✏ TRY IT!

1. 這個手勢在各國會有不同的意思。

_____

2. 郵差挨家挨戶遞送信件和包裹。

_____

3 Idols

提示 大多數的人都崇拜過偶像，可能是歌手、演員或運動員。請以 "Idols" 為題寫一篇英文短文，文分二段，第一段舉出自己或他人喜愛的一位偶像及如何喜愛這位偶像，第二段說明偶像的社會責任。

Sample 範文

[1]Many teenagers are crazy about their idols, and these idols have a great influence on their fans. [2]For instance, my sister likes a pop singer named Jolin very much. [3]She has gone to every one of Jolin's concerts and bought all of her albums. [4]She also tries to imitate the way Jolin dresses. [5]As a member of Jolin's fan club, my sister supports her idol with all her heart. [6]Once she even had a fight with my brother because he repeated a rumor he had heard about Jolin. [7]Without a doubt, Jolin is a really big influence on my sister.

[8]Since idols can influence young people so much, they should set good examples to their fans and remember that they have social responsibilities. [10]For example, pop idols can encourage their fans to work hard to accomplish their goals. [11]They can also donate money and participate in activities to raise money to help the poor and disadvantaged. [12]To sum up, idols should pay attention to their own behavior and make more positive contributions to society.

Writing Analysis 寫作精靈

主題：論偶像

時態：談論某人的現況或者現存的社會現象用現在簡單式，若說出某人過去做過的事則用過去簡單式。

鋪陳：1. 主旨句：很多青少年對偶像著迷，而這些偶像對他們的仰慕者影響很大。(Sentence 1)

    2. 第一段敘述妹妹喜愛偶像的方式，第二段延伸說明偶像的社會責任。(Sentence 2～11)

      (1)舉例說明：妹妹的偶像是流行歌手 Jolin。她參加 Jolin 每一場演唱會以及購買每一張專輯。她也嘗試模仿 Jolin 的穿著。身為歌迷會的一員，我妹妹全心全意支持她。有一次因為哥哥引述一則有關 Jolin 的謠言，妹妹就和他大吵一架。

      (2)社會責任：偶像對年輕人影響很大，所以應建立好榜樣，並謹記其社會責任。

          A. 偶像可以鼓勵歌迷努力達成目標

          B. 偶像也可以捐款或參與募款活動來幫助窮人或弱勢團體。

    3. 結論句：偶像應注意行為以及對社會做出正面的貢獻。(Sentence 12)

注意：若欲在一個段落裡重複提到同一個主詞數次，應避免從頭到尾都用代名詞指稱，才不會

與其他代名詞混淆。

🎯 Language Focus 語法重點

I. with all one's heart 全心全意地，衷心地　**set a good example** 做好榜樣

例 As a member of Jolin's fan club, my sister supports her idol <u>with all her heart</u>.

例 They wish <u>with all their hearts</u> that their teacher would recover soon.

例 They should <u>set good examples</u> to their fans and remember that they have social responsibilities.

例 You should set <u>an good example</u> to your sisters.

> 1. with all one's heart 用來強調內心強烈的感受，亦可改寫為 with all one's heart and soul。
> 2. set a good example 是指「以身作則，設立榜樣」，其中 good 可省略。

✏ TRY IT!

1. Mandy 全心全意愛著她的丈夫。

_____

2. 父母應該為自己的小孩做好榜樣。

_____

II. To sum up, S + V.... 總之，…

例 <u>To sum up</u>, idols should pay attention to their own behavior and make more positive contributions to society.

例 <u>To sum up</u>, the more you practice, the more skillful you will become.

> 1. 本句型可用於文章的結論句，總結之前提出的論點或陳述。
> 2. to sum up、in sum 以及 in short 都可以解釋為「總之，概括而言」。
> • To sum up/In sum/In short, the more you practice, the more skillful you will become.

✏ TRY IT!

1. 總之，你一旦設好目標，就要努力達成。

_____

2. 總之，你對未來要懷抱著樂觀的態度。

_____

主題寫作

主題句寫作

4 My Best and Worst Traits

提示 請以 "My Best and Worst Traits" 為題寫一篇英文作文，文分兩段，分別描述自己的優點與缺點。

Sample 範文

[1]I think being optimistic is my best trait. [2]No matter what situation I am in, I always try to look on the bright side. [3]For example, if I get a bad grade on a math test, I won't get upset myself. [4]Instead of shedding tears and feeling frustrated, I just try to learn from my mistakes and vow to study harder for the next exam.

[5]However, sometimes I am too optimistic, and I don't make good decisions because I have too much confidence in my abilities. [6]Take a recent unsuccessful interview as an example. [7]Last week, our school held interviews to select the students with the best English. [8]Thinking the interview would be a piece of cake, I didn't prepare for it at all. [9]Then, during the interview, when the teacher asked me questions, I can barely answer any of them. [10]It was no surprise that I was not one of the students chosen. [11]I should learn a lesson from this experience, and try to maintain my optimistic attitude and be more humble.

 ## Writing Analysis 寫作精靈

主題：我個人最大的優點與缺點

時態：談個性的優缺點宜用現在簡單式；若舉過去發生的事情為例，則用過去簡單式。

鋪陳：1. 主旨句：我想樂觀是我最大的優點。(Sentence 1)

    2. 細節發展：第一段說明樂觀是個人最大的優點，第二段則說明過於樂觀同時也是最大的缺點。(Sentence 2～10)

      (1)優點敘述：無論我處於何種狀況，我都會試著朝光明面看。

      (2)優點舉例：如果數學考不好時，我不會沮喪。我不會哭，也不會感到挫折，我反而會從錯誤中學習，立誓要為下一次的考試更加用功。

      (3)缺點敘述：有時我會太過樂觀，且因為對自己的能力太有自信，無法做出好決定。

      (4)缺點舉例：上週學校舉辦面試，要挑選英文程度最好的學生。我因為輕忽而完全沒有準備。面試時，當老師問我問題，我幾乎回答不出來。我沒被選上並不令人驚訝。

    3. 結論句：我應該要從這次的經驗學到教訓，一方面保持樂觀的態度，一方面也要更謙虛。(Sentence 11)

注意：有時候優點和缺點是一體兩面的，如果無法做到恰如其分，優點可能也會是缺點。

Language Focus 語法重點

I. No matter what + N + S₁ + V₁..., S₂ + V₂....　無論…，不管…

例 No matter what situation I am in, I always try to look on the bright side.

例 No matter what danger you are in, you should always keep calm.

> 1. what 在此作疑問形容詞用，後面須接名詞，名詞後面再接形容詞子句。
> 2. what 亦可作疑問代名詞用，如：
> • No matter what happens, I'll protect you.

TRY IT!

1. 無論你處於什麼樣的麻煩，我都會盡力幫你。

_____

2. 不管他送給你的禮物是什麼，你都應該要對他表達謝意。

_____

II. not...at all　一點也不…，根本不…

例 Thinking the interview would be a piece of cake, I didn't prepare for it at all.

例 I don't appreciate his help at all.

> 1. 強調一點都沒有，可用 not...at all 表示。另外，not...in the least 亦有相同的意思。
> • Thinking the interview would be a piece of cake, I didn't prepare for it at all.
>   → Thinking the interview would be a piece of cake, I didn't prepare for it in the least.
> 2. at all 若單獨使用於疑問句時，則用來強調所詢問的事情是否有一絲的可能性，解釋為「一點，究竟」。如：
> • Is it at all possible that you mistakenly set off the alarm?

TRY IT!

1. 想到你可能會生氣，我根本不敢說實話。

_____

2. 老實說，我一點都不贊成你。

_____

主題寫作

主題句寫作

5 What Makes a Good Friend?

提示 請以 "What Makes a Good Friend?" 為主題,寫一篇至少 120 個字的英文作文。第一段針對文章主題,說明什麼樣的朋友才算是「好朋友」,並在第二段舉自己的交友經驗為例,以印證第一段的說明。【93 年指考補考】

Sample 範文

¹A good friend is someone you can trust and someone who is always ready to give you a hand. ²He/She can listen to you and share in your happiness and sorrow. ³When you are upset, he/she will comfort and encourage you. ⁴When you are in need, he/she will be ready to help you. ⁵In other words, a true friend stands by you in every situation.

⁶Take something that happened to me recently, for example. ⁷I once got a very poor grade on an English test. ⁸I actually burst into tears when I got my test paper. ⁹My best friend, Julie, felt very sorry for me. ¹⁰She told me to calm down and look over the test paper again. ¹¹She pointed out that I hadn't really understood some of the grammar rules on the test. ¹²She suggested that I try to get more familiar with them before the next test. ¹³She even went with me to study at the library. ¹⁴With her encouragement and support, I did very well on the next English test. ¹⁵I really appreciate the help of my good friends.

Writing Analysis 寫作精靈

主題:談好朋友的定義與自身交友的經驗

時態:第一段下定義用現在簡單式,第二段舉過去與好友相處的例子,則用過去簡單式。

舖陳:1. 主旨句:好朋友是你可以信任的人,也是隨時準備幫忙的人。(Sentence 1)

2. 細節發展:第一段依據主旨句給予更詳細的定義,第二段則舉自己的交友經驗為例。
(Sentence 2~14)

   (1)詳細定義:好朋友能傾聽你說話,並分享你的快樂與憂傷。當你沮喪時,他 (她) 會安慰鼓勵你;你需要幫助時,他 (她) 隨時幫助你。換言之,真正的朋友會在任何狀況下不離不棄。

   (2)自身經驗:有一次英文測驗我考得很差,當我拿到考卷時,便放聲大哭。我最好的朋友 Julie 也替我難過,她告訴我要冷靜,並再把考卷看一遍。她指出我還不懂這次考試的一些文法規則,建議我在下次考試前要弄懂,她甚至和我到圖書館讀書。有了她的鼓勵與支持,我在下一次的英文考試考得很好。

3. 結論句:我真的很感激好友的幫忙。(Sentence 15)

注意:第一段撰寫好朋友的定義時,主旨句可以先下廣義,後面再接著詳加說明。可善用 "A

good friend is someone that..." 此句構。

 ## Language Focus 語法重點

I. sth. happened to sb. 某人發生什麼事

例 Take something that <u>happened to</u> me recently, for example.

例 What <u>happened to</u> Tom in the restaurant?

1. 若欲表達「某人發生什麼事」，中文語序習慣以人當主詞，但在英文中，happen to 的主詞必須是事件，寫作時須留意此特點。

2. happen 解釋為「(某事) 發生」，在大部分的情況下，happen 均可與 take place 以及 occur 互相替換。但須留意此三個動詞用法都不能用被動語態。如：
   • A serious car accident <u>happened</u> in front of my house this afternoon. (不能用 was happened)

TRY IT!

1. 當我恢復意識時，我不知道我發生了什麼事。

_____

2. 根據最新的消息，昨天在日本發生嚴重水災。

_____

II. S₁ + suggest + that + S₂ (+ should) + V.... 某人建議⋯

例 She <u>suggested</u> that I <u>try</u> to get more familiar with them before the next test.

例 The doctor <u>suggested</u> my father <u>give</u> up smoking.

1. suggest 表示「建議」時為意志性動詞，後接 that 子句時，助動詞 should 可省略，而動詞仍為原形。

2. 其他動詞如 recommend「推薦，建議」、advise「勸告，規勸」及 order「命令」等，皆適用於此句型。如：
   • The president <u>ordered</u> that all of the flood relief (should) <u>be</u> sent to the disaster area.

TRY IT!

1. 老師建議每個學生都應該輪流打掃教室。

_____

2. 這個推銷員推薦我父親買這輛棟豪華的別墅。

_____

主題寫作

主題句寫作

6 The Season I Like Best

提示 請以 "The Season I Like Best" 為題寫一篇英文作文，第一段說明理由，第二段描述該季節之景象或說明可從事的活動。

Sample 範文

¹Of all the four seasons, the one I like best is summer. ²For one thing, during the summer, I have a long summer vacation, and I can do the things I don't have time to do during the busy school semester. ³What's more, I can eat as much ice cream or as many Popsicles as I want in the summer. ⁴If it is hot, I can beat the heat by either enjoying the air conditioning at home or by going swimming at a nearby pool.

⁵Another reason I like summer is that all the lush green plants are full of life and vitality. ⁶I always feel full of energy when I see all the plants in bloom everywhere during the summer, and I also feel close to Mother Nature. ⁷Besides, my favorite summertime activity is swimming. ⁸In fact, I don't think anyone can resist the temptation to jump into a pool full of cool water on a hot summer day. ⁹I also sometimes enjoy working up a sweat doing outdoor sports, such as bicycling, inline skating, and hiking. ¹⁰Without a doubt, summer is my favorite season of all because I never feel bored at this time of year.

Writing Analysis 寫作精靈

主題：最喜歡的季節

時態：說明自己的喜愛用現在簡單式。

鋪陳：1. 主旨句：在所有季節中，我最愛夏季。(Sentence 1)

2. 細節發展：第一段說明喜歡夏季的理由，第二段描述夏季的景象與自己會從事的活動。
(Sentence 2～9)

(1)理由：A. 我可以在漫長的暑假中，做一些平常沒有時間做的事。

B. 夏天可以大吃冰淇淋和冰棒。

C. 天熱時，我待在家中吹冷氣或到附近的游泳池游泳。

(2)景象：綠油油的植物生氣蓬勃，讓我有活力，也覺得自己很接近大自然。這也是我喜歡夏季的另一個理由。

(3)活動：A. 我最愛的夏日活動就是游泳，我想沒人能抵擋在炎熱的夏日下，跳進冷水中的誘惑。

B. 我也喜歡會讓我流汗的戶外運動，例如騎腳踏車、溜直排輪和健行。

3. 結論句：因為每年的此時我從未感到無聊，所以夏季是我最喜愛的季節。(Sentence 10)

注意：戶外景色也可以是喜歡該季節的理由之一。舉本文為例，第二段前半部除了描述夏日景象外，同時也解釋了綠油油的景象亦是作者喜愛夏季的理由之一。

🫒 Language Focus 語法重點

> **I. Of all the + N, S + V....** 在所有的…中，…

🔘 Of all the four seasons, the one I like best is summer.

🔘 Of all the students, Martha is the smartest.

> 可用此句型說明在某一群體中，有某一個人或事物最為突出。注意主要子句須使用最高級的用法。

✏️ **TRY IT!**

1. 在所有戶外活動中，我最愛的是慢跑。

_____

2. 在所有的科目中，我最愛的是英文。

_____

> **II. as + much/many + N + as...** 儘量…，盡情…

🔘 What's more, I can eat as much ice cream or as many Popsicles as I want in the summer.

🔘 The robber took as much money as he could.

> 1. 本用法套用 as...as 的句型，表示「和…一樣多」，用來強調該名詞的數量。
> 2. 若欲強調的名詞為可數名詞，則用 many 修飾；若為不可數名詞，則用 much 修飾。

✏️ **TRY IT!**

1. 我們可以盡情唱歌。

_____

2. 在宴會上，你可以愛喝多少雞尾酒就喝多少。

_____

主題寫作

主題句寫作

7 The TV Program That I Enjoy Watching the Most

提示 請以 "The TV Program I Enjoy Watching the Most" 為題寫一篇英文作文，文分二段，第一段説明你最喜歡看的電視節目，簡單介紹其內容，第二段説明你喜歡它的理由。

Sample 範文

[1]*Who Wants to Be a Millionaire* is the TV program that I enjoy watching the most. [2]It is a quiz show, and the contestants on this show can win up to one million dollars if they are able to answer fifteen questions correctly. [3]The questions are asked one by one, and if a contestant answers incorrectly, then he or she loses the chance to win the million-dollar prize.

[4]I like this show because I can learn a lot by watching it. [5]I can learn everything from common-sense facts to professional information in different fields. [6]Another reason I enjoy watching this TV program is the host. [7]She likes to mislead the contestants, and she often tries to make them change their correct answers to wrong ones. [8]As a result, only those who are very certain about their answers are able to continue on in this game. [9]I actually think that the host does a good job of testing the players to see if they have what it takes to be the real winners of this quiz show. [10]In my opinion, *Who Wants to Be a Millionaire* is the best quiz show I have ever watched.

Writing Analysis 寫作精靈

主題：最喜愛的電視節目

時態：談論自己的喜好屬於事實的陳述，故應用現在簡單式。

鋪陳：1. 主旨句：我最愛看的電視節目是 *Who Wants to Be a Millionaire*。(Sentence 1)

　　　2. 細節發展：第一段簡單介紹本節目的內容，第二段則說明喜愛它的理由。

　　　(Sentence 2～8)

　　　(1)節目內容：這是一個益智的猜謎節目，參賽者只要連續答對十五個題目，即可獲得一百萬獎金。在本節目中，一次問一個問題，參賽者只要答錯，便喪失獲得百萬大獎的機會。

　　　(2)理由：A. 我喜歡這個節目是因為這個節目讓我獲益良多。從基本常識到各領域的專業知識，我可以學到任何東西。

　　　　　　　B. 另一個理由是主持人。她喜歡誤導參賽者，常常試著讓他們更換原本正確的答案。也因此只有對自己答案有把握的人才能繼續挑戰。我認為主持人表現優異，能測試參賽者是否有資格成為真正的優勝者。

3. 結論句：依我之見 *Who Wants to Be a Millionaire* 是我看過最棒的猜謎節目
   (Sentence 9)

注意：介紹電視節目的內容時，簡單扼要介紹即可，不需說明細微末節。

🫒 Language Focus 語法重點

I. S₁ + be + the + N(P) (+ that) + S₂ + V... + (the) most.... ···是某人最···的···

例 *Who Wants to Be a Millionaire* is the TV program (that) I like watching (the) most.

例 Basketball is the sport (that) I enjoy playing (the) most.

1. 本句型很適合做段落的主題句。
2. 後半段形容詞子句的 that 可省略，最高級 the most 前的 the 亦可省略。

✏ TRY IT!

1. 英文是我在學校中最喜歡的科目。

_____

2. 騎腳踏車是我空閒時最喜歡從事的活動。

_____

II. Another reason + S + V... + is/was + N(P)/that-clause.... 另外一個···的理由是···

例 Another reason I enjoy watching this TV program is the host.

例 Another reason I didn't call you was that the battery of my cell phone was dead.

1. 在段落中，若欲說明兩個理由，第二個理由可套用本句型。
2. 在本用法中，這個理由可以是名詞 (片語)，也可以是一個由 that 所引導的名詞子句。

✏ TRY IT!

1. 我喜歡 Paul 的另一個原因是他既友善又認真工作。

_____

2. 我不喜歡夏天的另一個理由是潮溼。

_____

主題寫作

主題句寫作

8 My Biggest Dream

提示 請以 "My Biggest Dream" 為題寫一篇英文作文。文中第一段針對文章主題，寫出你最大的夢想及解釋為何有此夢想。第二段舉出你將如何達成這個夢想。

Sample 範文

¹Dreams for people are like sunshine for living creatures—they are a necessary part of life. ²In my case, learning to speak different languages and then traveling by myself is my biggest dream. ³I am always longing to travel around the world. ⁴Therefore, if I had the ability to speak different languages, I could communicate with more people in the world. ⁵Furthermore, when it comes to finding a job, my ability to speak other languages will certainly be useful.

⁶To make my dream come true, I have spent a lot of time learning English and Japanese. ⁷When I go to college, I also plan to major in German. ⁸In all the languages I learn, I will focus on listening and speaking so that I can understand others and express myself clearly. ⁹In conclusion, I will work hard to make my dream come true in the near future.

Writing Analysis 寫作精靈

主題：我最大的夢想

時態：一般來說，說明自己的現況用現在簡單式。但因夢想是尚未達成的事，因此可穿插使用「與現在事實相反的假設句」。另外，若欲說明未來會做的努力，則用未來簡單式。

鋪陳：1. 主旨句：就我而言，學習多國語言並獨自出國旅行是我最大的夢想。(Sentence 2)

2. 細節發展：第一段說明為什麼會有這個夢想，第二段接著說明如何達成夢想。
   (Sentence 3～8)
   (1)原因：A. 我一直都渴望能環遊世界，因此如果我會說多國語言的話，就能和世界上更多的人溝通了。
   B. 會說多國語言的能力絕對有助於找工作。
   (2)努力的方向：A. 我花了很多時間學英語和日語。上大學時，我打算主修德語。
   B. 我會將學語言的重點放在聽與說的能力，以便可以了解他人的話並清楚地表達自己。

3. 結論句：我會努力讓我的夢想在不久的將來實現。(Sentence 9)

注意：1. 若文章需運用到兩種以上的時態時，撰寫文句時要特別小心，切勿混淆。

2. 所謂的「夢想」通常是指尚未實現的目標，因此假設夢想實現的情境，要使用與現在事實相反的假設語氣。

Language Focus 語法重點

I. If + S₁ + V₁-ed/were..., S₂ + could/should/would/might (+ not) + V₂....
如果…

例 If I had the ability to speak different languages, I could communicate with more people in the world.

例 If I were you, I would not open the box.

1. 本句型為與現在事實相反的假設語氣，強調所提的狀況現階段尚未發生。注意 if 子句中動詞用過去式，be 動詞則一律用 were，不可用 was；而主要子句中的助動詞也用過去式。
• If there were no air, there would be no life. (事實上現在有空氣，也有生命的存在。)
2. 若假設的情況是有可能發生的，則 if 子句和主要子句採直述法，動詞用現在簡單式。
• If you practice every day, you will win the race.

TRY IT!

1. 如果這個盲童有能力看得見，他想看看他的家人和朋友。

_____

2. 如果她是這個童話中的公主，她會逃離城堡去和心愛的人過幸福的生活。

_____

II. so that　為了，以便

例 I will focus on listening and speaking so that I can understand others and express myself clearly.

例 I turned on the lights so that I could see clearly.

1. 本連接詞片語用來連接兩個子句，表示第一個子句的發生是為了第二個子句，具有強調目的的口吻。
2. 本片語亦可解釋為「因此，所以」，用來連接兩個具有因果關係的子句，一般來說在 so that 前的子句為因，後者為果。
• It was very dark so that I couldn't see clearly.

TRY IT!

1. 他努力工作為了養家。

_____

2. Mary 沒有出席今天的會議，因此我們猜想她是不是生病了。

_____

主題寫作

主題句寫作

9 An Unforgettable Teacher

提示 寫一篇短文談談最令你難忘的老師。文分二段，第一段描述該師的特質或教學特色，第二段說明令你難忘的理由。

Sample 範文

¹To a student, a good teacher is as important as a lighthouse is to a ship. ²My English teacher in high school was such an inspiration. ³Her teaching was never dull, and she used materials that did not come from our textbook, such as movies, plays, and songs, to spark our interest in English. ⁴She taught us the language, and she taught us how to appreciate art and life as well.

⁵Unlike other teachers, this teacher asked us not only to focus our attention on the studies, but also to care about our society. ⁶I still remember how she once told us a story about several foreign priests who had founded a hospital to help the aborigines in Hualien. ⁷After hearing about this unselfish act of love, our class decided to donate some money to this charity. ⁸I will always remember this remarkable teacher, for no one has ever taught me so much.

Writing Analysis 寫作精靈

主題：一位難忘的師長

時態：描述現在的老師用現在簡單式，描述過去的一位師長用過去簡單式。

鋪陳：1. 主旨句：我高中的英文老師就是鼓舞我的明燈。(Sentence 2)

2. 細節發展：第一段描述老師的教學特色，第二段舉例說明令人難忘的原因。

(Sentence 3～7)

(1)教學特色：A. 她的教學從不無聊，她會使用非教科書的教學素材如電影、戲劇和歌曲等，來激發我們學英文的興趣。

B. 她教我們英文，也教我們如何欣賞藝術和體驗人生。

(2)難忘的理由：A. 和其他老師不同，老師要我們不只專注在課業上，同時也要關心社會。

B. 有一次她說了一個有關幾名外國傳教士的故事，他們在花蓮成立一間醫院來幫助原住民。聽完了這個無私的善舉，班上同學決定要捐一些錢給這個慈善機構。

3. 結論句：我永遠都會記得這個傑出的老師，沒人和她一樣教了我這麼多東西。

(Sentence 8)

注意：1. 第一段須設定好要描述的對象，切記只要針對寫作提示的要求來撰寫。此處使用到的

是描述技巧，針對教師的內在與教學特色做描述。

2. 類似的主題如「一位難忘的同學 (或朋友)」，也可以利用本範文架構來發展段落。

Language Focus 語法重點

I. as well　也，同樣地

例 She taught us the language, and she taught us how to appreciate art and life as well.

例 I would like to have a cup of tea and a bottle of juice as well.

---

1. as well 表示「(除了…之外) 還有…」的意思，通常置於句尾。另外 as well 不能用來連接兩個子句，需以連接詞 and 來連接。

• I would like to have a cup of tea and a bottle of juice as well.

2. as well as 的意思和 as well 相同，不過 as well as 通常置於句中，用來連接兩個名詞 (片語)。

• Mr. Wang will go to the post office as well as the bank this afternoon.

TRY IT!

1. 我喜歡打網球，也喜愛打棒球。

2. Ken 擁有一輛摩托車，還有一部汽車。

II. S₁ + V₁..., for + S₂ + V₂....　…因為…

例 I will always remember this remarkable teacher, for no one has ever taught me so much.

例 Jimmy would make a true leader, for he is the wisest person among all of us.

---

1. for 在此為連接詞，解釋為「因為」，用來連接兩個互為因果的子句。一般來說，表示結果的子句放前面，表示原因的子句放後面。

2. for 的前面一般都要加逗號。

TRY IT!

1. 我願意為父母做一切事情讓他們開心，因為我非常愛他們。

2. 我們應該投他一票，因為他是個有能力的人。

10 A Friend

提示 人的一生中經常會遇到困難。遇到困難時，身邊的朋友常會伸出援手，幫助我們轉憂為喜。請寫一篇短文，文分二段，第一段敘述你個人曾經遭遇的困境，第二段說明你的朋友如何幫助你解決問題，以及問題解決的過程。

Sample 範文

¹In my first year of senior high school, I was not doing well in school, especially in my math class. ²Desperate and anxious, I decided that I would do anything, even cheating, to pass my final exam in math. ³Fortunately, it was my friend Robert who saved me from making this big mistake.

⁴Instead of looking down on me, Robert persuaded me to give up on the idea of cheating. ⁵He also went with me to see our math teacher so that I could tell my teacher about my problems. ⁶In addition, Robert volunteered to help me review what had been covered in math class. ⁷Thanks to his help, I passed my math final exam. ⁸Without Robert's advice, I might have resorted to cheating to overcome the difficulties I was facing. ⁹This would have made me a dishonest person. ¹⁰Robert taught me the importance of honesty, and this is something I will never forget.

Writing Analysis 寫作精靈

主題：遭逢困境時朋友如何提供協助

時態：描述過去遭遇的困境及朋友適時伸出援手的過程，用過去簡單式。

鋪陳： 1. 主旨句：在我高一的時候，我在學校的表現很差，特別是數學課。(Sentence 1)

　　　　 2. 細節發展：第一段說明當時想到解決困難的方法，並點出是誰伸出援手；第二段說明朋友提供援助的過程及結果，並抒發對這件事的感想。(Sentence 2～9)

　　　　　(1)脫離困境的方式：我決定不惜一切，甚至是作弊，來讓數學期末考及格。

　　　　　(2)提供援助的朋友：是 Robert 幫我免於鑄下大錯。

　　　　　(3)提供援助的過程：A. 他沒有輕視我，他說服我放棄作弊的念頭。

　　　　　　　　　　　　　　　B. 他陪我去找老師，說出我的困難。

　　　　　　　　　　　　　　　C. 他自願協助我複習在數學課上學過的東西。

　　　　　(4)結果：幸虧有 Robert 的幫忙，我的數學期末考及格了。

　　　　　(5)感想：如果沒有 Robert 的忠告，我便會以作弊來解決當時遇到的困難，這會讓我成為一個不誠實的人。

　　　　 3. 結論句：Robert 教我誠實的重要性，而這也是我永遠不會忘記的一件事。(Sentence 10)

注意： 1. 敘述過去經驗以過去簡單式為主，但若欲在文中提出「設想」(要不是…)，則須以「與

過去事實相反的假設語氣」來描述。

2. 欲強調是某位友人伸出援手，可以用強調句型 "It + was + sb. + that...."。

🖋 Language Focus 語法重點

(I. Adj. and adj., S + V.... 在⋯與⋯之下，⋯)

例 Desperate and anxious, I decided that I would do anything, even cheating, to pass my final exam in math.

例 Hungry and thirsty, he decided to take a rest and grabbed something to eat.

1. 本句型是由兩個主詞相同的句子合併而成的。第一個句子的結構為 S + be + adj. and adj.，為求精簡，可省略主詞和 be 動詞，僅保留形容詞，和第二個句子以逗號隔開。
2. 前半句的形容詞用來說明主詞的狀態或狀況。

🖋 TRY IT!

1. 在絕望與無助之下，他決定盡一切努力來逃出火場。

_____

2. 既仁慈又慷慨，Brown 先生總是樂意幫助他人，不求任何回報。

_____

(II. S + would + have V-en... ⋯當時可能會⋯)

例 This would have made me a dishonest person.

例 It is a pity that you didn't take part in the race. You would have won it!

本句型為「與過去事實相反的假設法」，表示某個情況在過去是有可能發生的，但實際上並沒有發生。例：

• Why did you climb the tree? You would have fallen and have got hurt! (實際上動作者有爬樹，但沒有摔下來，也沒有受傷。)

🖋 TRY IT!

1. 如果沒有哥哥的勸告，我有可能就蹺家了。我當晚就會在街頭遊蕩了。

_____

2. Lisa 昨晚忘記帶錢包出門，不然她就會買那件漂亮的洋裝了。

_____

主題寫作

主題句寫作

11 Shopping

提示 人們有各種不同的理由去逛街、購物，相信你也有上街購物的經驗。寫一篇短文，文分二段，第一段說明你去購買的物品及理由，包括商店的所在地及所搭乘的交通工具，第二段敘述購物的經過，包括購買後是否滿意等。

Sample 範文

¹Shopping has always been my favorite pastime. ²Yesterday, in order to buy a birthday present for my younger sister, my best friend and I took the MRT to Ximending, a place where teenagers like us can always find the latest products. ³Because my younger sister likes Japanese cartoon characters, I planed to buy her something special with the character of "Hello Kitty" on it.

⁴Walking down the streets lined with all different kinds of shops in Ximending, I finally decided to buy a bag with a cute "Hello Kitty" design on it. ⁵I was sure that my sister would love it. ⁶I was also pleasantly surprised when the clerk gave me a 10 percent discount on the bag, since my friend had also decided to buy a necklace at the same store. ⁷When my sister received her present, she screamed in excitement. ⁸She loved that bag very much. ⁹Sometimes shopping not only brings me pleasure, but also makes my family members happy.

Writing Analysis 寫作精靈

主題：談論某次購物經驗

時態：談論經驗用過去簡單式。

鋪陳：1. 主旨句：購物一直都是我最愛的休閒活動。(Sentence 1)

　　　　2. 細節發展：第一段說明某次購物的地點、交通方式、購物的理由以及購買的商品；第二段敘述購物的經過，包括購買後是否滿意。(Sentence 2～8)

　　　　　(1)背景簡介：昨天為了買生日禮物給妹妹，我和好朋友一起搭捷運到西門町去。西門町是青少年可以買到最新流行產品的地方。因為妹妹喜歡日本卡通人物，所以我決定買有凱蒂貓圖案的產品。

　　　　　(2)購物經過：走在西門町上滿是商店的街道，我最後決定買個有凱蒂貓圖案的提包，我相信妹妹會很喜歡。此外，因為我朋友也決定要在這家店買一條項鍊，所以店員幫我打了九折，我既開心又驚訝。妹妹拿到禮物時，興奮地尖叫，她非常喜歡這個提包。

　　　　3. 結論句：有時候購物不僅能為我帶來樂趣，也能讓我的家人快樂。(Sentence 9)

注意：寫本文時須留意時態的運用。此外，敘述購物過程時，亦須依照時間順序來撰寫。

Language Focus 語法重點

I. N(P), a place where + S + V... ...這是一個...的地方

例 My best friend and I took the MRT to Ximending, a place where teenagers like us can always find the latest products.

例 Every winter, crowds of tourists flood in Hokkaido, a place where people can go skiing or take a bath in a hot spring.

> 後半句為一同位語,用來補充說明逗點前的地點。而同位語中,where 為關係副詞,用來連接後面的形容詞子句,以修飾前面的先行詞 a place。

TRY IT!

1. 每天數以千計的觀光客都會到台北 101 大樓參觀,該處是許多公司和機構的所在地。

2. 傍晚,我們抵達北韓,一個人們還在為取得足夠食物而掙扎的國家。

II. N(P) + V-en... 過去分詞片語

例 Walking down the streets lined with all different kinds of shops in Ximending, I finally decided to buy a bag with a cute "Hello Kitty" design on it.

例 The ivory dresser made in India is my mother's prized possession.

> 1. 本處表示被動的過去分詞片語用來修飾前面的先行詞 N(P),是省略關係代名詞與 be 動詞而來的。例:
> * The ivory dresser which was made in India is my mother's prized possession.
>   → The ivory dresser made in India is my mother's prized possession.
> 2. 若表示主動,則省略的只有關係代名詞,而動詞則改以現在分詞形式出現。
> * The old man tried hard to catch the cat which hid under the table.
>   → The old man tried hard to catch the cat hiding under the table.

TRY IT!

1. 逛完滿是各式各樣填充玩具的商店,我最後決定買這隻手上握著花的泰迪熊。

2. 她正和住在隔壁的女孩聊天。

主題寫作

主題句寫作

12 Garbage

提示 垃圾減量是當前環保的重要問題，請依此主題分兩段寫作。第一段說明垃圾增加的原因，第二段提出垃圾減量的方法。

Sample 範文

¹There are two reasons why there is more and more garbage in the world today. ²One reason is the growing population. ³As the earth's population increases, then the amount of garbage will surely increase as well. ⁴The other reason is that manufacturers are using more and more plastic packaging for their products, and people are not careful about recycling.

⁵Of course, it is not easy to control the size of the earth's population, but there are some things we can do to reduce the amount of garbage in the world. ⁶First, factories and stores should use as little plastic packaging as possible. ⁷Second, we should take reusable bags with us whenever we go shopping. ⁸Third, every family must start recycling. ⁹By doing these things, we will be able to decrease the amount of garbage in the world, reduce pollution, and protect the environment.

Writing Analysis 寫作精靈

主題：垃圾減量

時態：談論目前的問題用現在簡單式，若談遠景則可用未來簡單式。

鋪陳：1. 主旨句：造成今日世界上垃圾越來越多的原因有二。(Sentence 1)

　　　　2. 細節發展：第一段說明垃圾量增加的兩個原因為何，第二段則提出垃圾減量的方法。

　　　　　 (Sentence 2～8)

　　　　　 (1)原因：A. 世界人口增加。

　　　　　　　　　 B. 製造商使用越來越多的塑膠材料來包裝產品，另外人們也不仔細做好資源回收。

　　　　　 (2)解決之道：A. 工廠與商店應盡可能少用塑膠包裝材料。

　　　　　　　　　　　 B. 每次購物都應攜帶可重複使用的環保袋。

　　　　　　　　　　　 C. 家家戶戶開始資源回收。

　　　　3. 結論句：若能做到以上三點，則我們將能達成垃圾減量、減少污染及保護環境。

　　　　　 (Sentence 9)

注意：1. 寫作中探討某個問題的解決之道，建議至少提供二到三項的方法，較為恰當。

　　　　2. 近年來有關環保的議題逐漸受到重視，例如 air or water pollution、global warming 以及 energy crisis 等等。建議平常要多蒐集報章雜誌的資訊，以累積相關知識。

🌿 Language Focus 語法重點

I. One.... The other....　一個…另一個…

例 One reason is the growing population.... The other reason is that manufacturers are using more and more plastic packaging for their products....

例 Linda has two elder brothers. One is tall and thin, and the other is short and chubby.

> 一般而言，在本用法前的內文都會包含 two 或 both 等字詞，但有些名詞必定是「一雙，一對」的意思，例如 hands、feet 或 gloves 等，則可以不必特別再加註數量。例：
> • He held the knife in one hand, and the fork in the other.

✏ TRY IT!

1. Jamie 有一對雙胞胎女兒。一個精力充沛，另一個文靜但聰慧。

2. 在 Sam 匆忙跑出家後，他才突然發現他一腳穿球鞋，另一腳穿皮鞋。

II. First, ... Second, ... Third, ...　第一，…。第二，…。第三，…。

例 There are some things we can do to reduce the amount of garbage in the world. First, factries and stores should.... Second, we should.... Third, every family must....

例 You have to follow the classroom rules. First, keep your desk clean. Second, raise your hand before asking any questions. Third, no talking and eating in class.

> 1. 若提到某個問題有數項解決之道，此時便可善用轉折詞，讓文章更有條理。舉本範文為例，解決垃圾過多的方法有三項，可運用 first、second、third 等序數詞連接各個解決之道。
> 2. 序數詞亦可用來連接有先後順序的步驟。例：
> • Follow the three steps. First, mix the flour with sugar and milk. Second, add nuts to the mixture. Third, put the mixture in the oven and bake it for fifteen minutes.

✏ TRY IT!

1. 政府應立即採取一些措施。第一，建造一座臨時橋樑，讓災民能離開災區。第二，安頓災民於臨時避難所。第三，供應災民食物與水。

2. 在今年暑假結束前，我必須完成三項工作。第一，完成所有作業。第二，讀完五本小說。第三，寫二十篇英文作文。

主題寫作

主題句寫作

127

13 On My Way to School

提示 寫一篇短文敘述你上學途中看到、聽到或想到的事。文分兩段，第一段説明你上學途中的所見所聞，第二段説明對這些事的看法。

Sample 範文

¹I walk to school every morning, and sometimes I see unusual incidents on the way. ²For instance, last Monday on my way to school, I saw an old man lying alone on the side of the road. ³He was shivering and seemed very sick, but most people just quickly passed him by. ⁴All I could do was take out my cell phone and call 119, and then wait beside the old man until an ambulance came to take him to the hospital.

⁵I feel very sad about this incident. ⁶I don't know why the old man was left alone on the side of the road, and I don't understand why people are so indifferent to others. ⁷I think we should pay more attention to the elder, and the government should take care of those of them who are homeless. ⁸What's more, people should show more concern for those who are in need, or our society will become a cold and cruel one.

Writing Analysis 寫作精靈

主題：去學校路上發生的一件事

時態：説明一則故事用過去簡單式，抒發感想則用現在簡單式。

鋪陳： 1. 主旨句：我每天早上都走路上學，在路上我有時候會看見不尋常的事件。(Sentence 1)

    2. 細節發展：第一段説明事件的細節，第二段發表對這起事件的看法。(Sentence 2～7)

       (1)事件過程：上週一上學途中，我看到一個老人獨自躺在路邊。他全身發抖，似乎病得不輕，而大部分路過的人都不加理睬。我所能做的事就是拿出手機撥打 119，然後在旁陪伴他，直到救護車抵達並載他去醫院。

       (2)想法與見解：對於這次的事件，我感到很難過。我不知道為何這個老人獨自被遺留在路旁，也不了解為何人們如此冷漠。我們應更留意長者，政府也應照顧無家可歸的老人。

    3. 結論句：人們更應關心那些需要幫助的人，否則社會將會變得冷漠且殘酷。

    (Sentence 8)

注意： 1. 若欲在段落中敘述一起事件的經過，則應以簡單扼要為原則。舉本範文為例，作者以三句話便交代完整起事件，針對時 (last Monday)、地 (the side of the road)、人 (I, an old man) 以及事 (the old man: lying alone on the side of the road; I: calling 119 and waiting beside the old man) 等四大重點加以陳述。

    2. 即便是小故事亦有大啟示。若故事本身是負面消極的，記得在結論以正面積極的方式

思考，說明如何避免此類負面的事情再發生。

Language Focus 語法重點

I. All + S + can/could + do + is/was + V.... 某人能做的就是…

例 All I could do was take out my cell phone and call 119.

例 It is raining; all Cindy can do is stay at home and watch TV.

1. 本句型強調某人能做的事非常有限，帶有無奈的語氣。
2. 在 be 動詞後面的不定詞片語則是整句話的重點，而不定詞片語中的 to 通常會省略。
 • All I could do was (to) take out my cell phone and call 119.

TRY IT!

1. 當我下公車時，天空正下著大雨。因為我沒有帶傘，我只能趕緊衝回家。

2. 從腳踏車上摔下來後，這個小孩受了傷且無法站起。他所能做的就是大聲求救。

II. I don't know/understand + why + S + V.... 我不知道／不了解為何…

例 I don't know why the old man was left alone on the side of the road, and I don't understand why people are so indifferent to others.

例 I don't know why the building was on fire, and I don't understand why the firefighters arrived late.

1. 直接問句作為及物動詞的受詞時，即形成「間接問句」。需留意間接問句的語序為：疑問詞 + 主詞 + 動詞。
2. 範文運用 I don't know..., and I don't understand.... 之類的句型，雖然句子會顯得比較冗長，但在修辭上卻有加強語氣以及強調重點的效果，可以增加故事的條理與層次。

TRY IT!

1. 我不知道數學老師為什麼說我學習遲緩，而且我也搞不懂我為什麼無法專心於課業。

2. 我不了解為什麼很多名人一直試圖追求名利。

14 The First Time I Spoke English

提示 寫一篇短文敘述你第一次開口說英文的經歷。文分兩段，第一段說明你第一次說英文的經歷，第二段說明此次經歷所帶來的改變與影響。

Sample 範文

¹The first time I spoke English was around eight years ago in a cram school. ²My mother had sent me there to learn English. ³My teacher was named Steven, and he looked very nice and friendly. ⁴In the first class, he introduced himself and then began to teach us about the seasons. ⁵His explanation was interesting, and he even used colorful pictures. ⁶Although I didn't understand him well, I tried to follow along with what he was saying and imitate his pronunciation. ⁷Suddenly, he asked me a question, and I answered it correctly! ⁸He gave me a big smile, which really encouraged me.

⁹Since then, I have always liked to speak English. ¹⁰I am not afraid to express myself in English in front of others. ¹¹Little by little, I have gained more and more confidence. ¹²While traveling abroad, for example, I have used English to communicate easily with others and make new friends. ¹³Thanks to the positive experience, I have become fond of speaking English.

Writing Analysis 寫作精靈

主題： 第一次說英文的經驗

時態： 談論過去的經驗用過去簡單式。

鋪陳： 1. 主旨句：我第一次說英文是在八年前的一間補習班裡。(Sentence 1)

2. 細節發展：第一段敘述第一次開口說英文的過程，第二段則說明本次經歷所帶來的改變與影響。(Sentence 2～12)

(1)描述經歷：我的老師叫 Steven，他看起來人很好也很友善。在第一堂課中，老師自我介紹後，便開始教我們有關季節的題材。他的講解很有趣，而且甚至展示彩色的圖片。雖然我不是很了解，但我試著跟讀並模仿他的發音。突然間老師問了我一個問題，我答對了。他給了我一個燦爛的笑容，這真的鼓勵了我。

(2)改變與影響：從此我喜歡說英文，也不怕在別人面前用英文表達意見。漸漸地我越來越有自信。舉例來說，每當出國旅行時，我都能輕鬆地用英文與別人溝通，並結交新朋友。

3. 結論句：多虧有這次正面的經驗，我變得喜歡說英文。(Sentence 13)

注意： 本文旨在談論自身經驗，文章架構與行文方式可以套用到許多同類型的段落寫作中。作文題目如 An Unforgettable Experience、How I Learn English 或 One Thing I Learned in Senior High School 等，均可套用本文架構。

Language Focus 語法重點

I. ..., which... 關係代名詞的非限定用法

例 He gave me a big smile, which really encouraged me.

例 Uncle Joe showed up with a black mask, which really scared me.

1. 本用法中的關係代名詞不能用 that，且不可省略，與先行詞之間須以逗號隔開。另外，先行詞可以是字詞、片語或子句等。

2. 非限定用法對有明確意義的先行詞做附加說明，即便省略本附加說明，主句的語意仍完整。而限定用法旨在使先行詞的意義更加具體與明確，這類的子句不能省略，否則主句的意義便不完整。例：

• Fetch me the magazine which I put on the window desk. (形容詞子句限定說明是哪本雜誌)

TRY IT!

1. 有些學生常挑燈夜戰準備考試，這樣可能會有害身體健康。

_____

2. 姊姊為了減肥不吃早餐，這讓她無法專心上課。

_____

II. Since + 過去時間 , S + has/have + V-en.... 自從…，…

例 Since then, I have always liked to speak English.

例 Since last year, Rachel has been a member of this local yoga club.

1. 在本文中的 since 作介系詞用，後面可接時間名詞或一般名詞，而主要子句的時態為現在完成式，表示「從過去的某個時間點到現在，某人持續做某事或某事持續進行」。

• Since the war, the country has changed a lot.

2. since 亦可當連接詞用，後面接的子句為簡單過去式，而主要子句則為現在完成式。

• Since Lisa moved to Paris, I have never seen her.

TRY IT!

1. 從第一次遇見他開始，我就很喜歡和他下棋。

_____

2. 自從去年十月起，我就再也沒有收到她的來信或來電了。

_____

主題寫作　　主題句寫作

15 The Difficulties I Have in Learning English

提示 寫一篇兩段的短文描述你學習英文遇到的困難。第一段說明你遇到的困難，第二段說明你處理的過程及結果。

Sample 範文

¹Two of the biggest difficulties I have in learning English are listening and speaking, which I believe are the most important parts of communication. ²I used to feel nervous whenever I had to speak English because I was worried that my pronunciation wouldn't be correct and that I wouldn't be able to follow what others might say.

³In order to overcome these difficulties, I started to listen to the *Easy-to-Learn* radio program every day. ⁴In addition, I also tried not to read the Chinese subtitles whenever I watched movies in English. ⁵Moreover, I joined my school's English Conversation Club so that I can practice speaking English as often as possible. ⁶After doing all these things for two months, I found that my English listening and speaking skills have really improved. ⁷I believe that my English will get much better as long as I keep on working on it.

 ## Writing Analysis 寫作精靈

主題： 學習英文的經驗談

時態： 談學習英文的經驗用過去簡單式。

鋪陳： 1. 主旨句：我學習英文遇到的兩大困難是聽與說，而我相信這兩個要素是溝通上最重要的兩個環節。(Sentence 1)

 2. 細節發展：第一段簡述學英文遇到困難的狀況，第二段說明解決困難的方法與結果。
   (Sentence 2～6)

   ⑴困難：以前每當我必須開口說英文時，我都會很緊張，一則因為擔心發音不正確，再則怕跟不上他人說話的速度。

   ⑵解決之道：A. 為了克服這些困境，我開始每天聽《輕鬆學》的廣播節目。

   　　　　　　B. 每當我看英文電影時，會試著不看中文字幕。

   　　　　　　C. 我加入學校的英語會話社，儘可能常練習說英文。

   ⑶結果：持續兩個月之後，我發現我的聽力和口說能力確實改善了。

 3. 結論句：我相信只要我持之以恆，我的英文一定變得更好。(Sentence 7)

注意： 1. 為使文章內容充實，建議第一段可以寫兩項遇到的困難，而第二段至少也提出二至三項的解決方法。

 2. 轉折詞如 in addition 及 moreover 能讓內容的細節安排更有條理層次，可以多利用。

Language Focus 語法重點

I. used to + V 以前都會做某事…

例 I used to feel nervous whenever I had to speak English.

例 I used to play basketball with Frank on weekends.

> 1. used to 解釋為「以前…」，後面接原形動詞，表示「以前都會做某件事」。
> 2. be used to + V-ing 是指「習慣做某件事」，容易和 used to + V 混淆，須特別小心使用。
> • Mr. Wang is used to having a cup of coffee every morning before work.

TRY IT!

1. 我和祖父母住在鄉下時，每個週日都去河邊釣魚。

_____

2. Tony 以前週末都熬夜玩線上遊戲，這令他的父母生氣。

_____

II. S₁ + Aux. + V₁... as long as S₂ + V₂.... …只要…

例 I believe that my English will get much better as long as I keep on working on it.

例 You can use my car as long as you drive carefully.

> as long as 所連接的子句為條件子句，表示目前所提出的狀況，所以動詞時態用現在簡單式；而主要子句表示可能會發生的結果，可用未來簡單式或助動詞 can。

TRY IT!

1. 只要我們繼續努力工作，我相信我們的努力會讓經理印象深刻。

_____

2. 只要你對我有信心，我會盡全力完成任務。

_____

主題寫作

主題句寫作

16 Something That Must Be Done Before Graduation

提示 即將從高中畢業，你有沒有一件畢業前夕一定要完成的事。請寫一篇分兩段的短文，第一段說明想完成這件事的原因，第二段說明你要如何完成。

Sample 範文

¹One thing I want to do before my graduation is to apologize to my homeroom teacher. ²She used to care about me so much. ³However, things changed while she found out that I had a boyfriend when I should have been studying hard. ⁴When she tried to explain the disadvantages of this, I yelled at her, saying that she had no right to poke her nose into my business. ⁵As soon as these words had slipped out of my mouth, I realized how much I must have hurt her.

⁶Now that I'm going to graduate, I hope to make her understand how regretful I am. ⁷To do this, I will first make a card to express my gratitude for all she has done for me. ⁸Together with the card, I will give her a photo of us together, and then secretly place them on her desk. ⁹Finally, I plan to hug her at the graduation ceremony and apologize in person. ¹⁰I really hope that I can repair our broken relationship.

Writing Analysis 寫作精靈

主題：畢業前想做的事

時態：討論過去的事用過去簡單式；而說明未來如何完成此事則用未來簡單式。

鋪陳：1. 主旨句：在高中畢業前我想做的一件事就是向導師道歉。(Sentence 1)

　　　　2. 細節發展：第一段先交代原因，第二段則說明要如何完成此事。(Sentence 2～9)

　　　　　(1)原因：我的導師發現我交男朋友，而當時正是我應該認真讀書的時候。就當她試著解釋交男友的壞處時，我對她大吼，說她沒有權力管我的事。話一出口，我立刻意識到我傷她有多深。

　　　　　(2)計劃作法：A. 首先做一張卡片感謝她為我所做的一切。

　　　　　　　　　　　　B. 連同卡片，我會附上我倆的合照，接著偷偷放在她的桌上。

　　　　　　　　　　　　C. 最後，我計劃在畢業典禮上擁抱她，並當面向她道歉。

　　　　3. 結論句：我真的希望能修復我們破損的關係。(Sentence 10)

注意：1. 談到過去的憾事，記得時態使用過去簡單式，而助動詞可用 used to、would、could 或是 might。

　　　　2. 談到未來的打算，動詞時態用未來簡單式，常用 will + V 或 plan to + V (代表未來)。

Language Focus 語法重點

I. should + have V-en...　當時應該做… (但未做)

例 Things changed while she found out that I had a boyfriend when I <u>should have been</u> studying hard.

例 I <u>should have gone</u> to bed earlier last night, but I stayed up till 2 am.

1. should + have V-en... 是「與過去事實相反」的用法，表示過去本應該做某件事，但是其實未能做到。
2. 在範文的句子中，動詞為 study，而文章是指在那一段時間都應該認真讀書，故用完成進行式，來強調動作的持續性。

TRY IT!

1. Sam 昨天不應該讓他的女兒獨自一人待在家。

_____

2. 我們當時應該達成協議。我們真是愚蠢！

_____

II. must + have V-en...　當時一定…

例 As soon as these words had slipped out of my mouth, I realized how much I <u>must have hurt</u> her.

例 Father flew into a rage. He <u>must have known</u> the truth.

must + have V-en 是針對過去的事做出肯定的推測。而若欲對現在或未來做出肯定的推測，則應用 must + V/be。
- He didn't dare to look at me. He <u>must have lied</u>. (他當時一定說了謊)
- Jim's daughter <u>must be</u> ten years old now. (Jim 的女兒現在一定十歲了)

TRY IT!

1. 當媽媽不發一語走進臥室時，我知道她一定很難過。

_____

2. 你看起來很疲倦。你昨晚一定有熬夜。

_____

17 Stray Dogs

提示 請以流浪狗為題寫一篇文分兩段的短文，第一段敘述你對流浪狗的觀察與看法，第二段說明你認為要如何解決這樣的問題。

Sample 範文

¹A lot of people like to keep dogs as pets, but many of these dogs are eventually abandoned by their owners. ²These dogs then wander the streets and look for food in garbage dumps. ³I feel sorry for these animals because they are usually sick. ⁴Even worse, they sometimes spread diseases and attack passersby.

⁵The government has to deal with the problem of stray dogs. ⁶In my opinion, this problem can be solved in two ways. ⁷One way is for the government to enforce the ban on abandoning dogs. ⁸People should be fined heavily if they disobey this rule. ⁹The other way is for the government to establish a center where stray dogs can be taken care of and treated by vets. ¹⁰As long as these stray dogs are healthy, many people will be interested in adopting them. ¹¹If the government puts these two ideas into action, I believe that the number of stray dogs will gradually decrease.

Writing Analysis 寫作精靈

主題：流浪狗

時態：談論當前的社會問題用現在簡單式。

鋪陳：1. 主旨句：很多人喜歡養狗當寵物，但其中有很多狗最後都被飼主拋棄。(Sentence 1)

2. 細節發展：第一段先發表對流浪狗的觀察與想法，第二段提出解決之道。

(Sentence 2～10)

(1)觀察與想法：A. 這些被遺棄的狗兒流落街頭，在垃圾堆中覓食。

B. 因為牠們常常生病，我為牠們感到難過。更糟的是，牠們有時會傳播疾病或攻擊路人。

(2)解決之道：政府應該處理流浪狗的問題。

A. 政府需針對棄養狗兒這個問題來制定法條，違法者應繳交高額罰金。

B. 政府需成立棄養中心，在這邊流浪狗可以得到妥善的照顧，並能接受獸醫的治療。只要流浪狗是健康的，就會有很多人想收養牠們。

3. 結論句：如果政府將以上的兩點構想化為實際行動，我相信流浪狗的數量會逐漸減少。

(Sentence 11)

注意：1. 寫作提示要求對某社會問題提出個人的觀察時，一定要寫出具體現象，如範文中提到狗兒在街頭流浪、在垃圾場中覓食、會傳染疾病以及攻擊路人等。

2. 提出問題的解決之道時，可利用句型：One way is.... The other way is....。若提出三項
解決方式，則可用 First of all, ... In addition, ... Last but not the least, ... 表達。

🎯 Language Focus 語法重點

I. keep...as a pet　飼養…為寵物

例 A lot of people like to keep dogs as pets, but many of these dogs are eventually abandoned by their owners.

例 The little girl kept a rabbit as a pet.

> 1. keep 後面若接某種動物的話，解釋為「養，飼養」，範文中的用法即為此義。
> • This farmer kept a lot of chickens.
> 2. 若 keep 後面接人的話，則解釋為「供養，扶養」。

✏ TRY IT!

1. Jenny 想要養一隻狗當寵物，但是她的爸媽不准。

_____

2. 王先生沒辦法賺足夠的錢來養活自己和他的家人。

_____

II. In one's opinion, S + V....　依某人之見，…

例 In my opinion, this problem can be solved in two ways.

例 In Henry's opinion, we'd better stay inside waiting for Julie's phone call.

> 1. 表達「自我的意見」時，可用轉折詞 in my opinion，與主要子句用逗點隔開。
> 2. 本用法為習慣用語，opinion 一般都用單數，絕不可用複數。另外，my 亦可以與其他所有格替換，例如 her、Mary's 或 their 等。

✏ TRY IT!

1. 依我之見，你的問題有兩種方式可以解決。一是報告老師，二是向父母尋求幫助。

_____

2. 依林小姐之見，我們應該在天黑之前出發。

_____

_18_ **Exercise**

提示 運動有益健康是眾所皆知的。寫一篇分為兩段的短文，第一段說明運動的好處，第二段敘述你個人實際的運動經驗。

Sample 範文

¹Exercise can benefit us in many ways. ²For one thing, regular exercise can help a person build up a strong body and stay in good shape, which are two important keys to a healthy life. ³For another thing, exercise can help people relieve pressure from work or studies and even reenergize them. ⁴Exercise, therefore, can improve both our mental and physical health.

⁵Exercise has played an important role in my life ever since I was in elementary school. ⁶The first time my father took me to the swimming pool, I fell in love with this sport. ⁷During every summer vacation that followed, I went swimming two or three times a week. ⁸Besides, because I always felt so refreshed after swimming on a hot day, I discovered that I was also more active. ⁹In my opinion, people of all ages should get into the habit of exercise, so that they can enjoy a healthy life.

Writing Analysis 寫作精靈

主題：談論運動

時態：表達意見以及說明看法時用現在簡單式，舉過去運動的經驗用過去簡單式。

鋪陳：1. 主旨句：運動對我們帶來多方面的好處。(Sentence 1)

2. 細節發展：第一段點明運動有益身心健康，第二段敘述過去的運動經驗。

(Sentence 2～8)

(1)兩大好處：A. 規律運動可以幫助我們擁有強壯的身體與保持好身材。

B. 運動可以幫助我們紓解工作或讀書的壓力，並讓我們精力充沛。

(2)運動經驗：從國小開始，運動在我生命中就扮演了重要角色。

A. 經驗：就在我父親第一次帶我去游泳池時，我就愛上這項運動了。接下來的每年暑假，我每星期游泳二到三次。

B. 好處：在炎熱的天氣下游完泳，我覺得神清氣爽，也更有活力。

3. 結論句：依我之見，各個年齡層的人都應該養成運動的習慣，以享受健康的生活。

(Sentence 9)

注意：1. 若欲在第二段敘述自己過往運動的經驗，需特別留意段落之間的時態差異。

2. 為使各段落架構嚴謹，建議第一段在末尾做個小結論 (如範文中的第四句)，接著再發展第二段的個人經驗。

🌿 Language Focus 語法重點

I. For one thing, ... For another (thing), ...　　其中之一…。另外一個…。

例 Exercise can benefit us in many ways. <u>For one thing</u>, regular exercise can help a person build up.... <u>For another thing</u>, exercise can help people relieve pressure....

例 The MRT has benefited the development of Taipei City in many ways. <u>For one thing</u>, it helps developed a more solid transportation network. <u>For another</u>, it helps boost the local economy by appealing tourists from other cities or countries.

1. 在主題句中提及某事物有多樣益處，但受限於篇幅的關係，建議僅提出兩項說明即可。此時便可套用 For one thing, ... For another (thing), ... 的句型。
2. for one thing 表示「(多項中的) 其中之一」，故後面若欲再提出其中的另一項，則用 for another (thing)，而非 for the other (thing)。

✏ TRY IT!

1. Sally 決定不和同學一起去旅行。其中一個原因是她負擔不起，另外她也要照顧弟妹。

_____

2. Harry 是班上最受歡迎的學生。其中一個原因是他對每個人都很好，另外他長得又帥。

_____

II. a key to N/V-ing　　…的關鍵

例 Regular exercise can help a person build up a strong body and stay in good shape, which are two important <u>keys</u> to <u>a healthy life</u>.

例 Keeping early hours is <u>the key</u> to <u>staying healthy</u>.

1. 表示「某事件的關鍵」，可以用 a key to...。
2. 注意 to 之後接名詞，若為動詞則改為動名詞的形式。

✏ TRY IT!

1. 發現這三枚指紋是破了這件謀殺案的關鍵。

_____

2. 成功的關鍵是決心和準備。

_____

19 What Can Replace the TV in the Living Room?

提示 你家客廳擺了電視嗎？你認為客廳裡主要的活動就是看電視嗎？只有電視才能活絡家庭氣氛嗎？寫一篇兩段的短文，第一段簡單說明電視在你家客廳扮演何種角色，第二段建議一項或兩項以上可以代替電視營造良好家庭氣氛的物品，並說明其原因。

Sample 範文

¹Without a doubt, a television set plays an important part in almost every home these days. ²Like most other families, my family has our television in the living room, where everyone can sit and enjoy the TV programs. ³While watching TV, we talk about the programs we are viewing, and we also share what we did that day. ⁴In other words, the television serves as a stimulus to interaction among my family members.

⁵However, in my opinion, there are many other things that can take over the role that the television plays in our living room. ⁶For example, board games, card games, chess, puzzles, or even strategy computer games are all good for families to play together. ⁷By playing these games, families not only get to spend time together, but also have the chance to improve their relationships at the same time. ⁸Therefore, I think a television is not really a necessity in a family's living room—good interaction is.

Writing Analysis 寫作精靈

主題：可取代家中電視的物品或活動

時態：議論文一般都用現在簡單式。

鋪陳：1. 主旨句：電視機無疑在絕大部分的家庭裡扮演著重要的角色。(Sentence 1)

　　　　2. 細節發展：第一段舉自己的家庭為例，說明看電視時會有哪些活動。第二段則列舉一些可以替代電視的物品，並加以解釋。(Sentence 2〜7)

　　　　　(1)相關活動：我們看電視時，不只會討論電視節目，也會分享當天做了些什麼事。換句話說，電視扮演著促進家人之間互動的角色。

　　　　　(2)可替代性：有很多其他東西是可以取代電視在我們家客廳所扮演的角色。

　　　　　　A. 舉例：棋盤類遊戲、紙牌遊戲、西洋棋、解謎遊戲，甚至策略模擬電腦遊戲都很適合家人一起玩。

　　　　　　B. 功能：一起玩這些遊戲，家人既可共度時光，同時又可促進彼此間的關係。

　　　　3. 結論句：電視不是客廳裡的必需品，良好的互動才是必要的。(Sentence 8)

注意：此主題偏向結合個人生活經驗及議論事理的層面，寫作時以表達個人想法為重心。

✤ Language Focus 語法重點

I. Like + N(P), S + V....　和…一樣，…

例 <u>Like</u> <u>most other families</u>, my family has our television in the living room, where everyone can sit and enjoy the TV programs.

例 <u>Like</u> <u>many other girls</u>, I love shopping and going to the movies.

> 與某人或某事物有相同的狀況，可用 like + N(P)，而相同的狀況以句子型態呈現在後，中間以逗點隔開。若表示狀況不同，則改用 unlike。例：
> • <u>Unlike other animals</u>, humans can read and write.

✎ TRY IT!

1. 和許多其他女孩一樣，我無法抗拒購買漂亮衣服的誘惑。

2. 和多數其他的男生不一樣，Peter 喜歡做家事。

II. A serves as B　A 產生 B 的效果或結果，A 可用作 B

例 The television <u>serves as</u> a stimulus to interaction among my family members.

例 The sofa can <u>serve as</u> a bed.

> A serves as B 可解釋為「A 產生 B 的效果或結果」，屬於比較抽象的概念，範文的用法即屬此類；若解釋為「A 可用作 B」的話，則 A 和 B 一般都是具體的事物。

✎ TRY IT!

1. 老師說這個處罰對其他學生會有警告的效果。

2. 這間書房充當成爸爸的辦公室。

主題寫作

主題句寫作

20 Excuse Me

提示 Excuse me 和 Thank you 是日常生活中最常用的兩句話，挑選其中一句撰寫一篇短文，第一段說明你為何會用到它，第二段則寫出其結果。

Sample 範文

¹"Excuse me" is a common expression used to get someone's attention politely. ²I usually use it when I want to ask a question or ask someone to move so that I can pass by. ³Likewise, I use it when I do something embarrassing. ⁴When I have to leave a place earlier than others, for example, I will say, "Excuse me."

⁵Most of the time when I use this phrase, things usually turn out the way I want them to. ⁶However, there are times when a misunderstanding or even embarrassment is brought about by these words. ⁷For instance, I once asked someone to move so that I could walk through a crowd. ⁸Hearing my "excuse me," a lady turned around, looked at me, and said, "Yeah? You need help?" ⁹No matter what other people's responses might be, using the phrase "excuse me" is still a proper way to make others pay attention to you.

Writing Analysis 寫作精靈

主題：討論一日常用語

時態：針對一句話作說明用現在簡單式，舉出實際例子則用過去簡單式。

鋪陳：1. 主旨句：Excuse me 是一句為了禮貌地引起他人注意的常用語。(Sentence 1)

    2. 細節發展：第一段針對 Excuse me 此用語說明使用時機，第二段則舉一段過去發生的軼事為例，說明使用結果。(Sentence 2～8)

      ⑴使用時機：A. 我想問問題時。

               B. 要求他人借過。

               C. 做了一件尷尬的事，例如想提早離開某個地方。

      ⑵使用結果：使用該句話多半都能達成預期效果，但有時也會造成誤解或尷尬。例如有一次為了穿過人群，我請某人借過。一位女士聽到我說 Excuse me 之後，轉過頭來問我是不是需要幫忙。

    3. 結論句：無論他人的回應會是如何，使用 Excuse me 仍是引起他人注意的適當方法。
    (Sentence 9)

注意：在日常生活中，慣用語 Excuse me 的使用場合相當廣泛，若要以它為主題，建議在第一段列出其主要的使用時機，第二段則挑選其中之一發揮即可。

🖋 Language Focus 語法重點

I. likewise   也，亦

例 I usually use it when I want to ask a question or ask someone to move so that I can pass by. Likewise, I use it when I do something embarrassing.

例 The food was superb. Likewise, the wine (was superb).

> 1. 當兩個情況或概念很相似時，可用副詞 likewise，解釋為「同樣地，也」。Likewise 除了置於句首外，亦可置於句中。
> • Mary's second marriage was likewise unhappy.
> 2. likewise 可置於動詞之後，表示從事同樣的動作，可解釋為「同樣地，一樣地」。
> • I bought this CD and asked my cousin to do likewise.

🖊 TRY IT!

1. 他上次數學考試不及格，這次還是不及格。

2. 男生必須穿著正式服裝，例如西裝。女生亦要穿著正式服裝，例如套裝。

II. the way (that) S + V...   …的方式

例 Most of the time when I use this phrase, things usually turn out the way I want them to.

例 I don't like the way you talk to your parents.

> the way 解釋為「…的方式」，後面接形容詞子句加以補充說明。關係代名詞 that 可以省略。
> • Things usually turn out the way (that) I want them to turn out.

🖊 TRY IT!

1. 我不喜歡你處理這個問題的方式。

2. 這就是我們對待員工的方式。

21 My Room

提示 你擁有自己的房間嗎？或是與兄弟姐妹共用房間？寫一篇短文，文分二段，第一段介紹你房間的位置及擺設，第二段談談你在房間中的活動。

Sample 範文

¹My room is not only a place to study, but also a place to relax. ²I share my room with my sister, and we have tried our best to decorate it so that it is very comfortable. ³Inside, there are two separate desks with a big bed between them. ⁴Since we like novels and comics so much, there are many books in our room. ⁵A stereo and our collection of CDs can also be found next to the closet. ⁶Although my room is small, it is still an important place for studying, relaxing, and having fun.

⁷Listening to music while we study is one thing we like to do in our room. ⁸In addition to discussing our studies, my sister and I also often practice playing the guitar after we finished our schoolwork. ⁹We also enjoy reading books as we lie on the bed in this room. ¹⁰Though my room is neither big nor luxurious, it is, to me, the coziest place in the world.

Writing Analysis 寫作精靈

主題：我的房間

時態：介紹房間的位置及擺設用現在簡單式，介紹平常在房間中所做的活動亦用現在簡單式。

鋪陳：1. 主旨句：我的房間不只是讀書的地方，也是可以放鬆的地方。(Sentence 1)

    2. 細節發展：第一段除了點明房間是和妹妹共用，並簡介裡頭的擺設。第二段說明自己在房間會做的活動。(Sentence 2～9)

      (1)擺設與功能：A. 中間有一張大床，床的兩旁有兩張獨立書桌。房裡有許多書籍。在衣櫥旁邊，有音響和我們所收集的音樂光碟。

             B. 雖然房間小，但它仍是我們讀書、放鬆以及玩樂的地方。

      (2)活動：A. 在房間裡邊讀書邊聽音樂，是我們姐妹倆喜歡做的一件事。

          B. 除了討論課業外，在做完作業後，我和妹妹也常常練習彈吉他。

          C. 我們也喜歡躺在床上看書。

    3. 結論句：房間雖不大也不豪華，卻是最舒適的地方。(Sentence 10)

注意：在第一段介紹房間擺設時，點出房間內幾項重要的佈置或物品即可，切勿描寫太多細節，以避免文章頭重腳輕。

🎯 Language Focus 語法重點

I. a place + to V... 一個…的地方

例 My room is not only a place to study, but also a place to relax.

例 Let's find a place to hide.

> 1. 本用法中的不定詞具有形容詞的詞性，用來修飾前面的名詞 a place。須特別留意此處的不定詞後面一般都不帶任何的介系詞。
> 2. 和 place 不同的是，有些名詞後面的不定詞，必須再接介系詞，語法才算正確。例：
> - This is a good place to live. (to live 後面不用再接介系詞)
> - She is looking for an apartment to live in. (to live 後面一定要接介系詞，不可省略)

✏ TRY IT!

1. 我們的語言教室不僅是學英文的地方，也是開會的場所。

_____

2. 在這個空蕩蕩的房間裡，沒有床可以躺，也沒有沙發可以坐。

II. neither...nor... 既不…也不…

例 Though my room is neither big nor luxurious, it is, to me, the coziest place in the world.

例 The house on the hilltop is neither hers nor mine.

> 1. neither...nor... 為對等連接詞，解釋為「既不…也不…」，具有全盤否定的意思。須特別留意的是，受連接的兩個字詞，詞性必須相同。
> - Though my room is neither big nor luxurious, it is, to me, the coziest place in the world. (big 和 luxurious 均為形容詞)
> 2. 在正式用法中，若 neither...nor... 連接二個主詞，則該句的動詞形式以靠近的主詞決定。
> - Neither you nor he wants to go on the picnic. (動詞 want 的形式由主詞 he 決定)

✏ TRY IT!

1. 這個小男孩獨自坐在角落。他既不哭也不笑。

_____

2. 這顏色與設計都不是她的最愛。

_____

主題寫作

主題句寫作

22 The Most Important Value My Parents Have Taught Me

提示 身為子女，從小到大，你的父母必定教導及傳承許多價值觀，如獨立、誠實、心存感激或是勤奮工作等，舉出一個你認為最重要且影響你最大的價值觀來寫一篇英文作文。第一段簡單介紹此價值觀，並且說明它如何影響你的行為舉止。第二段說明你覺得此價值觀適當嗎？如果有一天為人父母，你會傳承給你子女相同的價值觀嗎？

Sample 範文

[1]My parents have always advised me: "Be open-minded, and you will get more out of life." [2]They have also taught me how important broad thinking is and encourage me to explore the world with an open mind. [3]Thus, I am always willing to try new things, and I am tolerant of different opinions. [4]To me, everything exists for a reason, and it is rewarding to learn about something from different perspectives. [5]Being open-minded enables me to make judgments without prejudice and experience new things by exposing myself to a variety of people and ideas.

[6]As far as I am concerned, being open-minded is the proper attitude toward life. [7]Since this world is diverse and always changing, only by keeping an open mind will I be able to make new discoveries every day. [8]If I have my own children some day, I will teach them how important it is to be open-minded.

Writing Analysis 寫作精靈

主題：影響自己的價值觀

時態：以現在自我的觀點去討論父母所教導的價值觀，仍用現在簡單式。

鋪陳：1. 主旨句：我父母總是勸告我思想要開明，如此我將會從生命中獲得更多。(Sentence 1)

2. 細節發展：第一段說明這個價值觀如何影響自己的想法與行為，第二段發表自己對這個價值觀的評價。(Sentence 2～7)

　(1)影響：A. 父母教我廣泛思考的重要性，並鼓勵我以自由開放的心胸去探索世界。因此我樂意嘗試新事物，並接納不同的意見。

　　　　　 B. 對我而言，萬物都有存在的理由，而且從不同的角度去學習是好的。擁有開放自由的胸襟使我能公正地做出判斷，也能藉由接觸不同的人事物而擁有新體驗。

　(2)評價：就我而言，開放自由的胸襟是一項適當的處世態度。因為世界大不同，而且每天都在改變，唯有敞開心胸每天才能都有新發現。

3. 結論句：如果將來我有了自己的孩子，我也會教導他們擁有自由開放的心胸是多麼的重要。(Sentence 8)

注意：在本篇的寫作提示中，有幾項重點是以問句呈現的。寫好文章後，務必檢查文章內容是否都包含這些問題的解答，切勿遺漏任何一個。

🎯 Language Focus 語法重點

I. Be/V..., and S + will + V.... ⋯，就會⋯

例 Be open-minded, and you will get more out of life.

例 Open the box, and you will see your present.

1. 祈使句後面接 and 或 or 所引導的子句時，祈使句便帶有「假設狀況」的性質，而後面的子句則表示「由此得出的推論或結果」，故須用未來簡單式。
2. 本用法可以與直述法的 if 條件句互換。例：
- Be open-minded, and you will get more out of life.
  → If you are open-minded, you will get more out of life.

✏️ TRY IT!

1. 順著這條街走兩個街口，你就會看到轉角處有家銀行。

_____

2. 每天閱讀英文報紙，一個月後你的英文閱讀能力將大大增強。

_____

II. Only... + Aux. + S + be/V.... 只有⋯才⋯

例 Only by keeping an open mind will I be able to make new discoveries every day.

例 Only then did I realize what my father meant.

1. only 後面可接介系詞片語、副詞或副詞片語，置於句首具有強調的功能。注意該句須使用部份倒裝語序，也就是將助動詞提至主詞前面。
2. 將某些倒裝句還原成正常語序時，須留意句中動詞的變化。
- Only then did I realize what my father meant.
  → I realized what my father meant only then.

✏️ TRY IT!

1. 只有這樣，我們才能準時完成任務。

_____

2. 只有透過訓練和練習，我們才有機會贏得這次的比賽。

_____

23 Becoming a Senior in High School

提示 請寫一篇英文作文，在第一段說明升上高三後，面對升學挑戰，有什麼樣的感想。第二段寫出你如何規劃高三生活，以邁向大學之路。

Sample 範文

¹Time certainly does fly. ²Two years of my high school life have passed, and now I'm faced with a great challenge—the College Entrance Examination. ³I am quite nervous and a little scared because there are piles of books I have to review and I don't have much time to do this. ⁴I've always been determined to ensure I am well-prepared for the exam. ⁵After all, this exam is very important; it may greatly affect my future.

⁶In order to focus on studying, I've decided to give up my favorite forms of entertainment, such as watching TV and surfing the Internet. ⁷Also, to stay healthy and energetic, I will exercise every day. ⁸Furthermore, leading a regular life will help me maintain a steady state of mind. ⁹Most importantly, I will make a study plan and put it into practice step by step. ¹⁰By doing all these things, I am sure that I will be ready when the exam comes.

Writing Analysis 寫作精靈

主題：談高三生活與計畫

時態：討論現況用現在簡單式，若提到未來的規劃則用未來簡單式。

鋪陳：1. 主旨句：前兩年的高中生涯已經過了，現在我正面臨大學入學考試的重大挑戰。
(Sentence 2)

2. 細節發展：第一段說明自己面對眼前挑戰的心情與想法，第二段簡述自己對高三生活的規劃。(Sentence 3～9)

　　(1)我的現況：A. 因為有很多書要複習，但時間所剩不多了，我感到既緊張又害怕。

　　　　　　　　B. 我已下定決心要全力以赴，以確定我準備充分。畢竟，這次的考試非常重要，它也許對我的將來有很大的影響。

　　(2)我的計畫：A. 為了專心讀書，我決定放棄我最喜歡的娛樂活動，如看電視和上網。

　　　　　　　　B. 為了保持健康和精力充沛，我會每天運動。

　　　　　　　　C. 過規律的生活會幫助我保持穩定的心理狀態。

　　　　　　　　D. 最重要的是，我會訂定讀書計畫，並逐步實踐。

3. 結論句：藉由執行以上的計畫，等到考試來臨時，我一定會是準備充分的。
(Sentence 10)

注意：在寫作的技巧中，若欲提出多項的作法或概念時，一般都會將最重要的一項放在最後面，

以加深讀者印象。為求強調，還可以在該項前面加上轉折詞 most importantly。

🖋 Language Focus 語法重點

I. Agreement of Subject and Verb　主詞與動詞的一致性

例 Two years of my high school life have passed.

例 He thinks that ten years is a long time.

> 1. 一般來說，當主詞是表示時間、重量、金額或距離等名詞的複數形時，會被視為一個整體，因此通常搭配單數動詞。
> - Two million dollars is a large sum of money for many people. (表示金額)
> - One hundred miles is not very far. (表示距離)
> 2. 須特別留意的是，在某些情況下，表示時間的名詞並非被視為一個整體，例如強調許多時間的流逝等。此時複數的時間主詞則須搭配複數動詞。
> - So far, ten months have passed.

🖋 TRY IT!

1. 就許多高中生而言，一萬元是一筆大錢。

2. 自從我在巴黎巧遇 Smith 先生，至今已經過了五年。

II. N by N　逐…地，一…一…地

例 Most importantly, I will make a study plan and put it into practice step by step.

例 The patient is getting worse day by day.

> 1. by 可以用來連接兩個相同的可數名詞，表示「逐…地，一…一…地」之意。此兩個名詞均使用單數形，不需冠詞。
> 2. 此用法的常見片語有：year by year (逐年地)、word by word (逐字地)、page by page (逐頁地)、one by one (一個一個地)、day by day (逐日地)。

🖋 TRY IT!

1. 我祖母開始一點一滴地喪失記憶力了。

2. 學生們排好隊後，便開始一個一個進入語言教室。

主題寫作

主題句寫作

24 A Slogan That Impresses Me the Most

提示 商業廣告為了深植人心常常會提出極具吸引力的口號，寫一篇短文介紹一則最令你心動或難忘的廣告口號，説明它吸引你的原因及其效果。

Sample 範文

¹The slogan that impresses me the most is Heineken's "Just Heineken" slogan. ²In fact, all of the recent Heineken commercials on TV end with this slogan. ³In one commercial, a young man puts his hand into a big barrel of ice water and endures the freezing water for a long time, just to find a bottle of Heineken from among all the other different beers. ⁴At the end of this commercial, the slogan "Just Heineken" appears, and it gives me the impression that "Heineken" is something that people just want. ⁵In other words, people will do whatever it takes to get a bottle of Heineken. ⁶This slogan seems to have become very popular among beer drinkers. ⁷Whenever they want to have a beer, Heineken is probably the first one that comes to mind.

Writing Analysis 寫作精靈

主題：一則廣告標語

時態：敘述目前的想法、廣告內容及其影響，宜用現在簡單式。

鋪陳：1. 主旨句：讓我印象最深的廣告標語是海尼根的「就是要海尼根」。(Sentence 1)

2. 細節發展：挑選一則海尼根的廣告為例，描述完廣告內容之後，最後説明它的影響及效果。(Sentence 2～6)

　　(1)廣告簡介：一名年輕男子將手伸進充滿冰水的桶子裡，他忍受寒冷的冰水好一陣子，就只是為了從不同品牌的啤酒中，找出一瓶海尼根啤酒。

　　(2)標語效果：在廣告結尾出現了標語「就是要海尼根」，這給我一種人們非海尼根啤酒不喝的印象。這個廣告標語在愛喝啤酒的人之中，似乎廣為流傳。

3. 結論句：只要他們想喝啤酒時，海尼根也許是第一個進入腦海的啤酒產品。(Sentence 7)

注意：1. commercial 指的是電視或電台廣告，而 advertisement 除了指電視或電台廣告之外，也可以指報章雜誌上的廣告。使用時要特別留意兩者的差別。

2. 要能清楚地描述廣告內容，如同説故事一般，人、事、物等三大元素缺一不可。

Language Focus 語法重點

I. S₁ + V₁ + whatever + S₂ + V₂.... ⋯任何⋯的事物⋯

例 In other words, people will do <u>whatever</u> it takes to get a bottle of Heineken.

例 You can eat <u>whatever</u> you want.

> 1. whatever 解釋為「任何⋯的事物」。作此解釋時，一般都置於句中，後面接名詞子句，範文即屬於此用法。此時，whatever 可與 anything that 互相替換，例：
> - In other words, people will do <u>whatever/anything that</u> it takes to get a bottle of Heineken.
> 2. whatever 解釋為「無論什麼⋯」。作此解釋時，whatever 具有連接詞的性質，用來連接兩個子句。此時，whatever 可與 no matter what 互相替換，例：
> - <u>Whatever/No matter what</u> you do, I will support you.

TRY IT!

1. 我會做你要我做的任何事。

_____

2. 無論你怎麼說，我都不認為他是個誠實的人。

_____

II. Whenever + S₁ + V₁..., S₂ + V₂.... 每當⋯，⋯

例 <u>Whenever</u> they want to have a beer, Heineken is probably the first one that comes to mind.

例 <u>Whenever</u> I see my English teacher, I feel very nervous.

> 1. whenever 解釋為「每當⋯」。作此解釋時，whenever 具有連接詞的性質，一般都置於句首，範文即屬於此用法。此時，whenever 可與 every time (that) 互相替換，例：
> - <u>Whenever</u>/<u>Every time (that)</u> they want to have a beer, Heineken is probably the first one that comes to mind.
> 2. whenever 解釋為「無論何時」。作此解釋時。一般都置於句中，後面接副詞子句。此時，whenever 可與 no matter when 互相替換，例：
> - You will be welcome <u>whenever/no matter when</u> you come.

TRY IT!

1. 每當我生病的時候，媽媽都會照顧我。

_____

2. 無論你什麼時候來拜訪，我都會在家。

_____

主題寫作

主題句寫作

25 A Library

提示 圖書館是學生們經常前往的場所，其重要性不言可喻。針對校內或校外任何一間圖書館，寫一篇短文談談你對它的看法。

Sample 範文

¹The library is one of my favorite places in my school. ²In addition to all the different books available there, the library is also a very important place for students. ³Whenever there is a report assignment, the library is the best place for us to look up the information we need. ⁴It is also a quiet place for us to study or prepare for our exams.

⁵In the library, we can browse through different newspapers and magazines. ⁶In addition, we can read or borrow books that we are interested in, so that we can learn new things and broaden our minds. ⁷Most importantly, all of these resources in the library are free. ⁸Anyone can go into the library and find the information he or she needs. ⁹To me, our school's library is truly the most wonderful place in the world.

Writing Analysis 寫作精靈

主題：對圖書館的看法

時態：提出對某事物的看法或意見用現在簡單式。

鋪陳：1. 主旨句：圖書館是我在學校裡最喜歡的地方之一。(Sentence 1)

   2. 細節發展：第一段說明圖書館對學校的重要性為何，第二段則進一步介紹圖書館的功能。(Sentence 2～8)

    (1)重要性：A. 每當我們有報告作業要交的時候，圖書館是查閱所需資料最好的地方。

        B. 圖書館是個安靜的地方，適合我們讀書或準備考試。

    (2)功能：A. 我們可以瀏覽各種不同的報章雜誌。

       B. 我們可以借閱有興趣的書籍，學習新知並開闊眼界。

       C. 最重要的是，所有館內的資源都是免費的。任何人都可以進去圖書館，找尋自己所需的資料。

   3. 結論句：對我來說，我們學校的圖書館是世界上最棒的地方。(Sentence 9)

注意：建議本篇的文章架構可以分成兩大部份，第一部分是說明圖書館為什麼很重要，寫出二到三個理由；第二部分是圖書館的功能，也可列舉出二或三項功能。

Language Focus 語法重點

I. In addition to + N(P)/V-ing, S + V.... 除了⋯之外，還有⋯

例 In addition to all the different books available there, the library is also a very important place for students.

例 In addition to Chinese calligraphy, she is adept at embroidery.

1. 表示除了第一種狀況外，第二種狀況也包含在內，就可用 in addition to 來連接。
2. in addition to 為介系詞片語，故後面應接名詞 (片語)，若遇到動詞，則應改為動名詞。

TRY IT!

1. 除了各種不同的飲料外，這家便利商店也販賣三明治和零食。

2. 除了參觀博物館之外，我們也去了主題樂園，在那裡玩了一整個下午。

II. In addition, S + V.... 此外，⋯

例 In addition, we can read or borrow books that we are interested in, so that we can learn new things and broaden our minds.

例 Jane is a talented musician. In addition, she is also a famous painter.

1. 欲為前面所提過的某人或某事物增加額外資訊，可使用 in addition 來連接此兩個資訊。
2. in addition 可以置於句首，以逗點與後面的子句隔開。另外也可以置於句中，前後各以一個逗號與前後的字詞隔開。
- We can, in addition, read or borrow books that we are interested in, so that we can learn new things and broaden our minds.

TRY IT!

1. 你必須閱讀老師所指定的資料。此外，你也必須寫一篇英文作文。

2. 當老師在講課時你應該要專心。此外，如果有必要時要做筆記。

主題寫作

主題句寫作

26 The Best Coffee Shop in My Town

提示 每個人對自己生活的城鎮都有相當程度的了解與認識，包括當地的餐廳、商店、電影院等，寫一篇短文介紹你所居住城鎮上最值得推薦的地點，請寫出二至三項的優點或特色。

Sample 範文

¹Corner is the best coffee shop in my town. ²It is located on the corner of a street. ³Though it is not big, Corner is still great. ⁴The coffee served there has the best taste, and the cakes are delicious. ⁵If you prefer tea, there are also many kinds of scented tea available there; each one has a different and delicate smell. ⁶What's more, Corner has a great atmosphere. ⁷It is never noisy, and the owner always plays soft music in the coffee shop. ⁸Whenever I go into Corner, I immediately start to feel calm and relaxed. ⁹Sitting in a comfortable chair, I can read a book, appreciate the paintings from foreign countries on the wall, or just hang out there, with a cup of coffee and a piece of cake. ¹⁰I love Corner so much because it provides me with a peaceful place to go to in this busy world.

Writing Analysis 寫作精靈

主題： 地點的介紹

時態： 介紹目前的某個地點用簡單現在式。

鋪陳： 1. 主旨句：鎮上最棒的咖啡屋是 Corner。(Sentence 1)

2. 細節發展：先簡介咖啡屋的地點與規模，接著說明商品與環境的優點，最後分享自己會在咖啡屋從事的活動。(Sentence 2～9)

　　(1)地點與規模：它位於某個街道的轉角處，規模雖不大，但仍是很棒的咖啡屋。

　　(2)商品美味：咖啡味道好，蛋糕也很美味。另外，對於喜歡喝茶的人，Corner 也有供應多種不同口味的香料茶，每一種都有獨特的美妙香味。

　　(3)氣氛優雅：裡面的氣氛很好，一點都不嘈雜，另外老闆都會播放輕柔的音樂。

　　(4)從事的活動：我每次一進到咖啡屋，我立刻就覺得平靜且輕鬆。坐在舒適的椅子上，我可以看書、欣賞牆上的異國畫作或者只是待在那邊喝杯咖啡和吃塊蛋糕。

3. 結論句：我之所以會喜歡 Corner 是因為在這個忙碌的世界裡，它提供我一處僻靜之所。(Sentence 10)

注意： 1. 寫作提示提出幾個地點為例，切記從中選擇一項說明即可，勿挑選二個以上的地點。

2. 推薦某一場所時，建議由外而內介紹，也就是先介紹外觀，其次是室內陳設，最後再提到氣氛或給人的感受。

🌿 Language Focus 語法重點

I. What's more, S + V.... 此外，…

例 The coffee served there has the best taste, and the cakes are delicious.... What's more, Corner has a great atmosphere.

例 Through instant messaging, you can quickly reach your friends. What's more, it doesn't cost any money.

> 1. 表示除了前面所提到的，還有進一步的說明時，可用轉折詞如 What's more、In addition、Besides、Furthermore 以及 Moreover。
> 2. 使用轉折詞時，注意後面要加上逗點與主要子句隔開。

✏ TRY IT!

1. Beethoven 是一位才華洋溢的作曲家。此外，他非常熱愛音樂。

_____

2. 媽媽挖空南瓜來製作南瓜燈籠。此外，她用裡面的果肉烤了一個派。

II. A, B, or C A、B 或者 C

例 Sitting in a comfortable chair, I can read a book, appreciate the paintings from foreign countries on the wall, or just hang out there, with a cup of coffee and a piece of cake.

例 You can go to the zoo by car, by bus, or by train.

> 1. or 為對等連接詞，用來連接相同詞性的字詞、片語或具有相同結構的子句。
> 2. 連接兩個字串時，or 前面一般不加逗號。
> • If you feel dizzy or sick, consult your doctor as soon as possible.
> 3. 連接三個字串時，第一和第二個字串後面應加逗號，而 or 則擺在第三個字串前面。

✏ TRY IT!

1. 假日時你可以沿著河邊騎腳踏車、在公園裡慢跑或者在沙灘上散步。

_____

2. 如果我們去加州旅遊的話，我們可以去洛杉磯的迪士尼樂園玩，或是到舊金山的惡魔島 (Alcatraz) 參觀。

_____

主題寫作

主題句寫作

27 A Camera Cell Phone

提示 近年來電訊通信進步神速，人與人之間的聯絡方式也有卓越的變革。在今日，有著數位相機功能的手機十分流行，也許你也會想要擁有一台。請寫一篇英文作文說明為什麼你想要或不想要一台具有數位相機功能的手機。

Sample 範文

¹If I could choose, I would want to have a cell phone with a digital-camera function. ²The reason is simple: I could take pictures whenever I wanted to, and I wouldn't need to carry a camera with me. ³Once I met a friend I had not seen for a long time. ⁴After a long talk, it occurred to me that we should take a picture together to remind us of the moment. ⁵However, I hadn't brought my camera with me, and my cell phone did not have a camera function. ⁶I was so disappointed. ⁷Fortunately, my friend happened to have the newest style of cell phone with a camera. ⁸Therefore, we took the photo with my friend's phone. ⁹After this incident, I realized how useful a cell phone with a camera function really can be.

Writing Analysis 寫作精靈

主題：談論是否想擁有照相手機

時態：針對某假設狀況表達自己的看法，應使用與現在事實相反的假設法；舉過去發生的事件為例，用過去簡單式。

鋪陳：1. 主旨句：如果我能選擇，我想擁有一台有照相功能的手機。(Sentence 1)

2. 細節發展：說明理由之後，舉自身經驗為例，支持自己的說法。(Sentence 2～8)

   ⑴理由：每當我想拍照時，我不需帶手機就能照相。

   ⑵經驗：有一次我遇到久未謀面的朋友，長談之後，我突然想到我們兩個應該一起拍照留念。但是我沒帶相機，手機也沒有照相功能，這讓我很失望。所幸我朋友碰巧有最新款的照相手機，因此我們就用它拍了照。

3. 結論句：在此事件之後，我了解有照相功能的手機真的很好用。(Sentence 9)

注意：1. 在假設的情況中，敘述自己可能的作法或行為，此時應用與現在事實相反的假設法。

2. 寫作表達自己的意見時，除了說明理由之外，也應舉例說明，以增加說服力。

🎯 **Language Focus** 語法重點

> **I. If + S + could + V..., S + would + V....** 如果能 (與現在事實相反的假設法)

例 If I could choose, I would want to have a cell phone with a digital-camera function.

例 If he could study abroad, he would go to Italy.

> 1. 表示現在的狀況不可能發生或是純屬假設，則可利用「與現在事實相反」的假設法。
> • If I could fly, I would fly to France to visit my sister. (但事實上我不能飛)
> 2. 注意從屬子句與主要子句的助動詞都用過去式。

✏ **TRY IT!**

1. 如果我能到外國旅遊的話，我想要到巴西去。

2. 如果我現在能見到去世三年的父親，我會緊緊抱住他，並告訴他我有多愛他。

> **II. It occurred to sb. that S + V....** 某人突然想起…

例 It occurred to me that we should take a picture together to remind us of the moment.

例 It occurred to him that he forgot to bring a bottle of water with him.

> 1. 若某人與子句中的主詞是同一人，加上 that 子句含有「某人應該要做某事」的意味時，that 子句便可和不定詞片語互相代換，如：
> • It occurred to me that I should take an umbrella with me.
>   → It occurred to me to take an umbrella with me.
> 2. 動詞 strike 與片語 occur to 都解釋為「突然想起」，因此可以互相代換。
> • It occurred to me that we should take a picture together to remind us of the moment.
>   → It struck me that we should take a picture together to remind us of the moment.

✏ **TRY IT!**

1. 上了公車後，我突然想起我出門前沒關窗。

2. 望著天上的星星，她突然想到應該打個電話給父母。

主題寫作

主題句寫作

28 Making Money or Leading a Simple Life

提示 有些人覺得拼命賺大錢很重要，然而有些人覺得滿足於簡單的生活就好。你的意見是什麼？你覺得哪一個比較重要？請說明理由。

Sample 範文

¹For many people, earning a lot of money is important, but in my opinion, leading a simple life is far more significant. ²Money may bring you wealth, fame, and social status. ³However, in the pursuit of wealth, you may lose some things that are irreplaceable, such as your family, your friends, or your health. ⁴Usually, rich people have a lot of things to worry about. ⁵They cannot spend much time with their families and, therefore, find it difficult to get along with their spouses or children. ⁶It is also hard for them to find true friends because so many people covet their wealth. ⁷Worse still, when they are busy making their fortune, rich people often do not pay attention to their own health and may end up with serious health problems. ⁸For these reasons, I prefer to live a life without such worries. ⁹I will be content with whatever kind of life my income can support. ¹⁰After all, compared with money, there are many other things that should be cherished more in life.

Writing Analysis 寫作精靈

主題：選擇賺大錢或過簡單的生活

時態：談論事理用現在簡單式。

鋪陳：1. 主旨句：許多人認為賺大錢是重要的，但依我之見，過簡單生活更有意義。
(Sentence 1)

2. 細節發展：說明追求財富可能會讓人們失去更珍貴的東西，最後再次強調自己想過簡單生活。(Sentence 2～9)

(1)追求財富的壞處：金錢可帶來財富、名聲和社會地位，但在追求財富的同時，你可能會失去一些無法取代的東西，例如家庭、朋友或健康。

　　A. 有錢人日理萬機，他們無法撥出很多時間和家人相處，因此很難和配偶或小孩和睦相處。

　　B. 他們也很難找到真正的朋友，因為有很多人都是貪圖他們的財富。

　　C. 更糟的是，他們忙著賺錢時，常不注意健康，終致健康出了嚴重的問題。

(2)自己的抉擇：基於以上這些理由，我寧可過著沒有這些煩惱的生活。無論我的收入能維持那一種生活，我都會滿足。

3. 結論句：畢竟，與金錢相較之下，生命中還有許多更值得珍惜的東西。(Sentence 10)

注意：作者以反向思考的方式來行文，先指出追求財富的所有壞處，讓讀者了解追求財富並不是個好選擇，最後再次強調自己比較想過簡單的生活。

🌿 **Language Focus 語法重點**

I. find + it + adj. + to V...　　覺得…，認為…

例 They cannot spend much time with their families and, therefore, find it difficult to get along with their spouses or children.

例 He found it impossible to finish this project in one week.

> 1. 在本用法中，it 為虛受詞，真正的受詞是後面的不定詞片語，而形容詞則是用來形容受詞。
> 2. make 也有類似的用法，句型列法為 make + it + adj. + to V...，解釋為「使某事…」。
> • Computers and the Internet have made it possible to work at home.

✏TRY IT!

1. 我很少花時間讀書，因此覺得要得到成績好是困難的事。

_____

2. 他總是準備充分，因此覺得處理每件事都很容易。

_____

II. Compared with + N(P)/V-ing..., S + V....　　和…相較之下，…

例 Compared with money, there are many other things that should be cherished more in life.

例 Compared with watching movies, reading novels is more interesting for me.

> 1. 注意 compared with 後面要接名詞或名詞片語，若遇到動詞，則要改成動名詞。
> 2. 本用法亦可與片語 in/by comparison with 互相代換。
> • Compared with my sister, Sally is more elegant.
> 　→ Sally is more elegant in/by comparison with my sister.

✏TRY IT!

1. 與你在科學上的成就相較之下，我的成功似乎是無足輕重。

_____

2. 與你哥哥相較之下，你體貼多了。

_____

主題寫作

主題句寫作

29 How SARS Affected My Life

提示 請以 "How SARS Affected My Life" 為題，敘述 SARS 對你個人生活的影響，以及你因此所做的調適與改變。個人生活可以涵蓋你的日常生活及個人感受。

Sample 範文

¹When SARS broke out, it not only caused people to worry about becoming infected with it, but it also made many people inconvenient in their daily lives. ²Take me, for example. ³In addition to wearing a mask, I washed my hands all the time and cleaned my desk at school with alcohol three times a day. ⁴Unfortunately, the smell of alcohol always made me feel nauseous. ⁵What's worse, I started to suspect that others had SARS whenever I heard people coughing. ⁶Worried about becoming infected, I decided to stop going to public areas so often. ⁷Since there was no sign that our fight against SARS would come to an end quickly, I told myself I had to accustom myself to these inconveniences. ⁸After all, anything, even these procedures, could become a habit over time. ⁹Thanks to these precautions, I was never infected with SARS.

Writing Analysis 寫作精靈

主題：談一種曾經流行的疾病

時態：描述曾經發生的事件一律用過去簡單式。

鋪陳：1. 主旨句：當 SARS 爆發流行時，它不但讓人們擔心受到感染，還造成許多人在日常生活上的不方便。(Sentence 1)

　　　　2. 細節發展：舉自己為例，描述當時所做的預防措施及心理調適。(Sentence 2～8)

　　　　　(1)預防措施：A. 除了戴口罩以外，我隨時洗手，並用酒精消毒學校的書桌，一天三次。不幸的是，酒精味每次都讓我想吐。

　　　　　　　　　　　B. 更糟的是，每當我聽到人們咳嗽，我就懷疑他們感染了 SARS。擔心受到感染，我決定少到公共場所去。

　　　　　(2)心理調適：因為當時沒有跡象顯示對抗 SARS 的戰爭很快就會結束，所以我告訴自己要習慣這些不方便。畢竟時間一久，任何事都有可能會變成習慣。

　　　　3. 結論句：因為上述的預防措施，我從來沒受到感染。(Sentence 9)

注意：寫作提示已經將文章內容限制在描寫個人經驗與抒發個人感想，因此切勿離題描述別人的經驗或感想。

✏️ Language Focus 語法重點

I. once/twice/three times/... a day   一天一次／一天兩次／一天三次／…

例 I washed my hands all the time and cleaned my desk at school with alcohol <u>three times a day</u>.

例 The patient should take medicine <u>twice a day</u>.

> 1. 本用法表示某事「在一天之內規律地發生一次或兩次以上」。注意一次的說法是 once，兩次的說法是 twice，而三次和三次以上的說法則是數字後面加上 times，如 five times。
> 2. 其他時間名詞如 week、month、year 或 century 等，都適用於本用法中。
> • These managers meet <u>twice a month</u>.
> 3. 若欲強調某事在某個時間單位內每每規律發生，則可用 every 連接時間名詞，如 twice every Wednesday 或 ten times every month 等。

✏️ TRY IT!

1. 在醫院工作時，這名護士隨時洗手，並一天兩次清潔她的桌子。

_____

2. Anna 每週日都打三次電話給她的男朋友。

_____

II. thanks to   幸虧，由於

例 <u>Thanks to</u> these precautions, I was never infected with SARS.

例 <u>Thanks to</u> his timely help, we didn't lose a lot of money.

> 1. thanks to 是介系詞片語，後接名詞或名詞片語。
> 2. thanks to 後面的名詞表示原因，主要子句便為結果。在大部分的情況下，thanks to 所接的原因都有正面的幫助，故有好結果；但也可以接帶有負面影響的原因，具有諷刺意味。
> • <u>Thanks to</u> you, I was fired!
> 3. 其他片語如 because of 和 due to 也表示說明某種原因，其後都接名詞或名詞片語。
> • I was late for the meeting due to/because of the heavy traffic.

✏️ TRY IT!

1. 多虧有持續的醫療照護，這個老人很快地就從心臟病發復原。

_____

2. 因為你的愚蠢決定，我們喪失了賺大錢的機會！

_____

30 My Ambition

提示 寫一篇英文短文說明你的志願，包括未來想從事的行業是什麼？是什麼原因促使你做出這種選擇？你打算做何種準備以達成你的目標？

Sample 範文

¹My ambition for the future is to become a successful interpreter. ²I have always liked learning languages because I think it is interesting to learn about the cultures behind the languages. ³For me, being an interpreter would <u>enable me to help people from different cultures communicate with each other.</u>

⁴To make my dream come true, I first need to have a good command of English, Chinese, and perhaps even another foreign language. ⁵I must master every area of these languages, including reading, writing, speaking, and listening. ⁶That way, I will be able to translate correctly and fluently from one language to another. ⁷Second, I must read extensively and absorb all kinds of information so that I will be able to quickly understand the basic background of whatever I am interpreting.

⁸<u>I am confident that by doing these things I will be able to attain my goal of becoming an interpreter one day.</u>

Writing Analysis 寫作精靈

主題：我的志願

時態：說明想當口譯員的原因以及如何達成目標，用簡單現在式。

鋪陳：1. 主旨句：我未來的志願就是成為一位成功的口譯員。(Sentence 1)

2. 細節發展：先說明為何有這樣的志願，接著再說明自己應如何努力以達成志願。

(Sentence 2～7)

⑴原因：我一直都喜歡學語言，因為我認為學習語言背後的文化是件有趣的事。對我來說，當口譯員可以讓我幫助不同文化背景的人互相溝通。

⑵努力的方向：A. 首先我應該要精通英文和中文，也許還要精通另一種外語。我必須精通每種語言的各種領域，包括聽說讀寫。如此，我才能正確且流利地翻譯。

B. 另外我必須要廣泛閱讀並吸收各種不同的資訊，如此一來才能快速了解口譯素材的基本內容。

3. 結論句：藉由達成上述的努力方向，我有把握終有一天我會成為口譯員。(Sentence 8)

注意：為使文章內容豐富且多樣化，說明自己應如何努力以達成目標時，建議描述兩到三項的努力方向。

Language Focus 語法重點

I. enable sb. to V... 讓某人能夠…

例 For me, being an interpreter would <u>enable</u> <u>me</u> <u>to help</u> people from different cultures communicate with each other.

例 My parents' support <u>enabled</u> <u>me</u> <u>to continue</u> working on this project.

1. 在本用法中，受詞的後面應該要接不定詞，而非動名詞。
2. 若將受詞 sb. 改為 sth.，則 enable sth. to V... 解釋為「使某事物能夠…」，而 enable sth. 則解釋為「使某事物成為可能，使某事物可行」。
- Gasoline <u>enables</u> <u>this car to move</u>.
- The new highway <u>enables</u> <u>easier access</u> to the island.

TRY IT!

1. 對我而言，出國讀書讓我能夠體驗另一個文化以及開闊眼界。

_____

2. 這一大筆錢能讓 George 在郊區買一棟豪華的別墅。

_____

II. S be confident that + S + V.... 某人有把握…

例 I am <u>confident</u> <u>that</u> by doing these things I will be able to attain my goal of becoming an interpreter one day.

例 The student was <u>confident</u> <u>that</u> he would pass the exam.

1. 若某人肯定某事會發生，則可以用 S be confident that + S + V.... 來表示，後面的 that 子句就代表肯定會發生的事情。
2. confidant 解釋為「知己，密友」，拼字和 confident 很相近，寫作時要特別注意拼寫，切勿混淆。

TRY IT!

1. 我有把握藉由做這些事情，終有一天我能夠讓我的夢想成真。

_____

2. Ted 有把握他能在中午之前抵達目的地。

_____

主題寫作

主題句寫作

31 Pocket Money

提示 根據統計資料得知，從十五歲到二十四歲的青少年學生當中，平均每個月的零用錢外加打工的收入為 4,589 元。根據你的現況，你認為零用錢多少才合理？並說明你如何支配運用你的零用錢。

Sample 範文

¹I think that NT$ 3,000 a month is the ideal amount of pocket money for me because this amount covers my expenses each month. ²To begin with, I divide my monthly expenses into three main parts: transportation, lunch, and entertainment. ³Since I take the bus to school, I have to pay around NT$40 in the bus fare each school day. ⁴Therefore, one-third of my pocket money must be used for transportation.

⁵Next, I have to spend one-third of my pocket money on my lunch. ⁶My mom is too busy to prepare my lunch, so I usually buy my lunch at school. ⁷Finally, the rest of my pocket money is used to buy CDs, books, movie tickets, or anything else I need. ⁸If I don't spend all of my money that month, I then deposit the rest of it in my bank account. ⁹Thus, it is clear that NT$3,000 a month is the perfect amount of pocket money for me.

Writing Analysis 寫作精靈

主題：零用錢

時態：討論個人對某件事物的看法用現在簡單式。

鋪陳：1. 主旨句：我認為一個月三千元的零用錢是理想的金額，因為這個數目足夠支付我每月的開銷。(Sentence 1)

2. 細節發展：說明每個月零用錢分成三個部份來使用，並說明結餘的去向。

   (Sentence 2～8)

   (1)交通費：我搭公車上學，每天的車資約 40 元，因此交通費佔了零用錢的三分之一。

   (2)午餐費：因為媽媽沒空幫我準備午餐，所以我通常在學校買午餐吃，這也佔了零用錢的三分之一。

   (3)娛樂費：其他的零用錢就是用來購買音樂光碟、書、電影票或是其他所需物品。

   (4)結餘去向：如果沒有花完當月的零用錢，我就會將剩下的錢存進銀行戶頭裡。

3. 結論句：由上清楚得知一個月三千元的零用錢是理想的金額。(Sentence 9)

注意：若欲針對某個主題分成三個部份解說時，記得運用轉折詞，如 first、second、third 或 to begin with、next、finally，如此能讓段落更加有組織。

Language Focus 語法重點

I. to begin with 首先

例 To begin with , I divide my monthly expenses into three main parts: transportation, lunch, and entertainment.

例 Here are three steps of making a banana smoothie. To begin with, peel three bananas.

1. 有許多常用的轉折詞為不定詞片語，這種片語一般多置於句首，後面必須搭配一主要子句，用逗點隔開。除了 to begin with 之外，片語如 to sum up「總而言之」、to make matters worse「更糟的是」、to be frank「坦白說」等，均適用於此句構。
2. 寫作中善用轉折詞是加分的利器，使文意更見流暢。

TRY IT!

1. 如果你接近一匹馬，要遵守幾項簡單的規定。首先，不要走在馬的後方。

_____

2. 我今天不想出去。坦白說，我寧願待在家裡看電視。

_____

II. too adj. + to V... 太…而無法…

例 My mom is too busy to prepare my lunch, so I usually buy my lunch at school.

例 Brian was too tired to move. He didn't want to answer the door.

1. 注意句型 too adj. + to V... 具有否定之意，解釋為「太…而無法…」，可以與另一個句型 so adj. + that + S + can't/couldn't + V... 互相代換。
- My mom is too busy to prepare my lunch.
   → My mom is so busy that she can't prepare my lunch.
2. 若主詞是物件，又 to V 有明確的動作產生者，則可以在 to V 前面加上 for + 人。
- The juice is too sweet for me to drink.

TRY IT!

1. 那個小孩太害怕了而無法跑走，他只是一動也不動地站著，嘴巴張得大大的。

_____

2. 這個工作太困難，我無法準時完成，所以我需要多幾天的時間。

_____

主題寫作

主題句寫作

32 One Thing I Feel Regretful About

提示 即將畢業的你，回想高中三年來的生活點滴，是否有什麼遺憾的事呢？描述高中歲月裡一件令你遺憾的事，並說明你的感想及可能的彌補方式。

Sample 範文

¹My three years of senior high school have been wonderful, but there is one thing I regret.

²When I was a freshman, I had a group of close friends in my class. ³We shared our deepest secrets as well as our joys and sorrows with one another. ⁴However, after we were separated into different classes in our sophomore year, I found it hard to maintain these close friendships. ⁵My friends had their own lives and busy schedules, and so did I. ⁶Therefore, we didn't have many chances to get together during our last two years of senior high school. ⁷This really made me sad.

⁸Consequently, I have decided to get together with my old friends after the College Entrance Exam. ⁹At that time, we will all be done with our schoolwork. ¹⁰I plan to have a sleepover at my house, and I can't wait for this reunion. ¹¹I believe that we can become close friends again.

Writing Analysis 寫作精靈

主題：高中生活的一件憾事

時態：談及過往用過去簡單式，說明感想用現在簡單式，可能的彌補則用未來簡單式。

鋪陳：1. 主旨句：我的高中三年都很美好，但有一件憾事。(Sentence 1)

2. 細節發展：首先描述此件憾事，接著說明可能的彌補方式。(Sentence 2～10)

(1)憾事：高一時在班上我有一群死黨，彼此分享秘密、喜悅與憂傷。但是高二分班後，我覺得維持友誼變得困難。我和朋友都有自己的生活，也都很忙。因此在最後兩年的高中生涯中，我們沒有太多機會相處。這令我很傷心。

(2)彌補方式：我決定在大學入學考試之後，和老朋友相聚。屆時我們已經完成學業了，我計劃在我家舉辦過夜派對，而且我迫不及待和他們重聚。

3. 結論句：我相信我們能再次成為親密的好友。(Sentence 11)

注意：就大部分的高中生而言，快樂的回憶應多於遺憾的事，所以第一句寫下 My three years of senior high school have been wonderful, but there is one thing I regret. 可強化自己樂觀的人格特質。

🌿 Language Focus 語法重點

I. A as well as B　　A 以及 B

例 We shared our deepest secrets as well as our joys and sorrows with one another.

例 Anyone who is handsome as well as intelligent has a chance to date Monica.

> 1. 寫作中使用 and 的機會很多，但過多時則顯呆板無趣，無法突顯用字的變化。此時可以與 as well as 或 not only... but also... 交替運用。
> * John is intelligent and energetic.
>   → John is intelligent as well as energetic.
>   → John is not only intelligent but also energetic.
> 2. 如果用 as well as 連接二個主詞時，因重點在於強調前者，所以動詞單複數應由第一個主詞決定。
> * Mary as well as her brothers goes to school by bus every day.

✏️ TRY IT!

1. 你必須付飲料和電影票的錢，總數是新臺幣三百元。

_____

2. 來自外國的學生及牧師聚在教堂裡，一起慶祝耶誕節。

_____

II. S₁ (+ Aux.) + V/be..., and so + Aux./be + S₂.　　…，…也是

例 My friends had their own lives and busy schedules, and so did I.

例 I am good at playing the piano, and so is my sister.

> 1. 副詞 so 解釋為「也，亦」，表示第二個子句的主詞和第一個子句的主詞有相同的情況。注意此兩個子句皆為肯定句，so 之後務必形成倒裝句。(否定則用 neither)
> 2. 若第一個子句的動詞前面有助動詞時，則第二個子句須根據其主詞選擇適當的助動詞；若第一個子句僅有一般動詞，則第二個子句須依照其主詞選用助動詞 does、do 或是 did。若第一個子句的動詞為 be 動詞，則第二個子句須根據其主詞選擇適當的 be 動詞。

✏️ TRY IT!

1. 大象對老鼠說：「如果你能保密，我也能做到。」

_____

2. Sandy 已有大量的回家作業要做，我也是。

_____

33 My Idol

提示 請以 "My Idol" 為題寫一篇英文作文，說明自己所崇拜的偶像是誰，以及為什麼會崇拜他／她？

Sample 範文

¹My idol is my physics teacher, Mr. Yang. ²He has been my teacher for three years, and I admire him for several reasons. ³First, he is a very intelligent and creative teacher. ⁴Whenever we are puzzled by a physics problem, he always comes up with a brilliant method to help us understand and solve the problem.

⁵In addition, Mr. Yang is an open-minded person. ⁶He often shares his experiences with us and encourages us to discuss our problems in class. ⁷Finally, I admire Mr. Yang because he is committed to learning. ⁸Every time I see him, he is always reading the latest physics journal. ⁹He also often tells us that we should never stop learning, especially in today's era of ever-changing technology. ¹⁰Without a doubt, Mr. Yang is my idol as well as one of the best teachers I have ever had.

Writing Analysis 寫作精靈

主角：崇拜的偶像

時態：若偶像為當今存活人物用現在簡單式，已作古之古人則用過去簡單式說明其成就。

鋪陳：1. 主旨句：我的偶像是我的物理老師，也就是楊老師。(Sentence 1)

2. 細節發展：說明崇拜物理老師的三大理由。(Sentence 2～9)

　(1)理由一：楊老師聰明有創意，每當我們遇到物理問題，感到困惑不解時，他總是能想出很棒的方法幫我們解惑。

　(2)理由二：楊老師思想開明，他常在課堂上與我們分享經驗，並鼓勵我們在課堂上討論自己的問題。

　(3)理由三：楊老師勤學，每次我看到他，他總是在閱讀最新的物理期刊。他也告訴我們不要停止學習，尤其是在當今科技日新月異的時代。

3. 結論句：無疑地，楊老師不僅是我遇過最棒的老師，他也是我的偶像。(Sentence 10)

注意：寫作提示未限定段落數目時，寫一段或二段都無妨。若要分二段時，各段落的篇幅要儘量一致。舉本範文為例，若因第一段只說出所崇拜的對象就分段會太單薄，若將崇拜的原因都集結成一段又顯得太多，此時可利用轉折詞 first、in addition、finally，說明第二項理由時用 in addition 分段即可。

🎯 Language Focus 語法重點

I. S + V..., especially.... …，特別是…

例 He also often tells us that we should never stop learning, <u>especially</u> in today's era of ever-changing technology.

例 I like all kinds of vegetables, <u>especially</u> mushrooms and lettuce.

> 1. 陳述事實或情況時，可以用 especially 連接更符合此陳述的狀況。
> 2. especially 可以用來連接許多不同詞類的字詞，如介系詞片語、名詞、形容詞或副詞子句等，此時 especially 會放在主要子句後面，並以逗號隔開，範文例句便屬此種句構。
> 3. 當 especially 和主詞有關時，則應置於主詞的後面，前後以逗號與主詞和其他字詞隔開。
> • All my family love reading. My mother, <u>especially</u>, reads as many books as she can.

✏️ TRY IT!

1. 這隻狗不時搖尾巴，特別是當牠的主人輕輕拍牠的頭。

_____

2. 我和爸媽都愛吃海鮮。特別是我，外出用餐時總是點蝦子吃。

_____

II. Without a doubt, S + V.... 毫無疑問地，…

例 <u>Without a doubt</u>, Mr. Yang is my idol as well as one of the best teachers I have ever had.

例 <u>Without a doubt</u>, *Snow White and the Seven Dwarfs* is one of the most well-known fairy tales in the world.

> 1. 寫作中為了強化結論句的可信度，可以使用轉折詞 without a doubt 來增加說服力。
> 2. without a doubt 和 without doubt 都解釋為「毫無疑問地」，兩者可以互相替換。另外，without a doubt 亦可以與 there is no doubt that 互相替換。
> • <u>There is no doubt that</u> Mr. Yang is my idol as well as one of the be st teachers I have ever had.

✏️ TRY IT!

1. 無疑地，《魔戒》是我曾經閱讀過最棒的書之一。

_____

2. 無疑地，我們會在下一次會議中再次討論這些重要的議題。

_____

34 My Favorite Book

提示 介紹你最喜愛的一位作家或一本書，說明其作品特色或該書內容，及對你的影響。

Sample 範文

[1]My favorite book is *The Present*. [2]It tells the story of a young man looking for the true meaning of life. [3]At first, this man was upset and frustrated because of the many difficulties in his life. [4]Then, he visited an old man. [5]The old man told the young man that if he changed the way he looked at life, he would find the happiness he longed for.

[6]When the young man did this, he realized that the "present" was the present, not the past or the future. [7]Only when he focused on what he was doing at the present moment could he truly enjoy himself, and this led him to success and happiness.

[8]This story has made a great impression on me. [9]I now do understand if I am stuck in the past or worrying about the future, I will fail to grasp the present. [10]In other words, I should appreciate and enjoy the moment I am in. [11]Therefore, whenever I feel nervous or distressed, I always think of *The Present* and the valuable lesson this book has taught me.

Writing Analysis 寫作精靈

主題：最喜愛的一本書

時態：簡介故事內容用過去簡單式，說明本書對自己的影響用現在簡單式。

鋪陳：1. 主旨句：我最喜愛的書是 *The Present*。(Sentence 1)

　　　　2. 細節發展：先簡述本書大意，接著說明書中故事帶給自己的影響與啟示。

　　　　　(Sentence 2～10)

　　　　　(1)本書大意：此書敘述一個年輕人尋找生命真諦的故事。

　　　　　　A. 一開始這個年輕人因人生遭遇許多困難而感到沮喪氣餒，他去拜訪一位長者，這位長者告訴他如果他能換一種方式來面對人生，就會找到他所渴求的快樂。

　　　　　　B. 年輕人依照指示而行，他了解到真正的「禮物」就是現在，不是過去也不是未來。唯有專心於當下所為，才能活得快樂，進而找到成功與幸福。

　　　　　(2)影響啟發：我了解到如果我執著於過去或擔心未來，我便無法抓住現在。換言之，我應該要活在當下。

　　　　3. 結論句：每當我緊張焦慮時，我總會想起 *The Present* 這本書，還有此書教我寶貴的一課。(Sentence 11)

注意：寫作提示中是提到一本書「或」一位作家，可自己選擇熟悉且有所準備的部分下手。

✎ Language Focus 語法重點

I. do/does/did + V 　真的⋯

例 I now <u>do understand</u> if I am stuck in the past or worrying about the future, I will fail to grasp the present.

例 After a three-hour meeting, I <u>did feel</u> tired and exhausted.

1. 助動詞 do、does、did 若出現在肯定句中，後接原形動詞，這是一種加強語氣的用法。
2. 本用法適用於強調動詞的部份，若欲強調名詞，則可用 the very + N，解釋為「就是⋯」。
• *The Lover in Harvard* is <u>the very</u> movie that I want to watch.
3. 如果要強調時間副詞或地方副詞時可用句型 It is... + that....。
• It was on his sixtieth birthday <u>that</u> he won a million dollars in the lottery.

✐ TRY IT!

1. 我真的說了實話，但是沒有人相信我。

_____

2. 不用擔心我。我現在真的覺得好多了。

_____

II. In other words, S + V.... 　換句話說，⋯

例 <u>In other words</u> , I should appreciate and enjoy the moment I am in.

例 She asked John to leave. <u>In other words</u>, he was fired.

1. 接在 in other words 後面的子句，通常是針對前面較冗長且較不明確的陳述，以簡單扼要的方式再次陳述。
2. 一般來說，in other words 後面都有逗號，藉此與主要子句隔開。

✐ TRY IT!

1. 這個男孩是第一個通過終點線的跑者。換句話說，他贏了這次賽跑比賽。

_____

2. 他帶著困惑的表情看著她。換句話說，他不了解她的意思。

_____

主題寫作

主題句寫作

35 The Life of a Senior High School Student

提示 你個人覺得高中生的生活有趣或枯燥？為什麼有趣？為何枯燥？請以 "The Life of a Senior High School Student" 為題，說明你的看法。

Sample 範文

¹In my opinion, the life of a senior high school student is very interesting. ²We not only learn many new things in our lectures but also have a lot of fun doing different activities.

³In my science classes, for example, I have done several experiments to test the theories we have learned in physics, biology, and chemistry. ⁴I once even cut a frog open to examine its organs and vessels. ⁵Activities such as these really motivate me to study more.

⁶Extracurricular activities also make life at school more interesting. ⁷Usually, after school we are quite busy practicing singing, playing sports, and organizing events. ⁸Extracurricular activities like these enable my classmates and I to develop close friendships.

⁹In conclusion, the life of a senior high school student is interesting, since students can learn new things and do different activities.

Writing Analysis 寫作精靈

主題：高中生活

時態：討論現況用現在簡單式。

鋪陳：1. 主旨句：依我之見，高中生的生活是非常有趣的。(Sentence 1)

2. 細節發展：解釋為何有這樣的見解，並舉自己的高中生活為例，分成課堂上和課外兩大部分說明。(Sentence 2～8)

　　(1)原因：我們不止在課堂上學會很多新事物，參與活動時也玩得很開心。

　　(2)課堂活動：在科學課裡，我做了幾個實驗，以驗證所學的物理、生物及化學理論。我有一次甚至解剖青蛙，檢視其器官與血管。像這類的課堂活動讓我更想學習。

　　(3)課外活動：課外活動也讓學校生活更有趣。放學後我們常常忙著練歌、運動以及籌辦活動。像這些課外活動讓我和班上同學發展更親密的友誼。

3. 結論句：高中生的生活很有趣，因為學生可以學到新事物和從事不同的活動。
　 (Sentence 9)

注意：寫作提示要求對高中生活提出個人的看法，「有趣 (interesting)」或「枯燥 (boring)」只能選擇其中一種寫下看法，千萬不要二者都談，會突顯個人缺乏獨立思考能力。

Language Focus 語法重點

I. have fun + V-ing... ⋯玩得開心

例 We not only learn many new things in our lectures but also have a lot of fun doing different activities.

例 The boy had much fun playing with the toys.

> 1. have fun 是指「玩得開心」，後面接動名詞，表示從事某個活動玩得開心。另外，have fun 亦可單獨使用。
> • I didn't have fun at the party last night. It was very boring.
> 2. fun 的前面也可以接 a lot of、much、great 以及 good 等字詞，強調開心的程度。

TRY IT!

1. Tom 上週六和同學一起玩撲克牌，玩得很開心。

_____

2. 昨天我在姐姐的婚禮派對上玩得很開心。我還喝了很多雞尾酒。

_____

II. S₁ + V₁..., since S₂ + V₂.... ⋯，因為⋯

例 The life of a senior high school student is interesting, since students can learn new things and do different activities.

例 Michael decided to move to Paris, since he hoped to experience the French culture.

> 1. 寫作時若須使用許多表示因果的子句時，除了連接詞 because 之外，也可以用 since 和 as，交替使用才能顯出文字的活潑性。
> 2. since 可以置於句中，後面接表示原因的子句，前面則加上逗號，與表示結果的子句隔開。另外，since 亦可置於句首，與表示結果的子句以逗號隔開。
> • Since he hoped to experience the French culture, Michael decided to move to Paris.

TRY IT!

1. 因為我今天早上上學遲到，我放學後必須打掃教室，當作處罰。

_____

2. 因為這個青少年不是故意打破櫥窗的，這家店的老闆決定不報警。

_____

主題寫作

主題句寫作

36 After I Pass the College Entrance Examination...

提示 如果你順利通過大學入學考試，你希望得到父母或親友什麼樣的禮物或獎勵？為什麼？

Sample 範文

¹After I pass the College Entrance Examination, I hope my parents will buy a new computer for me.

²I'd like to receive a new computer for several reasons. ³For one thing, I could use the computer anytime I wanted. ⁴At present, I share a computer with my brother, and sometimes I have to wait long before I can use it. ⁵Once, we both had an important report to hand in the next day; however, my brother got to use the computer first, and I couldn't work on my report until midnight.

⁶Another reason I need my own computer is that our computer is too old and too slow to process a large amount of data. ⁷Besides, its hard drive is not large enough to store all of my photos.

⁸Most important of all, I will definitely need my own computer if I leave home for college.

⁹I really hope that I will do well on the exam, so that my dream of having my own computer will finally come true.

Writing Analysis 寫作精靈

主題：通過大學入學考試後希望得到的禮物或獎勵

時態：討論未來可能發生的事情用一般假設法，說明理由用現在簡單式。

鋪陳：1. 主旨句：順利通過大學入學考試之後，我希望父母買部新電腦給我。(Sentence 1)

2. 細節發展：說明會有這個願望的理由。(Sentence 2～8)

(1)理由一：我可以隨時使用電腦。目前我和哥哥共用電腦，有時候我得等很久才輪到我用。有一次，我們二人隔天都要交一份重要的報告，但是，我哥哥先用了電腦，而我直到半夜才能開始進行。

(2)理由二：我們的電腦太舊且速度緩慢，無法處理龐大的資料。另外，它的硬碟空間不足以儲存我全部的照片。

(3)理由三：更重要的是，如果我離家上大學，一定要有自己的電腦。

3. 結論句：我真的希望自己能考好，才能實現擁有電腦的夢想。(Sentence 9)

注意：寫作中提到未來有可能會發生或實現的事件要用 if 的句型，帶出有可能性的假設句。

🌿 **Language Focus** 語法重點

I. not...until... 直到…才…

例 My brother got to use the computer first, and I couldn't work on my report until midnight.

例 People usually don't realize the importance of health until they lose it.

> 1. 注意主要子句中的 not 在中文翻譯中是不存在的。
> 2. until 後面除了可以接時間副詞之外,也可以接子句。
> 3. until 所接的子句,動詞時態可以用現在簡單式代表未來時態。
> • I won't leave until this child's parents get here.

✏ TRY IT!

1. 有一次,Mary 下午三點理應在電影院和我碰面;但是,她一直到四點才現身。

_____

2. 直到我看到她手指上的鑽戒,我才知道她已經結婚了。

_____

II. S + be (+ not) + adj. + enough + to V.... …(不) 夠…去…

例 Besides, its hard drive is not large enough to store all of my photos.

例 Sue is old enough to ride a scooter or (to) drive a car.

> 1. 一般來說,副詞都是放在形容詞前面修飾,但 enough 雖為副詞,卻一定要放在形容詞後面修飾,須特別留意此特點。
> 2. 有時 enough 後面可以加上 for sb.,表示「某人 (不) 夠…去做某事」。
> • Besides, its hard drive is not large enough for me to store all of my photos.
> 3. enough 除了修飾形容詞外,亦可修飾副詞。如:
> • Sammy didn't run fast enough to win this race.

✏ TRY IT!

1. 這間辦公室沒有足夠的空間擺放這些桌椅。

_____

2. 這支手機小到可以讓我把它放進口袋。

_____

主題寫作

主題句寫作

37 Being Polite

 有禮貌的人通常是受人歡迎的，請以 "Being Polite" 寫一篇短文，說明禮貌的重要性。

Sample 範文

[1]The importance of politeness cannot be overemphasized, since being polite can help you improve your self-image and your relationships with others. [2]In today's busy, fast-paced world, contact between people is often reduced to brief exchanges of words or gestures. [3]Because people's impressions and judgments are often made after only a short interaction, just a single rude word or comment may forever label someone as an impolite person. [4]Therefore, being polite can help you make good impressions on others.

[5]Saying "thank you" and "sorry" in the proper situations will have a great impact on your relationships when communicating with others. [6]By saying "thank you," we can show our respect to whoever offers us a favor, service, or assistance. [7]Likewise, making an apology can help relieve the tension. [8]It is clear that being polite can make every encounter as pleasant as possible and lead to better relationships with others.

Writing Analysis 寫作精靈

主題：談禮貌

時態：論述一項觀念用現在簡單式。

鋪陳：1. 主旨句：禮貌的重要性不言可喻，因為禮貌有助改善個人形象與人際關係。
　　　(Sentence 1)

　　　2. 細節發展：說明為何禮貌有助於改善個人形象以及人際關係。(Sentence 2～7)

　　　　(1)改善形象：在現今步調快速的忙碌世界中，人與人之間的接觸常常只剩下簡短的言語或手勢。很多時候僅透過短暫的互動，人們就留下印象或評價，所以一句粗魯的言語就可能永遠被冠上不禮貌的標籤。因此有禮貌會讓你留給他人好印象。

　　　　(2)改善人際關係：與人溝通時，在適當的情況下道謝或致歉會大大影響你與他人的關係。藉由說聲「謝謝」，我們可以對幫助、服務或協助我們的人表示敬意。同樣地，道歉有助於減緩緊張的氣氛。

　　　3. 結論句：很明顯地，大家都清楚禮貌能儘可能讓每次接觸都愉悅，並改善我們與其他人的關係。(Sentence 8)

注意：在寫作中強調某件事物的重要性，可善用句型：The importance of... cannot be overemphasized，並利用連接詞 since 說明原因。

🎯 Language Focus 語法重點

I. The importance of...cannot be overemphasized. ...再重要不過了。

例 The importance of politeness <u>cannot be overemphasized</u>.

例 To a model, the importance of keeping in shape <u>cannot be overemphasized</u>.

1. 本句型是指「某事十分重要」，可以解釋為「某事再重要不過了」。the importance of 後面可以是名詞、名詞片語或動名詞片語。
2. 本句型可以與 We cannot overemphasize N(P)/V-ing.... 以及 We cannot emphasize N(P)/V-ing... too much. 等兩個用法互相代換。
   - The importance of politeness <u>cannot be overemphasized</u>.
     → We <u>cannot overemphasize</u> the importance of politeness.
     → We <u>cannot emphasize</u> the importance of politeness <u>too much</u>.

✏️ TRY IT!

1. 對一個二十幾歲的年輕男子而言，實現自己夢想再重要不過了。

2. 再怎麼強調規律運動的重要性都不為過。

II. It is clear + that + S + V.... 大家都清楚...

例 <u>It is clear</u> <u>that</u> being polite can make every encounter as pleasant as possible and lead to better relationships with others.

例 <u>It is clear</u> <u>that</u> every student in this school should follow the regulations, or they might be punished.

1. 本句型表示所說的內容很清楚或不容懷疑，適合做為文章的主旨句或結論句，表示該論述是普世價值，或人人都認可的。
2. it 為虛主詞，真正的主詞乃是 that 後面的名詞子句。

✏️ TRY IT!

1. 大家都清楚爭執會導致我們與朋友之間的關係變差。

2. 大家都清楚我們只有一個地球，而且環保再重要不過了。

主題寫作

主題句寫作

38 A Great Person in Human History

提示 人類史上有過無數偉大的人物，有發明家、藝術家、政治家、甚至作家，請寫一篇短文介紹一位你所知道的歷史人物，並說明其貢獻。

Sample 範文

[1]Mother Teresa is the person I admire most in human history. [2]When she was only twelve, she decided to help the poor. [3]At the age of eighteen, Mother Teresa went to India to help the people there. [4]She moved to one of the poorest places in India so that she could take care of the homeless and accompany the dying there.

[5]Mother Teresa dedicated nearly all of her life to helping the poorest of the poor and the sickest of the sick, regardless of their race, religion, or beliefs. [6]Her selfless dedication inspired compassion and support from people all over the world, and many people tried to follow her example by giving a hand to those in need. [7]Though Mother Teresa passed away in 1997, I believe that people will always remember her and the great love that she gave to the world.

Writing Analysis 寫作精靈

主題：歷史上的偉人

時態：談論歷史偉人的事蹟要用過去簡單式。

鋪陳：1. 主旨句：德蕾莎修女是我最景仰的歷史人物。(Sentence 1)

2. 細節發展：第一段簡介德蕾莎修女的事蹟，第二段則說明她的奉獻對世界帶來的影響。
   (Sentence 2～6)

   (1)事蹟：當德蕾莎修女只有十二歲的時候，就決定要幫助窮人。在十八歲的時候，她到印度去幫助當地的人。她搬到印度最貧困的地區，如此她便能照顧無家可歸的人並陪伴垂死的人。

   (2)影響：德蕾莎修女一生幾乎都在幫助窮困不堪以及病入膏肓的人，不分種族、宗教或信仰。她無私的奉獻激發世人，許多人追隨她的腳步，向需要幫助的人伸出援手。

3. 結論句：雖然德蕾莎修女死於 1997 年，我相信世人會永遠記住她以及她獻給這世界偉大的愛。(Sentence 7)

注意：1. 我們從小閱讀歷史偉人的故事，也曾用中文介紹過這些人物，卻少有機會用英文來陳述，所以藉此範文練習介紹一位歷史人物。通常介紹其生平時，會提到出生與死亡的年代，或是出生地，若不能正確記住則可省略不談。

2. 介紹偉人時要提到其重要事蹟，例如對世界的重大貢獻或對世人的影響，以彰顯他(她)在你心目中的偉大。

Language Focus 語法重點

I. the + adj. 以部分代全體的用法

例 When she was only twelve, she decided to help the poor.

例 She moved to one of the poorest places in India so that she could take care of the homeless and accompany the dying there.

> 1. the + adj. 是以部分代全體的用法，也就是以此形容詞來代稱所有擁有此特性的人。如：
>   the rich = rich people、the homeless = homeless people、the sick = sick people。注意後面的動詞要用複數形。
> 2. the + adj. 也可以指某一個限定範圍內條件符合的人。
> • The injured were immediately rushed to hospital after the accident.

TRY IT!

1. 當我只有十歲大時，我就決定要致力於幫助無家可歸的人和窮苦人家。

_____

2. 在她的童年時期，她的父母常常邀請鎮上的有錢人到家中吃晚餐。

_____

II. dedicate sth. to + V-ing.../N(P) 奉獻某事物於…

例 Mother Teresa dedicated nearly all of her life to helping the poorest of the poor and the sickest of the sick.

例 The scientist has dedicated most of his time to his research.

> 1. dedicate 搭配的介系詞為 to，後接動名詞片語或名詞、名詞片語。
> 2. devote 的解釋與用法皆與 dedicate 相似，故一般來說可以互相代換。

TRY IT!

1. 雖然他工作忙碌，但是仍奉獻週末的時間到附近的孤兒院照顧孤兒。

_____

2. 身為志工，她奉獻所有的力量去看護社區的老人。

_____

主題寫作

主題句寫作

39 My Cell Phone and I

提示 你可能擁有電腦、手機、照相機，甚至是寵物，如狗、貓、鳥、魚等。請以 "My _____ and I" 為題寫一篇英文短文，描述它 (牠) 在你的生活中所扮演的角色，以及它 (牠) 帶給你的好處或壞處。

Sample 範文

¹My cell phone plays an important role in my life. ²I can't imagine what my life would be like if I didn't have it. ³With my cell phone, I can not only communicate with others, but also send messages to anyone, if necessary. ⁴My cell phone can also serve as a digital camera that I can use to take pictures, so I will never miss out on any chance to record a memorable scene.

⁵Moreover, I can update and save my schedule or any important information in my cell phone. ⁶For example, I can check my phone to see whether I have forgotten one of my friends' birthday. ⁷In addition, my cell phone also provides me with fun and entertainment. ⁸It has many games, and I can easily kill time by playing these games when I am bored.

⁹The only disadvantage of my cell phone is its price. ¹⁰Actually, the cost of the cell phone and the telephone fee are more expensive than I can really afford. ¹¹However, even though I have to pay that much, my cell phone is still a very useful gadget that I can't live without.

Writing Analysis 寫作精靈

主題：自己與某件物品的關係

時態：討論目前的狀態用現在簡單式。

鋪陳：1. 主旨句：手機在我的生活中扮演重要的角色。(Sentence 1)

2. 細節發展：分項說明手機的好處及壞處。(Sentence 2～10)

(1)好處：A. 可以聯繫他人，如有必要也可以傳簡訊給任何人。

B. 充當數位相機，如此便不會錯失任何值得記錄的景象。

C. 在手機中更新、儲存行程或重要資訊。例如我可以查看手機，看看是否忘了朋友的生日。

D. 手機也提供樂趣與娛樂，裡面有很多遊戲，當我無聊的時候，就可以玩這些遊戲打發時間。

(2)壞處：手機唯一的缺點就是價錢。事實上，手機本身和通話費都超出我所能負擔的範圍。

3. 結論句：雖然得付很多錢，我的手機還是一項非常實用且不可或缺的電子產品。

(Sentence 11)

注意：半開放式的寫作中，應選擇一項與自己關係密切的物品或動物，下筆時才能呈現真實情感。

Language Focus 語法重點

I. if necessary　如果有必要的話

例 With my cell phone, I can not only communicate with others, but also send messages to anyone, if necessary.

例 I'll call you at once, if necessary.

1. if necessary 常見於完整子句之後，省略主詞和 be 動詞。
2. 除了 if necessary 之外，類似句型尚有 if anything = if there is anything「即便有」、if possible = if it is possible「如果有可能」、if in doubt = if sb. is/was in doubt「如有疑慮」。

TRY IT!

1. 有了電腦，我不僅可以上網查所需要的資料，如果有必要的話，也可以在網路上購物。

2. 如果可能的話，警方希望在月底前能找回這名失蹤少年。

II. Actually, S + V....　事實上，…

例 Actually, the cost of the cell phone and the telephone fee are more expensive than I can really afford.

例 Actually, no one else could solve this tough problem except Mary.

1. 表達目前的實際狀況，可在完整字句之前加上 actually 做轉折詞。
2. actually 可與以下片語代換：in reality、in actuality、in effect、as a matter of fact。

TRY IT!

1. 事實上，機票錢加上旅行的其他費用比我原先預期的超出很多。

2. 事實上，他並沒有發現我早已偷偷地從窗戶溜出房間。

主題寫作

主題句寫作

40 Should the Lottery Be Abolished?

提示 臺灣發行彩券引發許多社會現象與社會問題，你是否贊成停止彩券發行？請以 "Should the Lottery Be Abolished?" 為題寫一篇英文作文，說明你贊成的原因或反對的理由。

Sample 範文

[1]The advantages and disadvantages of the lottery have been widely discussed. [2]As far as I am concerned, its benefits outweigh its drawbacks.

[3]First of all, a portion of lottery-ticket sales is set aside to promote the welfare of minorities, who can be better cared for, as a result. [4]At the same time, lottery-ticket buyers can feel that they have contributed a little to charity, even if they end up winning nothing. [5]Second, the lottery provides ordinary people with the hope that they might become rich overnight. [6]Though the chances of winning the lottery are quite slim, the lottery still gives people a sense of hope. [7]Finally, the lottery can add a little fun to our boring lives. [8]Those who play the lottery are kept in suspense until the winning numbers are announced. [9]Many people feel that this excitement is the most enjoyable part of the lottery.

[10]All in all, the lottery has more advantages than disadvantages. [11]In my opinion, it should not be abolished.

Writing Analysis 寫作精靈

主題：彩券是否應停止發行

時態：探討現況用現在簡單式。

鋪陳：1. 主旨句：我個人認為彩券的優點勝於缺點。(Sentence 2)
  2. 細節鋪陳：分項說明彩券的優點，以強調彩券的優點比缺點還重要。(Sentence 3～10)
    (1)優點一：一定比例的彩券營收用於提升弱勢族群的福利，讓他們得到較好的照顧。而買彩券的人即便最後什麼獎都沒得到，也覺得幫助了慈善機構。
    (2)優點二：彩券給人們帶來希望，他們可能一夜致富，雖然中獎機率微乎其微，卻也提供人們一絲希望。
    (3)優點三：彩券為枯燥的生活增添一點樂趣，玩彩券者直到中獎號碼宣布之前，心都懸在半空中，許多人認為這種刺激是彩券最有樂趣的部份。
  3. 結論句：依我之見，彩券不應廢除。(Sentence 11)

注意：本寫作主題旨在讓同學發表自己的意見，說明是否贊成廢除彩券。無論贊成或反對，都應寫出理由，建議寫兩項到三項的理由，讓文章內容更豐富。

🎯 Language Focus 語法重點

I. S₁ feel that + S₂ + V.... …覺得…，…認為…

例 At the same time, lottery-ticket buyers can <u>feel that</u> they have contributed a little to charity.

例 <u>Many people feel that</u> this excitement is the most enjoyable part of the lottery.

> feel 在此解釋為「覺得，認為」，後面接 that 子句。feel 雖然可以用來表達意見，但是多半都是基於自己的感覺或情緒，而非事實或證據。

✒ TRY IT!

1. 我覺得政府並沒有盡力解決這個問題。

_____

2. 我認為這部電影是我看過最棒的喜劇片之一。

_____

II. end up + V-ing... 最後以…收場

例 At the same time, lottery-ticket buyers can feel that they have contributed a little to charity, even if they <u>end up</u> <u>winning</u> nothing.

例 If you don't work hard, you'll <u>end up</u> <u>losing</u> everything.

> 1. 指出某人最後的下場，可用片語 end up。此片語常用來描述不好的結果或下場。
> 2. 若結果或下場是以 be 動詞為首，則在改為 being 之後，通常都會省略。
> • You should be much more careful, or you might <u>end up</u> <u>(being)</u> in serious trouble.

✒ TRY IT!

1. 這位富有但自私的國王最後一人獨居大城堡中。

_____

2. 如果你當時搶了那位老婆婆的錢，你最後一定會落得坐牢的下場。

_____

主題寫作

主題句寫作

41 War and Peace

提示 有人說戰爭是和平的手段，也有人說最壞的和平也勝過最好的戰爭。請以 "War and Peace" 為題，敘述你對戰爭與和平的觀點或意見。

Sample 範文

[1]When it comes to world peace, people hold different views about it. [2]Some people think that the only way to achieve peace is to defeat their enemies through war and bring them under control. [3]Others feel the best way to promote world peace is to communicate with others and learn how to respect them.

[4]As far as I am concerned, declaring war on someone else is the worst thing in the world. [5]In a war, civilizations are destroyed, people are killed, and families are broken up. [6]What's worse, hatred grows. [7]How can we expect to have a better world this way?

[8]The most important thing of all, in my opinion, is that people of all races and religions learn to respect one another and start to handle conflicts with communication. [9]Sometimes two opposing groups have to meet each other halfway to solve a problem. [10]Why don't we just learn to be tolerant of different voices to ensure peace?

Writing Analysis 寫作精靈

主題：戰爭與和平

時態：就事論事用現在簡單式。

鋪陳： 1. 主旨句：人們對世界和平持有不同的看法。(Sentence 1)

    2. 細節鋪陳：第一段介紹達到世界和平的兩種看法，第二段說明自己認為戰爭並非良策，第三段則進一步解釋尊重與溝通才是真正達成和平的作法。(Sentence 2～9)

      (1)兩種看法：A. 達到和平的方法是透過戰爭打敗敵人並加以控制。

               B. 促進和平最佳之道是彼此溝通並學會尊重他人。

      (2)自己對戰爭的看法：對我來說，向他人宣戰是世界上最糟糕的事。戰爭破壞文明，人們慘遭殺害，而且家庭破碎。更糟的是，仇恨滋長。這樣我們如何期待一個更好的世界呢？

      (3)正確作法：依我之見，最重要的是各個種族或宗教的人都應學會彼此尊重，並以溝通處理衝突，有時持相反意見者要妥協以解決問題。

    3. 結論句：何不學著包容不同的聲音以確保和平？(Sentence 10)

注意：寫作時，為了使文句更有變化，除了使用複合句之外，亦可以採用問句，讓文章看起來更加活潑。

🎯 **Language Focus** 語法重點

I. Some.... Others.... 有些…。另一些…。

例 Some people think that the only way to achieve peace is.... Others feel the best way to promote world peace is....

例 Some students go to school by bus. Others take the MRT.

> some、others 是指非限定的兩個族群，尚有其他族群未被提出。而 some、the others 則是指限定的兩個族群，解釋為「有些…其餘的…」。
> - Some people will mop the floor. Others will wash the windows. (有三個以上的族群)
> - Some people will mop the floor. The others will wash the windows. (僅有兩個族群)

✏️ **TRY IT!**

1. 一談到彩券，人們抱持著不同的想法。有些人相信彩券的部份營收幫助了弱勢族群過更好的生活，有些人則認為彩券只會給社會帶來負面的影響。

_____

2. 在週末時，有些人待在家看電視，有些人則偏好從事戶外活動。

_____

II. one another; each other 互相

例 The most important thing of all, in my opinion, is that people of all races and religions learn to respect one another and start to handle conflicts with communication.

例 Sometimes two opposing groups have to meet each other halfway to solve a problem.

> one another 以及 each other 均代表相互關係。在傳統用法中，one another 是指「三者或三者以上的相互關係」，而 each other 則是指「兩者之間的相互關係」，兩者用法略有不同。雖然在現代英語中，兩者已經沒有差別了，但作文乃為正式文體，因此建議按照傳統用法。

✏️ **TRY IT!**

1. 我想 Mary 和 Ted 是誤會彼此了。

_____

2. 這個社區的居民都互相尊重，因此衝突並不多。

_____

42 The Best Teacher That I Have Ever Met

提示 截至目前為止的學生生活，誰是你遇到過最好的老師？請以 "The Best Teacher That I Have Ever Met" 為題，舉出具體的例子說明。

Sample 範文

¹My senior high school geography teacher is the best teacher that I have ever met. ²She is my role model not only because she is knowledgeable, but also because she has such a great philosophy about life. ³As a geography teacher, she teaches us a lot about different places around the world, including everything from the economies and health problems of these places to their climates, plants, and animals. ⁴I have learned a lot from her clear and detailed explanations.

⁵In addition, her philosophy about life can be seen in her attitude toward her students. ⁶She never asks us to study hard just to get good grades, but instead wants us to understand what we are studying. ⁷According to my teacher, only those who know what they want can make their dreams come true. ⁸My geography teacher is a knowledgeable teacher and also a good friend, and she always encourages us to set and accomplish our goals. ⁹Someday, I hope to be as great a teacher as she is.

Writing Analysis 寫作精靈

主題：最好的老師

時態：舉現在的例子說明用現在簡單式。

鋪陳：1. 主旨句：高中地理老師是我遇到過最好的老師。(Sentence 1)

2. 細節發展：說明地理老師為何是心目中最好的老師，最後說明她在自己生命中所扮演
   的角色。(Sentence 2～8)

   (1)知識淵博：身為地理老師，她教導我們世界各地的相關知識，主題從經濟、健康問
      題，一直到氣候、植物和動物。從她清楚且詳細的解說中，我學到很多東西。

   (2)人生觀：她的人生觀反映在對學生的態度上。她從不要求我們為考高分而學習，而
      要我們明白自己在學什麼。她認為只有知道自己要什麼的人才會實現夢想。

   (3)扮演的角色：我的地理老師不僅學識淵博，也是一位好朋友，她總是鼓勵我們設定
      並達成目標。

3. 結論句：希望有一天我能成為像她一樣的好老師。(Sentence 9)

注意：舉例說明時，要解釋他 (她) 為何是心目中最好的老師，描述他 (她) 的個人特色、偉大事
   蹟、價值觀等等，這些細節最後都可以歸納成對自己的影響。

🖋 Language Focus 語法重點

I. as + 身分／職業　身為…

例 As a geography teacher, she teaches us a lot about different places around the world.

例 As seniors in high school, we should focus on our studies.

> 1. as 當介系詞用，後接名詞表示一種身分或職業。
> 2. 除了置於句首外，as + N(P) 亦常放在某些動詞後面，解釋為「從事…，打扮成…」。
> - Samuel works as a reporter.
> - This old man dressed as Santa Claus, trying to please his grandchildren.

🖋 TRY IT!

1. 身為家中的獨子，他必須努力工作養家。

_____

2. 身為一名士兵，他必須聽從指揮官的命令，並為國家奮戰。

_____

II. as + adj. + a(n) + N + as...　和…一樣…

例 Someday, I hope to be as great a teacher as she is.

例 I have as good a voice as the singer.

> as...as... 屬於同級比較，第一個 as 後面是接形容詞或副詞，如：This apple is as big as that one. 或是 I can run as fast as you.。而本句型乃是進階用法，要比較的字詞是有形容詞修飾的名詞。
> - The singer has a good voice. I have a good voice, too.
>   → I have as good a voice as the singer.

🖋 TRY IT!

1. Nancy 和她姊姊一樣都是有名的舞者。

_____

2. 我擁有的房子和你的一樣大。

_____

主題寫作

主題句寫作

43 My Advice on How to Make Good Use of Your Time in High School

提示 高中生活將接近尾聲，想必充滿酸甜苦辣，有歡笑、有榮耀或有些遺憾。請以 "My Advice on How to Make Good Use of Your Time in High School" 為題，寫一篇文章鼓勵學弟妹能善用時間。

Sample 範文

[1]Based on my experiences during the past three years of senior high school, I'd like to provide some advice for freshmen and juniors about how to make good use of your time in high school.

[2]First of all, you should strike a balance between schoolwork and extracurricular activities. [3]Taking part in various activities can enrich your life and enlarge your circle of friends, but don't forget that your school work should be your first priority. [4]In addition, read as many books as possible. [5]Since books are a major source of knowledge, you can learn from others' experiences by reading extensively. [6]Most important of all, try to learn more about yourself by exploring what your interests are and figuring out what you can do well. [7]Only by doing this will you be able to set a reasonable goal and make the right choices for yourself.

[8]I sincerely hope you will take my advice. [9]If you do, you will definitely have an interesting and fulfilling time in high school.

Writing Analysis 寫作精靈

主題：給學弟妹的忠告

時態：以目前的身分，提出未來的建議或期許用祈使句或未來簡單式為宜。

鋪陳：1. 主旨句：以自己高中三年的經驗為基礎，我想提供一些有關如何善用時間的忠告給高一和高二的學弟妹。(Sentence 1)

2. 細節發展：提出自己給學弟妹的三項忠告，最後再強調自己非常希望學弟妹們可以聽從。(Sentence 2～8)

    (1)忠告一：學業與課外活動取得平衡。參與各種活動可充實生活並擴大交友圈，但別忘了學業才應該是優先。

    (2)忠告二：盡量多閱讀。因為書籍是知識的主要來源，透過廣泛閱讀可以從他人經驗中獲得智慧。

    (3)忠告三：最重要的一點是，藉由探索自己的興趣以及發掘自己的長才，試著多了解自己。只有如此才能設定合理的目標，進而為自己做出正確的決定。

3. 結論句：如果你能做到，高中生活一定很有趣而且很充實。(Sentence 9)

注意：忠告是勸告某人要遵從自己的意見，所以在英文中多為祈使句。

🖋 Language Focus 語法重點

I. Based on + N(P), S + V....　依據…，…

例 Based on my experiences during the past three years of senior high school, I'd like to provide some advice for freshmen and juniors about how to make good use of your time in high school.

例 Based on a true story, this film urges viewers to face the problem of global warming.

> based on 解釋為「依據…，以…為基礎」，後面可以接名詞或名詞片語，表示主要子句是依照此延伸而來的。而另一個相似的片語 according to 則解釋為「根據，依照」，後面一樣可以接名詞或名詞片語，表示主要子句的內容是完全按照此而來的。

🖋 TRY IT!

1. 依據我的經驗，我確定你的狗一定是病了。

_____

2. 根據這則新聞報導，犯罪率已逐漸減少。

_____

II. have a(n)...time　過得…，玩得…

例 If you do, you will definitely have an interesting and fulfilling time in high school.

例 The children had a good time playing hide-and-seek.

> 1. time 的前面會加上形容詞，如 good、great、wonderful 等等，表示擁有愉快的時光。
> 2. 本片語後面除了接地方副詞之外，若接某個動作時，須將一般動詞改為動名詞。

🖋 TRY IT!

1. 如果你停止想那些讓你討厭的麻煩，你一定可以在派對上玩得開心。

_____

2. 我和 Mandy 在咖啡廳聊我們最喜歡的動畫片，聊得很愉快。

_____

主題寫作

主題句寫作

44 Preparing for a Year Abroad

提示 在忙碌課業之餘，你曾想過打包行李，出國一年，去親身體驗自己有興趣的事物嗎？請以 "Preparing for a Year Abroad" 為題，描述在此一年中，你會選擇什麼地點，進行什麼樣的活動？你又會以什麼樣的態度來度過在異鄉的這一年？

Sample 範文

[1]If I ever had the opportunity to study abroad for a year, I would definitely go to the city of London. [2]From *King Arthur* to *King Lear*, I have always been fascinated by English literature. [3]I would study English literature and the language in London, where I could walk around historical sites and experience what life must have been like a long time ago.

[4]In addition, I would choose to live with a homestay family so that I could learn more about the people, life, and food in England. [5]I think with a positive attitude and an open mind, I could adjust to any cultural differences I might encounter. [6]After all, only by accepting and embracing these cultural differences will I be able to broaden my horizons and learn something from others.

Writing Analysis 寫作精靈

主題：假想自己在國外度過一年

時態：假設目前不可能發生的情況，用「與現在事實相反」的假設句。

鋪陳：1. 主旨句：如果我有機會出國讀書一年，我一定會選擇到倫敦市。(Sentence 1)

　　　2. 細節鋪陳：先說明自己的學習方向，接著描述自己在異國的生活。(Sentence 2～5)

　　　　(1)學習方向：從《亞瑟王》到《李爾王》，我一直都對英國文學著迷。我會在倫敦學習英國文學和語言，在那邊我可以探訪歷史古蹟，並體驗一下很久以前的生活是怎麼樣的。

　　　　(2)生活概況：我會選擇住在寄宿家庭中，以便了解當地居民、生活與食物。我認為採取積極的態度以及開闊的心胸，便可以適應文化差異。

　　　3. 結論句：畢竟唯有欣然接納這些文化差異，我才能增廣見聞，從他人身上學到更多。
　　　　(Sentence 6)

注意：1. 全篇使用「假設法」，所以助動詞都採用過去式，如 would、could、should、might。

　　　2. 使用倒裝句作為結論具有強調重點的效果。

🌿 **Language Focus** 語法重點

I. S + have/has been + V-en (+ by + O)　現在完成被動式

例 From *King Arthur* to *King Lear*, I have always been fascinated by English literature.

例 She has been taken good care of by her parents.

> 1. 表示從過去一直到現在都持續發生的經驗用現在完成式，若句子為被動語態，則在過去分詞前加上 been。
>
> 2. 在本用法中，主詞 (S) 是動作的承受者，而 by 後面的受詞才是動作的執行者。在某些情況中，動作的執行者是未知的，或是不具有重要性，則可省略不提。

📝 TRY IT!

1. 從鄉村音樂到流行歌曲，我一直著迷於英文歌曲。

_____

2. Karen 是父母的掌上明珠。她一直都被小心地保護著。

_____

II. ...ago　…以前

例 I would study English literature and the language in London, where I could walk around historical sites and experience what life must have been like a long time ago.

例 I moved to Italy ten years ago.

> 1. ago 前面一般是表示時間的名詞，如 three years、a week、two decades 等。
>
> 2. ago 和 before 都可以用來表示「某段時間以前」，但使用時機卻不相同。例如，ten years ago 和 ten years before 雖然都解釋為「十年前」，但 ten years ago 是「從現在時刻」往前推算十年，而 ten years before 是指「從過去某個時刻」再往前推算十年。因此 ago 多用於過去簡單式或現在完成式，而 before 多用於過去完成式。
>
> • When I talked to John, I found out that his wife had been my classmate ten years before.

📝 TRY IT!

1. 很久以前人們相信地球是宇宙的中心。

_____

2. 當我回到這個五年前我離開的小鎮時，我發現一切都沒有改變。

_____

45 Learning in the Age of Technology

提示 隨著電腦及網路的普及，未來的學生或許可以不用像現在一樣天天到學校上課。相反的，他們可以待在家中，靠著各種多媒體設備來自我學習、與老師溝通、繳交作業或考試，進而完成課業。在這二種學習方式中，你比較喜歡哪一種？為什麼？

Sample 範文

¹As technology advances, traditional ways of learning have been greatly transformed. ²While it is true that direct eye contact with teachers and face-to-face discussions with classmates are important, I still prefer to learn by using the Internet and multimedia equipment.

³For one thing, this way of learning is very convenient. ⁴All I need is a computer, and I can get all the useful information I need. ⁵Moreover, this way of learning can help save a lot of our natural resources. ⁶For example, if assignments are given out and turned in by e-mail, no paper will be printed out or wasted. ⁷Furthermore, multimedia learning activities are more interactive and full of variety than traditional learning activities of the past. ⁸With video conferencing and instant messaging, opinions and ideas can be expressed or shared as if people were in the same room. ⁹In fact, questions can be asked and answers at any time. ¹⁰What's best, with this method of learning, I can learn new things through fun games.

¹¹All in all, using new technology and multimedia devices to learn can have many benefits, and that is why I prefer it to the traditional ways of learning.

Writing Analysis 寫作精靈

主題：科技時代的學習方法

時態：談論目前世代的話題用現在簡單式。

鋪陳：1. 主旨句：雖然與老師眼神的接觸以及面對面的討論很重要，但我仍偏好使用網路與多媒體設備來學習。(Sentence 2)

2. 細節發展：說明自己有此偏好的三項理由。(Sentence 3～10)

(1)理由一：這種學習法非常方便。我只需一台電腦就可取得所有我想要的實用資料。

(2)理由二：這種學習方式可以幫助節省自然資源。例如，如果作業都是以電子郵件發送和遞交，便不需使用到紙張。

(3)理由三：多媒體學習活動遠比過去傳統的學習活動更具有互動性與變化。有了視訊會議與即時通訊，意見和想法可以傳遞與分享，猶如大家都同處一室。更棒的是，有了這個學習方法，我可以透過有趣的遊戲學到新事物。

3. 結論句：因為好處多，所以我喜歡運用新科技及多媒體裝置學習。(Sentence 11)

注意： 由於現今科技發達，翻譯題或是作文的題材很可能會與電腦或網路相關，因此平時要多接觸相關詞彙，例如 video conferencing 和 instant messaging 等字詞。

Language Focus 語法重點

> **I. S₁ + V₁... as if + S₂ + were/V₂-ed....** $\cdots$就像$\cdots$

例 Opinions and ideas can be expressed or shared as if people were in the same room.

例 Mary looks as if she knew John. In fact, she has never seen him before.

> as if 解釋為「就好像，彷彿」，用來連接兩個子句。as if 後面接的子句有兩種情形，第一種是描述的情況有可能發生，則此子句的原動詞時態不需做任何調整。第二種是描述的情況與現在事實相反，則此子句的動詞時態要改為簡單過去式。若為 be 動詞，則改為 were，若為一般動詞則改為過去式。
> - It looks as if it is going to rain. (的確有可能下雨)
> - Opinions and ideas can be expressed or shared as if people were in the same room. (事實上人們並不在同一個房間裡)

🖊 TRY IT!

1. 這個員工講起話來好像他是經理似的。

_____

2. 別裝作你不知道我的祕密。我知道 Jessica 已經告訴你所有的事了。

_____

> **II. what's best** 最棒的是

例 What's best, with this method of learning, I can learn new things through fun games.

例 What's best, I can stand on the top of the Eiffel Tower.

> 1. 說明好的理由，第一點用 first of all，第二點用 what's better，最後用 what's best。
> 2. 若說明壞的理由，則可用 what's worse 和 what's worst。

🖊 TRY IT!

1. 最棒的是，你在欣賞完景色之後，還可以到附近的餐廳用晚餐。

_____

2. 最棒的是，當你走出畫廊時，可以看到輝煌的夕陽。

_____

主題寫作

主題句寫作

46 Lottery

提示 請寫一篇短文以 "If I won two million dollars in the lottery, I would help..." 為開頭敘述如果你中了樂透頭獎後，最想幫助的人或是機構，並寫出相關的理由。【91 年指考】

Sample 範文

¹If I won two million dollars in the lottery, I would help my schoolmates in senior high school. ²First, I would <u>donate money to the poor students in my school.</u> ³These days, more and more students are unable to pay their tuition and buy their meals. ⁴I still clearly remember what happened to one of my classmates in second grade. ⁵One day, she burst into tears because she couldn't buy anything nutritious for her little brother. ⁶Sadly, she and her brother only had NT$100 to buy their meals each day.

⁷Second, I would help my school improve its facilities so that the campus would be more suitable for the disabled students. ⁸If these changes were made, then they could receive education in a convenient and comfortable environment. ⁹Although two million dollars would not be a large enough amount to help everyone, I still hope that I would be able to do something for my schoolmates.

Writing Analysis 寫作精靈

主題：贏得兩百萬彩券後

時態：與現在事實相反的假設法。

鋪陳：1. 主旨句：如果我贏得兩百萬彩券，我首先會幫助高中的同學。(Sentence 1)

　　　　2. 細節鋪陳：分兩段解釋自己會採取那些方法來幫助同學。 (Sentence 2～8)

　　　　　(1)捐錢給同學：我會捐錢給學校裡的窮苦學生。最近越來越多學生付不出學費和餐費，我記得高二時有位同學因為無法給弟弟買營養品而放聲大哭，令人難過的是，他們兩人每天的餐費只有一百元。

　　　　　(2)捐錢給學校：我會幫助學校改善設備，如此校園會更適合身障學生就讀。如果校園改善了，那麼這些身障學生便能在一個方便且舒適的環境下接受教育。

　　　　3. 結論句：雖然兩百萬不足以幫助每一個人，我仍希望能為同學做些事。(Sentence 9)

注意：1. 寫作提示中提到自己「最想幫助的人或是機構」，所以一定要以此為重點去寫作，以免偏離主題。

　　　　2. 從提示句可看出本文是一種虛擬情境，所以要用「與現在事實相反」的假設法。

Language Focus 語法重點

I. donate sth. to... 捐某物給⋯

例 First, I would <u>donate</u> <u>money</u> <u>to</u> <u>the poor students</u> in my school.

例 The volunteer has <u>donated</u> <u>a lot of his free time</u> <u>to</u> <u>local charities</u>.

> 1. 除了錢財和物資之外，donate 後面也可以接時間。
> 2. 捐獻的對象可以是人、機構、醫學或科學研究。

✎ TRY IT!

1. 許多人捐贈了白米和衣物給這個窮苦的家庭。

_____

2. 這個生意人捐了一百萬給癌症研究。

_____

II. Sadly, S + V.... 令人難過地，⋯

例 <u>Sadly</u>, she and her brother only had NT$100 to buy their meals each day.

例 <u>Sadly</u>, he still failed the test even if he had studied really hard.

> 1. 副詞除了可以用來修飾形容詞之外，亦可以用來修飾一個句子，也就是本用法。
> 2. 修飾句子的副詞除了放在句首外，亦可以放在句中或句尾。
> - <u>Surprisingly</u>, his boss agreed to his request for a pay raise right away.
>   - → His boss, <u>surprisingly</u>, agreed to his request for a pay raise right away.
>   - → His boss agreed to his request for a pay raise right away, <u>surprisingly</u>.

✎ TRY IT!

1. 令人難過地，這位父親負擔不起他兒子的學費。

_____

2. 顯然地，這位部長涉及了這件醜聞。

_____

47 Mother

提示 請以 "I will never forget something happened between ＿＿＿ and me when I was ＿＿＿." 開始，文分兩段敘述從小到大你與長輩 (如父母親) 間難忘的一件事，並在第二段敘述此事對你的影響。

Sample 範文

¹I will never forget something happened between my mother and me when I was twelve. ²At that time, I was preparing for my final exam, and my mom was sitting beside me, ready to help. ³At first, everything went well. ⁴However, my mother then started to criticize my poor handwriting and complain that I was too slow when I was working on my math problems. ⁵I became so upset that I started to talk back, and I even yelled at her. ⁶A few minutes later, my mom left without saying a word.

⁷I felt triumphant in the beginning, but I soon regretted what I had done. ⁸When I later apologized to my mother, to my surprise, she also apologized and explained why she had criticized me. ⁹Then, we made up and had a good talk. ¹⁰From that day on, my mom has treated me like an adult, and our trust in each other has grown. ¹¹Without a doubt, this incident really brought my mom and me closer.

Writing Analysis 寫作精靈

主題：我的母親

時態：敘述過去難忘的一件事用過去簡單式。

鋪陳：1. 主旨句：我永遠也忘不了在我十二歲那年，我跟母親間發生的一件事。(Sentence 1)

　　　　2. 細節發展：第一段說明這件事發生的過程，第二段提供結局，以及這起事件對我的影響。(Sentence 2～10)

　　　　　(1)過程：那時我正在準備期末考，媽媽在我身旁準備幫助我。一開始都很順利，後來媽媽開始批評我字寫不好，又抱怨我解數學題目的動作太慢，我很沮喪所以就回嘴，甚至對媽媽吼叫。

　　　　　(2)結局：一開始我感到洋洋得意，不久就後悔了。後來當我向媽媽道歉時，出乎我意料之外，媽媽也向我道歉，並解釋批評我的理由。後來我們合好，相談甚歡。

　　　　　(3)事件影響：從那天起，媽媽待我如大人，而我們也越來越信任彼此。

　　　　3. 結論句：這次事件無疑讓我們更加親密。(Sentence 11)

注意：請依提示所提供的主題句發展文章。而畫線部分的字可依中文提示找出你可以發揮的主題，建議找你最熟悉且不會拼錯的字，如本文可寫 my father、my English teacher 等。

🎯 Language Focus 語法重點

I. a few   有些，一些

例 A few minutes later, my mom left without saying a word.

例 He has a few friends working in this restaurant.

1. 注意 a few 和 few 雖然後面都是接可數名詞，但語意相當不同。a few 解釋為「有些，一些」，相近於 some；而 few 解釋為「很少，一點點」，表示幾乎沒有。

2. little 和 a little 後面是接不可數名詞，而兩者的區別同上。

🖉 TRY IT!

1. 影印這些文件需要花數分鐘的時間。

_____

2. 因為他在學校是獨行俠，所以他沒什麼朋友。

_____

II. to one's surprise   令某人驚訝的是

例 When I later apologized to my mother, to my surprise, she also apologized and explained why she had criticized me.

例 When he opened the envelope, to his surprise, there was a large amount of money inside.

1. 本用法表達某人的情緒反應，surprise 可改為其他表示情緒的抽象名詞，如 to one's amazement「令人驚喜的是」、to one's delight「令人開心的是」、to one's excitement「令人興奮的是」。

2. 如要更強化其效果，可在名詞前加 great，或在 to 之前加 much。

- To our great excitement, Wang led his team to victory.

  → Much to our excitement, Wang led his team to victory.

🖉 TRY IT!

1. 昨天 Tony 上班遲到。令他驚訝的是，他的老闆竟然沒有刁難他。

_____

2. 令我大吃一驚的是，導師同意我們所有的要求。

_____

主題寫作

主題句寫作

48 Finding Mr. or Ms. Right Through the Internet

提示 請以 "In my opinion, finding Mr. or Ms. Right through the Internet is (not) a good idea." 開始，寫一篇短文說明你是否贊成透過網路尋找理想情人，並說明理由。

Sample 範文

[1]In my opinion, finding Mr. or Ms. Right through the Internet is not a good idea. [2]To begin with, there are actually many hoaxes in cyberspace. [3]For example. it is impossible to know for certain the identity of anyone you meet on the Internet. [4]A person can lie about his or her name, age, or even sex to fool others. [5]It is not romantic to make friends with someone who might be lying about his or her background.

[6]Worst of all, the person may take advantage of your curiosity and ask you out on a date. [7]Then, that person might do something bad to you. [8]In some terrible cases, some teenage girls have even been raped or murdered. [9]Therefore, I strongly believe that finding Mr. or Ms. Right through the Internet is a bad idea, especially since it can be so unsafe.

Writing Analysis 寫作精靈

主題：透過網路尋找理想情人

時態：探討當前社會現象用現在簡單式。

鋪陳：1. 主旨句：依我之見，透過網路尋找理想情人並不是一個好主意。(Sentence 1)

　　　2. 細節發展：說明兩個理由支持自己的論點。(Sentence 2～8)

　　　　(1)理由一：網路上充斥著許多騙局。例如，要確定任何一個網友的身分是不可能的事，任何人都可以謊報姓名、年齡、甚至性別，藉此愚弄別人。和掩飾其背景的人做朋友並不浪漫。

　　　　(2)理由二：最糟的是，有心人士可能利用你的好奇心邀約你，做出對你不利的事。在某些可怕的案例中，有些青少女甚至被強暴或謀殺。

　　　3. 結論句：我堅決相信透過網路尋找理想情人是個壞主意，特別是因為這十分不安全。(Sentence 9)

注意：1. 寫作提示中限定第一句，基本上就是段落文章的主旨句，必須以此繼續發展文章內容。

　　　2. 注意第一句就要決定自己所持的意見是肯定的或否定的，而下結論句時也可以呼應主旨句的方式強化自己的論點。

🎯 **Language Focus** 語法重點

I. make friends with sb. 和某人做朋友

例 It is not romantic to <u>make friends with someone</u> who might be lying about his or her background.

例 When he visited New York last month, he <u>made friends with some Americans</u>.

> 1. 無論 with 後面是一個人或是兩個以上的人，一律都用 make friends。
> 2. make friends 亦可單獨使用，解釋為「結交朋友」。
> • I found it difficult to <u>make friends</u> at school.

✏️ TRY IT!

1. 和一個會欺凌他人的人做朋友並不睿智。

_____

2. 我不是來這裡交朋友的。相反地，我是來這邊學習新事物。

_____

II. I strongly believe that + S + V.... 我堅信…

例 I <u>strongly believe that</u> finding Mr. or Ms. Right through the Internet is a bad idea, especially since it can be so unsafe.

例 I <u>strongly believe that</u> Joseph will win the English composition contest.

> 1. 在寫作中，文章已經提出幾項可靠且有說服力的理由來佐證自己的看法，則結論句便可採用本句，以強調自己的信念。
> 2. 主詞亦可以替換成其他代名詞或人名；另外，strongly 和 believe 的位置亦可調換。
> 3. 若欲表達強烈的建議，則可將 believe 改為 suggest 或 advise。
> • The doctor <u>strongly suggested</u> that my father (should) quit smoking.

✏️ TRY IT!

1. 我堅信抽菸來提神是個壞主意，特別是因為這會傷害你的健康。

_____

2. 老師力勸他要努力用功，如此他才能就讀於嚮往的大學。

_____

49 A Short Story About Julie

提示 請發揮你的想像力自訂題目，以 "Julie got caught cheating on an English test last Friday." 為開頭寫一篇英文短篇故事。

Sample 範文

¹Julie got caught cheating on an English test last Friday. ²Because she had <u>been addicted to computer games</u>, she forgot to prepare for the test. ³When she came to school that day, she found that all of her classmates were studying. ⁴She thought that it would be impossible for her to learn so many new words and sentences by heart in such a short time. ⁵Thinking only of how angry her parents would be if she got a bad score, Julie decided to cheat on the test. ⁶After the test papers had been handed out, her teacher, Mr. Simon, seemed to focus his attention on his book. ⁷As a result, Julie put her textbook in her lap and quickly started to copy down the correct answers. ⁸Suddenly, Julie felt someone <u>patting her on the shoulder</u>. ⁹She turned around and saw Mr. Simon standing right behind her. ¹⁰The teacher told her to hand in her test and angrily informed her that she would receive a score of zero. ¹¹Julie burst into tears. ¹²If Julie had prepared for the test, this unfortunate situation would never have happened at all.

Writing Analysis 寫作精靈

主題：Julie 作弊被抓

時態：說故事用過去簡單式為宜，時而搭配過去完成式，以區隔不同動作發生的先後順序。

鋪陳：1. 主旨句：Julie 上星期五考英文時作弊被抓。(Sentence 1)

    2. 細節發展：交代故事背景以及說明事件經過，並提供故事結局。(Sentence 2～11)

      ⑴故事背景：她沉迷於電腦遊戲而忘了準備考試。在考試當天抵達學校時，她發現所有的同學都在讀書。她心想自己不可能在短時間內背好所有的生字和句子，而且如果成績不佳，父母不知道會有多生氣，她當下決定作弊。

      ⑵事件經過：在考試卷全都發完後，她的老師 Mr. Simon 似乎就專注在看書。因此 Julie 便將課本放在大腿上，很快地開始抄寫正確的答案。突然間，Julie 覺得有人拍她的肩膀，她轉頭看到 Mr. Simon 就站在她正後方。

      ⑶故事結局：老師要她交出試卷，並很生氣地告訴她要給她零分，Julie 放聲大哭。

    3. 結論句：如果 Julie 早有準備應試，這不幸的狀況根本不會發生。(Sentence 12)

注意：敘述故事的時態，以故事發生的「時間順序」為段落發展的架構。

🖋 Language Focus 語法重點

I. be/get addicted to + N(P)/V-ing...　沉迷於…，對…上癮

例 Because she had been addicted to computer games, she forgot to prepare for the test.

例 This mother is trying hard to prevent her children from getting addicted to surfing the Internet.

1. 表示對某件事情的沉迷，通常指負面的事。另外，to 的後面可以接名詞、名詞片語或是動名詞片語。
2. 以人為主詞，並有同樣用法的動詞片語尚有 be/get used to「習慣於」和 be/get accustomed to「習慣於」。

🖋 TRY IT!

1. 自從妻子過世，他整日沉迷於酒中。

2. 暑假期間，Nancy 沉迷於看漫畫書，她完全沒有做作業。

II. pat sb. on the shoulder/head/...　輕拍某人的肩膀／頭部／…

例 Suddenly, Julie felt someone patting her on the shoulder.

例 I patted Mary on the back, trying to comfort her.

1. 某些肢體動作要搭配特定的介系詞，例如 pat 屬於「拍打」動作，介系詞用 on。其他相關動作尚有 pet「輕輕撫摸 (小孩或動物)」。
• He petted the cat on the head.
2. 若為「抓握」的動詞，則介系詞用 by。如 grab「一把抓住」、grasp「緊抓」、catch「抓住」。
• The police officer grabbed the thief by the arm.

🖋 TRY IT!

1. 他輕拍她的肩膀，告訴她別哭了。

2. 因為嚇壞了，小女孩緊抓住媽媽的手腕。

主題寫作

主題句寫作

50 Exams

提示 請寫一篇英文作文，文分兩段，第一段以 "Exams of all kinds have become a necessary part of my high school life." 為主題句；第二段則以 "The most unforgettable exam I have ever taken is..." 開頭並加以發展。【92 年指考】

Sample 範文

¹Exams of all kinds have become a necessary part of my high school life. ²I think exams are actually a way to make students study hard. ³After taking an exam, I know what I have learned as well as what I might not have noticed before. ⁴In addition, exams allows me to feel that I can master something on my own.

⁵The most unforgettable exam I have ever taken is last semester's final exam. ⁶When I received the test sheets of math, I quickly went through all the pages, trying to find the easiest one. ⁷To my astonishment, though, I couldn't find any easy questions. ⁸I tried again, only to realize that I could not answer any of the questions. ⁹For the remaining seventy-five minutes of the test, I just sat there staring at the paper. ¹⁰That was the most terrible and unforgettable exam I have ever taken.

Writing Analysis 寫作精靈

主題：考試與高中生活

時態：第一段談現況用現在簡單式，第二段談過去經驗用過去簡單式。

鋪陳：1. 主旨句：各種考試都是我高中生活重要的一部份。(Sentence 1)

    2. 細節發展：第一段說明考試對自己的重要性，第二段則敘述自己最難忘的一次考試。

    (Sentence 2～9)

      (1)重要性：A. 我認為考試是一個迫使學生用功的途徑。考完試之後，我知道自己已經學會什麼以及哪些地方還不懂。

            B. 此外，考試讓我覺得我可以靠自己精通或熟悉某些事物。

      (2)難忘的考試：上學期的期末考，是我最難忘的考試。當我拿到數學考卷時，快速瀏覽過試卷，想找出最容易的題目。然而令我驚訝的是，我找不到任何簡單的題目。我又試了一次，才明白我一題也不會。剩下的七十五分鐘，我只能坐在那盯著考卷看。

    3. 結論句：這是我考過最糟糕也是最難忘的一次考試。(Sentence 10)

注意：依據主旨句發展第一段的內容時，要提出見解，以充分支持主旨句的論點。另外，敘述第二段的經歷事件時，內容要按照時間順序發展，多利用與時間相關的轉折詞讓段落更為清楚。

🖋 Language Focus 語法重點

I. only to + V... 卻…

📖 I tried again, only to realize that I could not answer any of the questions.

📖 She opened the door, only to find that there was no one in the office.

> 1. only to + V... 接在主要子句的後面，並以逗號隔開。注意 only to 後面只能接原形動詞，而原形動詞後面常常接 that 子句。
> 2. only to 用來表示隨後某事緊跟著發生，而這件事通常都使人感到驚訝或失望。

🖊 TRY IT!

1. 我抵達機場，卻發現飛機已經起飛了。

_____

2. 他打開書桌最上層的抽屜，卻發現裡面的錢全部不見了。

_____

II. sit...V-ing... 坐在…做…

📖 For the remaining seventy-five minutes of the test, I just sat there staring at the paper.

📖 My father sat on the couch watching his favorite TV program.

> 1. 本用法表示「某人坐在某個地方做某事」，注意第二個動作應以現在分詞的形式呈現。
> 2. 除了 sit 之外，肢體動作如 stand 和 lie 也有類似的用法。
> • The housewife stood on the sidewalk chatting with her friends.
> 3. 其他動詞如 come 和 go 也有相同的用法。
> • After having worked for ten hours, Jim came home feeling exhausted.

🖊 TRY IT!

1. 接下來的五個小時，我躺在床上盯著天花板。

_____

2. 不知道該做些什麼，他坐在書桌前望著黑板。

_____

主題寫作

主題句寫作

核心英文字彙力
2001～4500(三版)

丁雍嫻 邢雯桂
盧思嘉 應惠蕙　編著

◆ **最新字表！**

依據大學入學考試中心公布之「高中英文參考詞彙表 (111 學年度起適用)」
編寫，一起迎戰 108 新課綱。單字比對歷屆試題，依字頻平均分散各回。

◆ **符合學測範圍！**

收錄 Level 3~5 學測必備單字，規劃 100 回。聚焦關鍵核心字彙、備戰學測。
Level 3：40 回
Level 4：40 回
Level 5-1(精選 Level 5 高頻單字)：20 回

◆ **素養例句！**

精心撰寫各式情境例句，符合 108 新課綱素養精神。除了可以利用例句學習
單字用法、加深單字記憶，更能熟悉學測常見情境、為大考做好準備。

◆ **補充詳盡！**

常用搭配詞、介系詞、同反義字及片語等各項補充豐富，一起舉一反三、輕
鬆延伸學習範圍。

WORD UP 數位學習特惠販售中

英文素養寫作攻略

郭慧敏 編著

108 課綱英文素養寫作必備寶典

將寫作理論具象化，打造一套好理解的寫作方法！

本書特色

1. 了解大考英文作文素養命題重點，掌握正確審題、構思與布局要領。

2. 從認識文體、寫作思考串聯到掌握關鍵句型，逐步練好寫作基本功。

3. 提供大考各類寫作題型技巧剖析與範文佳句，全面提升英文寫作力。

PASS KEY TO

英語 *Make Me High* 系列

作文致勝關鍵：

寫作範例100

學科能力測驗適用

解答本

郭慧敏　編著

WRITING

100

BEST SAMPLES

三民書局

TRY IT! 翻譯練習參考解答

學測篇

1 **I.** 1. Susan is not only a talented pianist but also a famous painter.

2. Not only does Mr. Lin speak fluent English, but he also masters Spanish.

II. 1. In addition, I expose myself to nature as much as I can by jogging along the riverside after school every day and going hiking in the mountains on weekends.

2. Senior high school students should read as many Chinese classics as they can in their leisure time.

2 **I.** 1. This class consists of twenty-one boys and twenty-four girls.

2. This meal consisted of a glass of juice, a hamburger, and some French fries.

II. 1. Thank you for reminding me to turn off the lights. How considerate you are!

2. What a pity! You should have come to the party last night.

3 **I.** 1. Mrs. Wang is strict with her children. For example, she demands that they should get good grades in school.

2. Jason is not only a good father but also a good teacher. For example, he always teaches his daughter math with patience after work.

II. 1. Those who are mature enough should be able to know the difference between right and wrong.

2. Those who are under 18 are not allowed to drive cars.

4 **I.** 1. Even though no one agreed with my idea, I didn't feel discouraged.

2. I think nobody would believe me even if I told the truth then.

II. 1. During the summer vacation, I did many outdoor activities such as surfing, hiking, and fishing.

2. I like reading such inspiring novels as *The Old Man and the Sea*.

5 **I.** 1. With the final exam approaching, I can't do anything but stay at home and study hard.

2. After that accident, his parents couldn't choose but accept the harsh fact.

II. 1. It goes without saying that what attracts me most is the simplicity of the country life rather than the prosperity of a city.

2. I enjoy classical music rather than country music.

6 **I.** 1. I take it for granted that a good citizen should obey the law.

2. To my surprise, he took it for granted that we should help him out.

II. 1. Take myself for example. I know better than to cheat in exams.

2. My father takes the law seriously. He knows better than to rob a bank.

7 **I.** 1. My mother is so dedicated to community service that she is highly respected.

2. This is such a funny joke that the audience burst into laughter.

II. 1. Without my teacher's advice then, I wouldn't have made the correct decision.

2. Without the financial assistance offered by the government, this company could have went bankrupt.

8 I. 1. This postcard made me think of Australia, where I went horse-riding for the first time.

2. Listening to the soft music makes me (feel) sleepy.

II. 1. The moment the teacher opened the box, a frog jumped out and scared her to death.

2. The moment I got off the plane, I saw several police officers standing on the jet bridge.

9 I. 1. Sue passed me a note, asking me to pass it to Jenny.

2. I called my parents last week, informing them that I won't go home this weekend.

II. 1. Mom was in a rage and yelled at everyone in the living room, including Dad.

2. A lot of waste paper, including my final report, were thrown into the dump nearby.

10 I. 1. Since that accident, this little girl has never talked to anyone, including her family.

2. Laurence has traveled to many countries, and India is his favorite one.

II. 1. From this experience, I learned that I should be polite to strangers and that I should not say anything offensive to them.

2. Most important of all, from this experience, I learned that money can't buy anything and that family is the most precious thing in the world.

11 I. 1. It's normal for people to feel frustrated when they encounter difficulties, and I am no exception.

2. Most young people long to make a fortune, and I think you are no exception.

II. 1. After this incident, John and Mary reached an agreement to respect each other and, at the same time, learn to control their temper.

2. You'd better not do the math exercises and listen to the music at the same time.

12 I. 1. Though my mom was exhausted after work, she not only made dinner for me, but also helped me with my homework patiently.

2. Though it was pouring, the crowd stood still and sang the national anthem loudly.

II. 1. From this experience, I learned that having luck alone is not enough.

2. Being a good father requires a sense of responsibility and determination to protect his children.

13 I. 1. For the audience, this TV program is not instructional but entertaining.

2. For me, Mr. Smith is not an ambitious politician, but a great educator.

II. 1. I wish that these rumors were disappearing. However, it seems that it is impossible.

2. I wish that I owned a time machine that could let me go back to the past.

14 I. 1. It was Friday morning, and I was very nervous because I had a math test.

2. He hurried home because his family were waiting for him.

II. 1. Even though I got bad grades, Mom still considered me (to be) a good girl.

2. After he succeeded in solving this crisis, people in town considered him (to be) a hero.

15 **I.** 1. There were several guards standing in front of the bank.

2. Even though there are many obstacles standing in my way, I won't give up my dream.

II. 1. Needless to say, it is one of the most wonderful movies I have ever watched.

2. Needless to say, Chinese dishes are popular with many Westerners because they are very delicious.

16 **I.** 1. As far as I am concerned, I think that Michael's latest novel will be a best-seller.

2. As far as this play is concerned, she is indeed a talented musician.

II. 1. After graduating from senior high school, Paul didn't go abroad for further studies. Instead, he worked as a mechanic in a garage.

2. My parents didn't get angry when they saw the poor grades on my report card. Instead, they encouraged me to study harder.

17 **I.** 1. He stood up, grabbed me by the hand, and asked me not to leave.

2. The police warned everyone not to drink and drive.

II. 1. What impresses me most about Korea is Kimchi.

2. What impresses me most about this singer is her beautiful voice.

18 **I.** 1. I thought this rumor might let up, but to my disappointment, it became widespread.

2. When on earth will this rain let up?

II. 1. Just as she began to work, the alarm downstairs went off.

2. Just as I was to give up, Mom's inspiring words occurred to me.

19 **I.** 1. I left my umbrella in the back of your car.

2. Don't stand in back of the car. It's too dangerous!

II. 1. The little boy burst into tears when he saw this snake.

2. All the audience burst into laughter after hearing the joke.

20 **I.** 1. I liked the song composed by Jay in particular.

2. The houses on this street are expensive, especially the one at the corner.

II. 1. This teacher is very popular with his student because he has a sense of humor.

2. The reason why he was fired was that he had no sense of responsibility.

21 **I.** 1. A learned person is not always someone who earns a lot of money.

2. Food that looks good doesn't necessarily taste good.

II. 1. Having been busy working, Miller seldom has dinner with his wife.

2. She was busy feeding her baby, so she couldn't answer the phone.

22 **I.** 1. When the train was about to leave, he found his child missing.

2. Lauren suddenly fainted when all the other runners were about to sprint.

II. 1. Had you worked harder, you would have won the championship.

2. Had I not cheated in the math exam, I would not have been punished.

23 I. 1. It goes without saying that those who respect others will be respected.

2. It goes without saying that a good citizen should obey traffic laws.

II. 1. I wonder if he will arrive at the restaurant on time.

2. I wonder if I could leave earlier.

24 I. 1. I'll find the keys no matter where they are.

2. No matter where you go, be sure to inform us.

II. 1. During a test, anxiety may distract us from thinking carefully.

2. The noise outside the window distracted her from doing yoga.

25 I. 1. For Larry, the weekend is a time to keep company with his family.

2. For them, it is a time to broaden their horizons.

II. 1. He told me how pleasant it was to live in a small village with his wife.

2. The experience of traveling in Japan makes me understand how important it is to learn foreign languages.

26 I. 1. When it comes to failure, I will never forget the fact that I failed both of my English and math finals last semester.

2. When it comes to foreign food, I think that Japanese cuisine is very special.

II. 1. When he stood in front of the altar, six numbers suddenly came into his mind.

2. It occurred to me that I had left my umbrella on the bus this morning.

27 I. 1. If I find someone trying to cheat on the test, I'll try to stop him from making such a mistake.

2. Applying sunblock over your skin can protect it from being burned by the sun.

II. 1. His accent is very different from that of ours.

2. Books with green labels are more expensive than those with red ones.

28 I. 1. Consulting the doctor, Dad decided to take his advice and quit smoking.

2. Feeling nervous and scared, the little girl didn't dare to move at all.

II. 1. He burst into tears with his forehead laid between his knees.

2. Father dashed into the basement with the flashlight in his hand.

29 I. 1. Stunned and nervous, I could barely utter any words.

2. The next morning, the widow felt so sad that she could hardly stop crying.

II. 1. Staring at this naughty boy, Mrs. Li didn't lose her temper on the spot. Instead, she took her son away immediately.

2. The big guy lost his temper, and he wanted to hit me on the spot.

30 I. 1. Mr. and Mrs. Smith have been living in New York since their first son was born.

2. We have been playing basketball together since elementary school. It has been nine years already.

II. 1. Not long after lunch, she began to feel dizzy and felt like throwing up.

2. Not long after graduation from college, he successfully found a job.

31 I. 1. It was not long before the little girl had stopped crying and fell asleep with her teddy bear in her arms.

    2. It was not long before the angry man calmed down, sat down, and then lit a cigarette.

II. 1. The little boy could do nothing but just watch his sister take away his chocolate bar.

    2. Having discovered the truth, the man could do nothing but just leave quietly.

32 I. 1. In the chaos that followed, the clumsy father finally dressed the baby.

    2. In the chaos that followed, I accidentally broke the vase.

II. 1. Instead of being praised in public, Sam ended up being fired for telling lies.

    2. Instead of making a profit, he ended up bankrupting.

33 I. 1. Peter had finished his homework, while I didn't do it at all.

    2. Mary likes going to concerts, while her boyfriend likes doing outdoor activities.

II. 1. I am looking forward to your new novel. When will it be published?

    2. I look forward to visiting Paris with you next year.

34 I. 1. You should not burn the midnight oil, which will lead to lack of sleep.

    2. I will make every possible effort to protect you as long as you say yes.

II. 1. When it comes to my failing eyesight, I think of the life full of textbooks and tests.

    2. In the failing light, I could hardly see anything ahead.

35 I. 1. Mr. Wang is forgettable. His wife has to remind him to take medicine over and over again.

    2. Read the lyrics over and over again until you know it by heart.

II. 1. Several people walking by laughed at him, which made him embarrassed.

    2. A girl walking by smiled at him, and then wave goodbye to him.

36 I. 1. After having browsed through the books on the shelf, I took the thickest one.

    2. This red top doesn't go well with this green pants.

II. 1. He pushed me and made me kneel down to the ground.

    2. I knelt down on the mat and began to pray.

37 I. 1. I don't want to stay in the boiling heat outside. Let's go to the movies in the theater nearby!

    2. On a freezing cold night, his father passed away.

II. 1. I was more happy than surprised when I heard the good news.

    2. She is more confident than beautiful.

38 I. 1. Except for a shovel, we found nothing along the riverbank.

    2. Except for the driver, there is no one on the bus.

II. 1. We are behind our rival by three runs.

    2. The Yankees tied the game in the bottom of the second inning.

39 I. 1. Whenever I see Nancy, I always can't help blushing.

    2. Having seen Dad badly hurt, I couldn't help crying.

II. 1. To improve my listening ability, I made up my mind to listen to English radio programs every day from now on.

    2. Looking at his report card, Jack made up his mind not to fool around anymore.

40 I. 1. He had never returned to his hometown since moving to the United States.

    2. She had never spoken to her family since witnessing the murder.

II. 1. At eight-thirty, I got a phone call from my teacher, telling me it was time for me to e-mail my essay to him.

    2. It is time for us to fight for freedom!

41 I. 1. Before going to bed, I checked all the plugs to make sure that they had been pulled out.

    2. Call David to make sure that he has arrived at the destination safely.

II. 1. He turned on the light because it was very dark in the room.

    2. Don't forget to turn off the oven.

42 I. 1. On hearing the result of the competition, everyone cheered with excitement.

    2. Upon seeing her son come back safe and sound, the mother cried with joy.

II. 1. The child seemed to want to eat the cake on the table.

    2. The journalist seemed to know the secret behind this scandal.

43 I. 1. His parents tried hard to get him to quit drugs.

    2. You should try hard to quit your bad habits, and then you can turn over a new leaf.

II. 1. For the sake of their children's health, Mr. and Mrs. Wang decided to move to the country.

    2. For the sake of his family and his business, Allen bought a new van.

44 I. 1. He was so absorbed in comic books that he wasn't aware of someone approaching.

    2. Are you sure that the government has been aware of our problem?

II. 1. Having lost the game, we had no choice but to accept defeat.

    2. Now that she decided to leave, we had no choice but to wish her good luck.

45 I. 1. You should cherish what you have. After all, you are much luckier than many other people.

    2. Lucy was shocked to know where her parents were because she thought she was an orphan.

II. 1. The doctor suggested that I should take exercise as much as I could every day.

    2. Emma closed the textbook, took out her pencil, and answered all the questions as quickly as she could.

46 I. 1. In order to develop a new market, the manager asked the whole team to work harder.

    2. In order to expand your vocabulary, you have to read as many books as possible.

II. 1. At first he didn't like English, but English became his favorite subject in the end.

    2. I wonder why they loved each other at first, but they didn't get married in the end.

47 I. 1. It is important for everyone to keep regular hours.

    2. Is it convenient for you and David to come over to my house at seven this evening?

II. 1. I didn't regret lending him the money because I knew I had helped a promising young person.

2. I did regret telling lies. I should have thought twice.

48 **I.** 1. Last night, my father got angry with me because I broke his favorite cup accidentally.

2. After Linda got his son dressed, she took him out for breakfast.

II. 1. Tim held back his anger, which avoided a fight.

2. Susan held back her tears, and decided to take good care of those poor kids.

49 **I.** 1. It is impossible for me to read through all the textbooks before the exam.

2. Can you make sense of what the teacher is lecturing?

II. 1. We had been walking for some time, but no one wanted to stop for some rest.

2. I did meet him at the airport sometime last week.

50 **I.** 1. Mike found it difficult to get used to getting up at six o'clock in the morning.

2. I used to play tennis with my friends on weekends, but I don't have time for the sport now.

II. 1. Jack tries his best to earn money, hoping that he can accomplish his goal of traveling around the world before the age of fifty.

2. As long as you do your best, getting into the college of your choice is not difficult.

指考篇

1 **I.** 1. With digital cameras, people can take pictures quickly and easily without using film.

2. With her help, I finished this report in three days.

II. 1. If John gets addicted to comic books, he will spend less time studying.

2. I spent two months getting used to city life in Japan.

2 **I.** 1. Not until I stood at the top of Mt. Jade did I realize how tall it is.

2. Not until you have finished your homework can you watch TV.

II. 1. This gesture carries different meanings from country to country.

2. Mailmen go from door to door to deliver letters and packages.

3 **I.** 1. Mandy loves her husband with all her heart.

2. Parents should set (good) examples to their children.

II. 1. To sum up, once you set a goal, you should work hard to accomplish it.

2. To sum up, you should have a positive attitude toward your future.

4 **I.** 1. No matter what trouble you are in, I will try my best to help you.

2. No matter what gift he gives you, you should be grateful to him.

II. 1. Thinking that you would get angry, I didn't dare to tell the truth at all.

2. To be honest, I don't agree with you at all.

5 **I.** 1. When I regained consciousness, I didn't know what had happened to me.

2. According to the latest news, a severe flood happened in Japan yesterday.

II. 1. The teacher suggested that every student (should) take turns to clean the classroom.

2. The salesperson recommended that my father (should) buy this luxurious villa.

6   **I.**   1. Of all the outdoor activities, the one I like best is jogging.

         2. Of all the subjects, the one I like most is English.

    II.   1. We can sing as many songs as we want.

         2. At the party, you can drink as many cocktails as you like.

7   **I.**   1. English is the subject (that) I like (the) most in school.

         2. Bicycling is the activity (that) I enjoy doing (the) most in my free time.

    II.   1. Another reason I like Paul is that he is friendly and hard-working.

         2. Another reason I don't like summer is humidity.

8   **I.**   1. If the blind child had the ability to see, he would want to see his family and friends.

         2. If she were the princess in the fairy tale, she would run away from the castle to lead a happy life with someone she loved.

    II.   1. He worked hard so that he could support his family.

         2. Mary didn't attend today's meeting so that we wondered if she was sick.

9   **I.**   1. I like to play tennis, and I enjoy playing baseball as well.

         2. Ken owns a motorcycle and a car as well.

    II.   1. I will do anything to make my parents happy, for I love them very much.

         2. We should vote for him, for he is a capable man.

10   **I.**   1. Desperate and helpless, he decided to do whatever he could to escape from the fire.

         2. Kind and generous, Mr. Brown is always willing to help others without asking for any reward.

    II.   1. Without my brother's advice, I might have run away from home. I would have wandered the streets at that night.

         2. Lisa forgot to bring her purse last night, or else she would have bought that beautiful dress.

11   **I.**   1. Every day, thousands of tourists come to visit Taipei 101, a place where many companies and organizations are located in.

         2. In the evening, we arrived in North Korea, a country where people still struggle to obtain enough food.

    II.   1. Browsing around the shop filled with all different kinds of stuffed toys, I finally decided to buy this teddy bear with a flower in its hand.

         2. She was chatting with the girl living next door.

12   **I.**   1. Jamie has twin daughters. One is energetic, and the other (is) quiet but intelligent.

         2. After Sam rushed out of his house, he suddenly realized that one of his feet was in a sneaker, and the other (was) in a leather shoe.

    II.   1. The government should take some measures at once. First, build a temporary bridge so that the victims can leave the disaster area. Second, settle the victims in temporary shelters. Third, offer the victims food and water.

2. By the end of the summer vacation, I have to complete three tasks. First, finish all of my homework. Second, finish reading five novels. Third, write twenty English essays.

13 **I.** 1. When I got off the bus, it was raining heavily. Because I didn't take an umbrella with me, all I could do was rush back home.

2. Falling off the bike, the kid got hurt and couldn't stand up. All he could do was cry out for help.

II. 1. I don't know why the math teacher said I was slow, and I don't understand why I couldn't concentrate on my studies.

2. I don't understand why many celebrities have been attempting to pursue fame and fortune.

14 **I.** 1. Some students often burn the midnight oil preparing for tests, which may do harm to their health.

2. In order to lose weight, my sister skipped breakfast, which made her unable to concentrate in class.

II. 1. Since the first time I met him, I have always liked to play chess with him.

2. I haven't heard from her since last October.

15 **I.** 1. I used to go fishing by the river every Sunday when I lived with my grandparents in the countryside.

2. Tony used to stay up playing online games on weekends, which annoyed his parents.

II. 1. I believe that our effort will impress the manager as long as we keep on working hard.

2. I'll try my best to finish this task as long as you have confidence in me.

16 **I.** 1. Sam shouldn't have let his daughter stay at home alone yesterday.

2. We should have reached an agreement. How stupid we were!

II. 1. When my mom went into her bedroom without saying anything, I realized she must have been very upset.

2. You look very tired. You must have stayed up last night.

17 **I.** 1. Jenny wanted to keep a dog as a pet, but her parents didn't allow her to do so.

2. Mr. Wang isn't able to earn enough money to keep himself and his family.

II. 1. In my opinion, your problem can be solved in two ways. One way is to report it to your teacher. The other way is to turn to your parents for help.

2. In Ms. Lin's opinion, we should set off before it gets dark.

18 **I.** 1. Sally decided not to travel with her classmates. For one thing, she couldn't afford it. For another (thing), she had to take care of her brothers and sisters.

2. Harry is the most popular student in his class. For one thing, he is nice to everyone. For another (thing), he is very handsome.

II. 1. The discovery of the three fingerprints is the key to solving the murder.

2. The keys to success are determination and preparation.

19 **I.** 1. Like many other girls, I cannot resist the temptation to buy beautiful clothes.

2. Unlike most other boys, Peter likes to do chores.

II. 1. The teacher said that this punishment would serve as a warning to other students.

2. This study served as Father's office.

20 **I.** 1. He failed last math test. Likewise, he failed this time.

2. Boys must wear formal clothes such as suits. Likewise, girls have to wear formal clothes like dresses.

II. 1. I don't like the way (that) you deal with this problem.

2. It is the way (that) we treat our employees.

21 **I.** 1. Our language lab is not only a place to learn English, but also a place to hold meetings.

2. In this empty room, there is no bed to lie on, and no sofa to sit on, either.

II. 1. This boy sat in the corner alone. He neither cried nor smiled.

2. Neither the color nor the design is her favorite.

22 **I.** 1. Walk two blocks down this street, and you will find a bank on the corner.

2. Read English newspapers every day, and your English reading ability will improve a lot after one month.

II. 1. Only in this way can we finish this task on time.

2. Only by training and practice will we have a chance to win this game.

23 **I.** 1. As far as many senior high school students are concerned, ten thousand dollars is a large sum of money.

2. Five years have passed since I came across Mr. Smith in Paris.

II. 1. My grandmother began to lose her memory little by little.

2. After the students had lined up, they started to enter the language lab one by one.

24 **I.** 1. I will do whatever you want me to do.

2. Whatever you say, I don't think that he is an honest man.

II. 1. Whenever I am sick, my mother takes care of me.

2. I will be home whenever you drop by.

25 **I.** 1. In addition to all the different drinks, the convenience store also sell sandwiches and snacks.

2. In addition to visiting the museum, we also went to the theme park, spending the whole afternoon there.

II. 1. You have to read the materials the teacher assigned. In addition, you must write an English essay.

2. You should concentrate when the teacher is lecturing. In addition, make notes if necessary.

26 **I.** 1. Beethoven was a very talented composer. What's more, he had a passion for music.

2. Mother hollowed out a pumpkin to make a jack-o'-lantern. What's more, she baked a pie with the pulp.

II. 1. On holidays, you can ride your bike along the river, go jogging in the park, or take a walk on the beach.

  2. If we travel to California, we can go to Disneyland in Los Angeles or visit Alcatraz in San Francisco.

27 I. 1. If I could take a trip to a foreign country, I would like to go to Brazil.

  2. If now I could see my father, who has been dead for three years, I would hold him tight and tell him how much I love him.

II. 1. After I got on the bus, it occurred to me that I didn't close the windows before I left my house.

  2. Looking at the stars in the sky, it struck her that she should call her parents.

28 I. 1. I seldom spend time studying and, therefore, find it difficult to get good grades.

  2. He is always well-prepared and, therefore, finds it easy to deal with everything.

II. 1. Compared with your achievement in science, my success seems to be of little importance.

  2. Compared with your brother, you are much more considerate.

29 I. 1. When working at the hospital, the nurse washed her hands all the time and cleaned her desk twice a day.

  2. Anna calls her boyfriend three times every Sunday.

II. 1. Thanks to the constant medical care, the old man recovered from a heart attack quickly.

  2. Thanks to your stupid decision, we lost a chance to make a big fortune!

30 I. 1. For me, studying abroad would enable me to experience another culture and expand my horizons.

  2. This large sum of money enabled George to buy a luxurious villa in the suburbs.

II. 1. I am confident that by doing these things I will be able to make my dream come true one day.

  2. Ted was confident that he could reach his destination before noon.

31 I. 1. If you get close to a horse, you should follow a few simple rules. To begin with, don't walk behind the horse.

  2. I don't want to go out today. To be frank, I would rather stay home and watch TV.

II. 1. That kid was too scared to run away. He just stood still with his mouth wide open.

  2. The task is too difficult for me to complete on time, so I need a few more days.

32 I. 1. You have to pay for the drink as well as the movie ticket, and the total will be NT$300.

  2. Students from foreign countries as well as the minister were together in the church to celebrate Christmas.

II. 1. The elephant said to the mouse, "If you can keep a secret, so can I."

  2. Sandy has got a huge amount of homework to do, and so have I.

33 I. 1. The dog wagged its tail all the time, especially when his owner patted it on the head.

2. My parents and I love seafood. I, especially, always order shrimps when eating out.

II. 1. Without a doubt, *The Lord of the Rings* is one of the best novels I've ever read.

2. Without a doubt, we will discuss these important issues at the next meeting.

34 I. 1. I did tell the truth, but no one believed me.

2. Don't worry about me. I do feel better now.

II. 1. This boy was the first runner to cross the finish line. In other words, he won this race.

2. He stared at her with a puzzled expression on his face. In other words, he didn't understand what she meant.

35 I. 1. Tom had a lot of fun playing cards with his classmates last Saturday.

2. I had great fun at my sister's wedding party. I also drank a lot of cocktails.

II. 1. I had to clean the classroom as a punishment, since I was late for school this morning.

2. Since this teenager didn't break the display window on purpose, the owner of this shop decided not to call the police.

36 I. 1. Once, Mary was supposed to meet me at the theater at three o'clock; however, she didn't show up until four.

2. I didn't know she was married until I saw the diamond ring on her finger.

II. 1. This office is not large enough to place these tables and chairs.

2. This cell phone is small enough for me to put it in my pocket.

37 I. 1. To a young man in his twenties, the importance of realizing his own dream cannot be overemphasized.

2. The importance of regular exercise cannot be overemphasized.

II. 1. It is clear that arguments will lead to worse relationships with our friends.

2. It is clear that we only have one Earth, and the importance of environmental protection cannot be overemphasized.

38 I. 1. When I was only ten years old, I decided to devote myself to helping the homeless and the poor.

2. In her childhood, her parents often invited the rich in the town over for dinner.

II. 1. Although he is busy working, he still dedicates his time on weekends to looking after the orphans at the nearby orphanage.

2. As a volunteer, she dedicates all her effort to caring for the elderly people in the community.

39 I. 1. With my computer, I can not only search for the information I need on the Internet, but also do online shopping, if necessary.

2. The police hope that they can find the missing teenager by the end of this month, if possible.

II. 1. Actually, the airfares and the expenses in this trip are much higher than I expected.

2. Actually, he didn't discover that I had slipped out of the room through the window.

40 I. 1. I feel that the government didn't try hard to solve this problem.

2. I feel that this film is one of the best comedies I have ever seen.

II. 1. This rich but selfish king ended up living alone in a big castle.

2. If you had robbed the old lady of her money, you must have ended up in prison.

41 I. 1. When it comes to the lottery, people hold different views. Some people believe that a portion of lottery-ticket sales helps minorities to lead a better life. Others think that the lottery only bring negative effects on the society.

2. On weekends, some people stay at home and watch TV. Others prefer to do outdoor activities.

II. 1. I think that Mary and Ted have misunderstood each other.

2. The residents in this community respect one another. Therefore, there are not many conflicts.

42 I. 1. As the only son in his family, he has to work hard to support his family.

2. As a soldier, he has to obey his commander's orders and fight for his country.

II. 1. Nancy is as famous a dancer as her sister.

2. I have as big a house as you.

43 I. 1. Based on my experience, I am sure that your dog must be sick.

2. According to the news report, the crime rate is on the decline.

II. 1. If you stop thinking about those annoying problems, you will definitely have a great time at the party.

2. Mandy and I had a good time talking about our favorite animated films in the coffee shop.

44 I. 1. From country music to pop songs, I have always been fascinated by English songs.

2. Karen is the apple in her parents' eye. She has always been carefully protected.

II. 1. A long time ago, people believed that the Earth is the center of the universe.

2. When I returned to the small town I had left five years before, I found out that everything remained the same.

45 I. 1. This employee talks as if he were the manager.

2. Don't act as if you knew nothing about my secret. I know Jessica had told you everything.

II. 1. What's the best, after you admire the scenery, you can go to the nearby restaurant to have dinner.

2. What's best, a splendid sunset can be seen when you walk out the gallery.

46 I. 1. Many people donated rice and clothes to this poor family.

2. This businessman donated one million dollars to cancer research.

II. 1. Sadly, this father could not afford his son's tuition.

2. Obviously, the minister got involved in this scandal.

47 I. 1. It will take a few minutes to copy these documents.

     2. Because he is a loner in school, he has few friends.

II. 1. Tony was late for work yesterday. To his surprise, his boss didn't give him a hard time.

     2. To my great surprise, our homeroom teacher agreed with all of our requests.

48 I. 1. It is not wise to make friends with someone who will bully others.

     2. I am not here to make friends. Instead, I am here to learn new things.

II. 1. I strongly believe that refreshing yourself with a smoke is a bad idea, especially since it will do harm to your health.

     2. The teacher strongly advised him to study hard, so that he could study at the university of his dreams.

49 I. 1. He has been addicted to alcohol since his wife died.

     2. During the summer vacation, Nancy was addicted to reading comic books. She didn't do any homework.

II. 1. He patted her on the shoulder, telling her to stop crying.

     2. Because she was so scared, the little girl grasped her mother by the wrist.

50 I. 1. I arrived at the airport, only to find that the airplane had already taken off.

     2. He opened the top drawer of his desk, only to find that all the money has gone.

II. 1. For the following five hours, I lay on the bed staring at the ceiling.

     2. Not knowing what to do, he sat at the desk looking at the blackboard.

英文文法入門指引（全新改版）
Basic English Grammar Guide (New Edition)

呂香瑩 著

1. 十五個精心整理的章節，詳細介紹文法，讓你迅速掌握重點、提升英文程度。

2. 實用的內容、重點式的解析與即時的演練，幫你破解文法上的難關。

3. 清晰的表格整理，協助你綜合比較、釐清觀念。

4. 特別規劃「學習便利貼」單元，一眼抓住文法關鍵。